4-Books-in-1!

✳ ٠ ✳ ٠ ✳ ٠ ✳

4-Books-in-1!

All That Glitters
Purple Nails and Puppy Tails
Makeover Magic
True Colors

JILL SANTOPOLO

Aladdin

NEW YORK   LONDON   TORONTO   SYDNEY   NEW DELHI

ALADDIN

An imprint of Simon & Schuster Children's Publishing Division
1230 Avenue of the Americas, New York, New York 10020
This Aladdin hardcover edition March 2016
All That Glitters text copyright © 2014 by Simon & Schuster, Inc.
Purple Nails and Puppy Tails text copyright © 2014 by Simon & Schuster, Inc.
Makeover Magic text copyright © 2014 by Simon & Schuster, Inc.
True Colors text copyright © 2014 by Simon & Schuster, Inc.
Cover illustration copyright © 2014 by Cathi Mingus
For information about special discounts for bulk purchases, please contact Simon & Schuster Special Sales at 1-866-506-1949 or business@simonandschuster.com.
The Simon & Schuster Speakers Bureau can bring authors to your live event. For more information or to book an event contact the Simon & Schuster Speakers Bureau at 1-866-248-3049 or visit our website at www.simonspeakers.com.
Series designed by Jeanine Henderson
Cover designed by Jeanine Henderson and Steve Scott
Interior designed by Steve Scott
The text of this book was set in Adobe Caslon.
Manufactured in the United States of America 0216 FFG
10 9 8 7 6 5 4 3 2 1
Library of Congress Control Number 2015956322
ISBN 978-1-4814-7594-5
ISBN 978-1-4424-7382-9 (*All That Glitters* eBook)
ISBN 978-1-4424-7385-0 (*Purple Nails and Puppy Tails* eBook)
ISBN 978-1-4424-7388-1 (*Makeover Magic* eBook)
ISBN 978-1-4424-7391-1 (*True Colors* eBook)
These titles were previously published individually in hardcover and paperback by Aladdin.

Contents

All That Glitters

For my niece, Lily Paige May.

May your life be filled with love, happiness,

and more than a little bit of sparkle.

Special glittery thanks to Karen Nagel,

editrix extraordinaire, as well as to Marianna Baer,

Betsy Bird, Jessica Ann Carp, Andrea Cremer,

Kekla Magoon, Marie Rutkoski, and Eliot Schrefer,

all writers who glimmer and glow.

one

Under Watermelon

The school bell rang, and Aly raced out the door, holding on tight to her backpack straps.

"Slow down!" a hall monitor shouted after her, but Aly didn't listen. She made it to the steps at the front of the school in record time.

Her purple polka-dot watch said 3:07. Only eight minutes until Arnold the deliveryman arrived at her mom's nail salon. Aly *really* wanted to be there to meet him. All the new sparkle colors were supposed to come that day, and Mom had promised that Aly and her sister, Brooke, could test them out the minute they arrived.

Where *was* Brooke? It took exactly five minutes to walk to the nail salon, which was three and a half blocks from Auden Elementary. Now Aly's watch said 3:08. That meant they'd have two minutes to spare, if Brooke came right away.

Aly turned around, looking through the doorway into the school. When she squinted, she was pretty certain she saw Brooke, her long, braided ponytail swinging back and forth, skipping down the hall with three other third graders. This was not the time for skipping!

"Brooke!" Aly yelled.

Brooke looked up, broke away from the other skipping girls, and ran toward Aly. When she got to the door, she was out of breath. "The sparkles! I almost forgot!" she said. "They must've skipped right out of my head!"

Aly loved her sister a lot, but Brooke was not the best at remembering. She was good at a lot of things, like (1) being a nail polish tester and (2) guessing which colors would be popular. But Aly was better at remembering. She was also better at making lists. Lots of lists. They helped keep all her thoughts organized. Brooke's thoughts were hardly ever organized.

"How many minutes do we have?" Brooke asked, pushing her glasses up to the top of her nose.

Aly looked at her watch again. "Six!" she said. "Time for racewalking!"

The two girls took off, walking their fastest, pumping their arms back and forth to get extra speed. There was a man in their town who was an expert racewalker and always wore pink shorts and a pink T-shirt the exact color of Ready Set Flamingo nail polish. Aly and Brooke called him Mr. Flamingo and liked to walk the speedy way he did when they were in a hurry. Elbows were involved.

"Aly, did we end up ordering Cherry, Cherry Nice?" Brooke asked, panting a little as they race-walked past the pet store and the empty shop across from the salon that used to be the Candy Bar.

Aly knew all the colors by heart. She'd helped Mom put in the order. "No Cherry, Cherry Nice," she said. "We got Strawberry Sunday, Under Watermelon, Lemon Aid, Orange You Pretty, and We the Purple."

Brooke thought for a second. "I bet Lemon Aid will be the most popular."

"Lemon Aid?" Aly asked. True Colors was only a few doors down now. Aly could see the sign—light blue with pink and purple curlicue letters. It was 3:14. One minute until Arnold!

"Yes," Brooke said. "Lemon Aid. Yellow hasn't been popular before. It needs a turn."

Now that she was a fifth grader, Aly knew that just

because you hadn't been popular before didn't mean you'd ever get a turn. Suzy Davis, who was the meanest girl in her whole grade, had never been popular. She'd just been mean. Ever since kindergarten. But then again, yellow was a color, and colors couldn't be mean, so maybe it was different with nail polish.

The sisters reached the front door of True Colors at the exact same time Arnold did. He was holding a big box in his arms.

"Hi, Arnold! Are the sparkles here?" Brooke asked. She was tugging on her braid, which she always did when she was extra excited. Or extra nervous. This time, the pulling was definitely for excitement.

"Right here!" he said, bending over so Brooke could see the package. "Aly, can you sign for it, please?"

Aly nodded. It was a job her mom had given her last year, once she was able to write her name perfectly in script.

Arnold gave Aly his signing machine and a plastic thing that looked like a pen. She signed *Alyssa Tanner* on the screen in her most careful handwriting. Then he took back his machine and handed her the box.

Brooke jumped up and down. "Can I hold it, Aly? Pleeeaassee!" she begged.

"You know the rules," Aly said. "Carrying boxes of nail polish is a fifth-grade-and-older job."

Brooke picked up her backpack, which was covered in twirly pictures she'd drawn on with old nail polish colors. "I know. But it was worth a try," she said as she held the door open for her sister.

Door opening was a third-grade job. Actually, it was a first-grade job, but it was one you could keep doing until you graduated from elementary school and turned a million years old. In the nail salon there were a lot of rules about what you could and couldn't do based on how old you were.

The bells on top of the door jingled as it closed behind Aly. Everyone in the salon turned to look. The place was packed—even the six waiting-for-a-manicure chairs near the front window were filled.

"Hi, girls!" a few of the manicurists said.

"I have cookies for you two," said Joan, who was Aly and Brooke's favorite manicurist. "Raisin chocolate chip." Joan wanted to open her own bakery one day.

"Hi, sweeties," their mom said, looking up from manicure station number one. She carefully squeezed a rhinestone with a pair of tweezers, about to glue it on Miss Nina's left pinkie nail. Miss Nina was one of the dog groomers at the pet store down the street and was a True Colors regular. She loved getting rhinestones on her pinkies.

"We got the new sparkles," Brooke announced as she raced toward a room at the back of the salon.

"I signed for the package," Aly added. She passed

the row of five huge teal pedicure chairs—all filled—
and walked around the ten manicure stations. Joan's
was number seven. All those stations were filled too.

"That's great!" their mom called after them. "Pretzels
and juice are in the back. And if you're still hungry after
that, you can each have one of Joan's cookies."

"Whoo-hoo!" Brooke yelled.

The bell jingled again, and more people walked
in. Aly couldn't believe how busy the salon was.

While Aly and Brooke munched on their pretzels—
and Joan's cookies—Brooke decided she wanted rainbow sparkle toes. One new color on each toe, starting
with Strawberry Sunday on her big toe, followed by
Orange You Pretty, Lemon Aid, We the Purple, and,
on her baby toe, Under Watermelon.

It wasn't a regular rainbow, because there was no
blue or green and it ended in pink, but Aly could see how
it might look cool. Still, she wanted to double-check.

It was always good to double-check, just in case people changed their minds. Especially when they made fast decisions, like Brooke.

"Are you positively sure?" Aly asked. Whenever new colors arrived, Aly was usually the nail painter and Brooke was usually the tester. It worked well that way because Aly was a very careful painter and Brooke picked good combinations to try.

"Certain," Brooke answered. She left her napkin and cup on the table and ran over to one of the old pedicure chairs in the corner. The blue-green leather on the chairs was worn out in some places, so Mom had them moved to the back. Brooke hopped into the chair on the right and slipped off her sandals, and Aly got started.

Aly had been practicing her polishing skills since she was in kindergarten. Brooke had been practicing too, but Aly was the expert. Aly had taught Brooke:

- Keep the side of your hand resting on something steady for wobble-free polishing.
- Wipe extra polish off on the side of the bottle before you paint a nail.
- People's feet are very ticklish.
- Red polish stains white shorts.
- So does purple.

And Brooke had taught herself how to stay super still while she was getting her toes painted—even if Aly tickled her or dripped polish on her shorts.

One by one, Aly applied the glittery colors. "They look so beautiful," Brooke whispered. "I love the sparkles. They are so . . . so . . ."

"Sparkly?" Aly said, and they both started laughing.

Aly tucked her hair behind her ears. It had been cut too short to pull into a ponytail, perhaps not the best hairstyle for a manicurist. She kept worrying that it would fall in front of her eyes and that she'd paint Brooke's skin instead of her nails. Maybe she should ask Mom to buy her some headbands.

After she'd applied a second coat, Aly admired Brooke's toes herself. She had to admit, the rainbow look was awesome, especially with the sparkles.

"Let's go see if there's a spot at the drying station, Brookester."

Brooke stood up and hobbled on her heels, following Aly out of the back room and into the main salon.

"I am the Princess of Sparkles," Brooke announced. Brooke would say or do anything, Aly thought, to make people pay attention to her. Mostly Aly didn't mind, but sometimes it could get annoying.

"Come over here and show me your royal toes," Mom said. She was by the door, helping Miss Nina get her car keys out of her bag so she wouldn't smudge her new manicure.

"Nice color choices, Brookie. And nice job, Aly."

"Maybe you could do my nails next week." Miss Nina winked at Aly. "You're just as good as your mom."

Aly smiled as Miss Nina left the salon. She was *so* ready to be a real manicurist, but Mom said she had to wait until she was eighteen. School had to be her main job until then. After that, she could paint nails. Or go to college. Or do both. Aly wasn't sure what she would choose.

"Do you like the rainbow?" Aly asked.

"Very much," said Mom.

"What rainbow?"

Aly looked up. Sitting on one of the chairs in the waiting area was Jenica Posner. *The* Jenica Posner—a sixth grader who was the very best soccer player on the girls' team.

And this was the first time she had ever spoken to Aly.

two

Strawberry Sunday

Aly couldn't answer. Her mouth opened, but no words came out. She just stared at Jenica. But Brooke chattered away like Jenica was her very best friend.

"There's a rainbow of sparkle polish on my toes," Brooke told her. Brooke wasn't shy around anyone. Not even sixth graders. Not even Jenica Posner.

Jenica got up and walked across the nail salon. "These are totally cool!" She kneeled down and inspected Brooke's toes.

"Can I get mine done like that, Nana?" she asked. Jenica turned her head toward a woman with a long white ponytail sitting at station number two.

"If they have time for you, honey. You'll have to ask," the woman answered.

Aly and Brooke's mom flipped through the pages of the salon's appointment book. She looked at the people in the waiting area. There were now more people waiting than there were chairs for them to sit on.

"I'm so sorry, sweetie," she said to Jenica, "but we're all booked up. Maybe tomorrow?"

"Tomorrow I have a soccer game," Jenica said. "Too bad."

Brooke looked at Aly. She winked once with her left eye, then twice with her right, trying to send a Secret Sister Eye Message. But Aly was having trouble understanding it. Finally, Brooke blurted out, "Aly, Mom! Aly could do it!"

Aly felt a rush of excitement. But she knew the rules. Brooke must have forgotten. "I can't," Aly whispered to her sister. "Not till I'm eighteen."

But Jenica didn't hear Aly's whispers. "Could she?" Jenica asked Aly's mom.

Aly held her breath. What would Mom say?

"Well . . ." Mom looked at the crowded shop and then at Aly. "Maybe just this once. As long as it's okay with you, Aly. Same rules as when you do Brooke's nails—no clippers, no cuticle cutters, just emery boards and polish."

"It's okay with me," Aly said as calmly as she could. But her stomach was flipping around like it was doing somersaults off a diving board.

"This one's on the house," Aly heard her mom say to Jenica's nana.

Since all the pedicure chairs were full, Aly and Brooke took Jenica to the back room.

"Brooke, please turn on the water at pedicure station one," Aly said, pretending that she and Brooke gave pedicures every day. "Jenica, sit over there, please."

"Okay, but which is station one?" Brooke asked.

Aly rolled her eyes. "You know . . . the left one."

Brooke turned on the faucet, and as the basin filled with water, Aly removed Jenica's old—and very chipped—toenail polish.

"Soccer's rough on toenail polish," Jenica said, flexing her big toes.

"I know what you mean," Aly answered, even though she really didn't. Weren't Jenica's toes protected by cleats while she played soccer?

"I think the water's ready!" Brooke chirped, slipping under Aly's arm to turn off the faucet. "Do you play soccer a lot? What about other sports? Do you play them, too?"

"Just soccer," Jenica said to Brooke. "Do I put my feet in now?"

Aly nodded as she added a drop of special skin-softening oil to the water. "It should be nice and warm and feel—"

"YIKES!" Jenica yelled. She yanked her feet out of the water. "That's *freezing*! I can't put my feet in there!"

Aly dipped her hand in the water. It felt like the tub of melted ice that her dad stored drinks in at barbecues.

"Brooke! Did you adjust the temperature?"

Brooke shrugged. "I thought I did. Sorry!"

Didn't Brooke understand that this was Jenica Posner? And that they couldn't mess up her pedicure?

Aly let the water drain, adjusted the temperature, and refilled the basin.

Finally, when Jenica's feet were clean and dry—and warm!—Aly gripped the bottom of her foot, just like she held Brooke's when she painted her toenails. But Jenica apparently hadn't practiced sitting still the way Brooke had.

She started laughing. "I'm really ticklish!" she said. "You can't touch my foot like that!"

Aly took a deep breath. She wasn't sure how to fix this, and if Jenica kept laughing, there was no way this pedicure could ever happen. Even though she was still sort of annoyed at Brooke about the cold water, Aly looked at her sister and opened her eyes as wide as possible. Code for *Help!*

"I know how you can stop feeling tickly," Brooke said to Jenica. "It's the trick I use when Aly paints my nails." She paused for a second. "Bite on your tongue. Not so hard that it bleeds or anything, but just so you feel it. Then you think about your tongue and you don't think about your feet being ticklish. And the tickle feeling goes away. Like magic."

Brooke smiled. "I came up with that myself."

Jenica looked horrified. "You want me to bite my tongue?"

"Not *hard*," Brooke said. "Just a little bit. I promise it works."

Jenica looked at Aly. Aly shrugged. "She never laughs when I polish her toes."

"This is weird," Jenica said. "But I'll try it."

Jenica bit down on her tongue, and slowly and carefully, Aly lifted Jenica's foot and started painting her toes with two coats of rainbow-colored sparkles.

After two toes were done, Jenica said, "You're right, Brooke. It works—it doesn't tickle anymore." She held out her hand, and Brooke high-fived it.

Aly was just thankful that the trick had worked as she concentrated on the job in front of her. She'd gotten two more nails done when her hair slipped in front of her right eye. Dumb haircut.

"Did you just get that red on my actual toe?" Jenica asked, wiggling her foot.

Aly rested the polish brush on the floor and tucked her hair back behind her ear. Then she looked down. Oops!

"Sorry about that," she said. She grabbed a little wooden stick, dipped it in polish remover, and wiped the polish off Jenica's toe. "I think I need a headband to keep my hair back."

"You totally do," Brooke said. Then she turned to Jenica. "She totally does."

Jenica pulled an elastic out of her own hair and handed it to Aly. "Why don't you do a half-up with this? It'll keep it out of your eyes."

Jenica Posner, the superstar sixth-grade soccer player, was giving Aly an elastic right off her own head? Aly couldn't believe it, but she did what Jenica said, putting half of her hair up on top of her head.

Then she took a deep breath and kept painting. This was more nerve-wracking than being in the district-wide spelling bee, and that had been one of the most nerve-wracking days of Aly's life!

"You're actually good at this," Jenica said as, stroke by stroke, Aly transformed Jenica's toes into a sparkly rainbow. No more polish got on Jenica's skin. Not even a drop. And thanks to Brooke's tongue trick, Jenica didn't laugh or wriggle anymore.

"Aly's not just regular good," Brooke said, "she's especially, fabulously good. She polishes my nails all the time. And sometimes, at home, she polishes my cousins' nails, and once my grandma's, and when we were little, she polished our stuffed animals' nails, but she got in trouble for that."

Aly cringed. Why oh why did Brooke have to tell Jenica about the stuffed animals?

Jenica laughed. "I bet your mom wasn't too happy with that one."

"Nope, not at all. For her punishment—"

"Brooke, do we have clear polish back here?" Aly asked. She knew they did, but she *had* to do something to get Brooke to stop telling Jenica Posner such embarrassing things about her.

Brooke got the clear polish. Then she started talking about Arnold and how he delivered all the polish to True Colors.

Feeling much calmer, Aly added a clear coat on top of the colors—something she didn't do for Brooke. It was what the real manicurists did, though.

"All done!" Aly said, and smiled.

Jenica lifted her feet out in front of her. "I can't wait to show the girls on the soccer team. They're going to flip."

"Well, if you tell them to call for appointments,

my mom can schedule them for rainbow sparkle pedicures too," Aly said as she opened the basin's drain.

"Good idea," Jenica said, standing up. "Can I walk?"

"Really carefully," Aly told her. "Mostly on your
heels. To the toe-drying station out front. Brooke,
can you bring Jenica's flip-flops, please?"

After Jenica's polish was dry, she said to Aly, "I'm
going to tell the team to ask for you. This is the pret-
tiest pedicure I've ever had."

Aly couldn't stop a huge smile from spreading
across her face. Out of all of the days she'd spent at
True Colors—even with Jenica almost freezing her feet
off, and Brooke's humiliating stories, and Strawberry
Sunday just about sticking Jenica's toes together—Aly
was pretty sure this was the best one yet.

three

Go for the Gold

The next morning Aly, Brooke, and two Pop-Tarts—chocolate for Aly and strawberry for Brooke—were in the backseat of their mom's car. It was so early that Brooke had finished braiding only one side of her hair. The other side hung down almost to her waist.

True Colors was opening an hour earlier than usual. One of the Saturday regulars, Miss Lulu, was getting married in the afternoon. Twelve bridesmaids were coming with her to the salon for matching Just Peachy manicures and pedicures.

After Miss Lulu and her wedding party left, a birthday girl was scheduled to come in with her two sisters and three friends before her Sweet Sixteen party. This was all in addition to the Saturday regulars and whoever else called for an appointment.

"Stop wriggling, Brooke. This side is totally crooked. It looks like it's coming out of your ear," Aly said with a giggle, trying to braid Brooke's hair while holding her Pop-Tart between her knees.

"Please, girls, keep it down back there," Mom said, glancing in the rearview mirror. "I can barely keep my thoughts straight. There's so much to get done today. And Dad won't be home until tomorrow."

Aly looked at her watch: 7:50. Mom seemed exhausted already. Dad was supposed to have been home from his business trip by now, but his flight last night was canceled at the last minute.

At the next red light Mom twisted around to look

at the girls. "Brooke," she said, "you have an important job today."

Through a mouthful of Pop-Tart, Brooke mumbled, "I do?"

"It's going to be a busy Saturday. You know what that means: bottles of polish all over the salon. Can you keep an eye on the colors and make sure there aren't any purples in the red section or blues in the orange section—that kind of thing?"

"Sure, Mom," she answered. "That's easy."

Organizing polish colors was one of Brooke's favorite jobs—and the one she was best at. The colors would go slowly from red to orange to gold to yellow to green to blue to purple to silver to black to brown. When she was done, the arrangement would look like it belonged in an art museum. Brooke did the same thing to her crayons and to the clothes hanging in her closet. She even did it to the books on her bookshelves.

When the red light turned green, Aly asked, "What can I do to help?"

Usually, she had a bunch of small jobs:

- Making sure the manicurists had enough hot towels
- Signing for packages
- Playing with toddlers
- Emptying trash cans
- Sweeping the floor
- Helping customers with their car keys and purses
- Running over to the bank to trade a few twenty-dollar bills for a ton of one-dollar bills

"I need you to answer the phone and make appointments in the schedule book," Mom said, pulling the car into the parking lot behind the salon.

Aly couldn't believe it. She'd never done that before.

She'd figured that was a high school job for sure. Or eighth grade at least.

"Do you mean it, Mom?" she asked.

The three got out of the car and walked to the rear entrance together. "Let's see how it goes until we're done with Lulu's wedding. Then I'll take over. But I'm sure you'll do fine," Mom said, opening the door.

"No problem. I'll do my best," Aly told her mom. Aly thought Brooke would be a *much* better phone answerer because she never, ever stopped talking. Well, except when she was eating a Pop-Tart.

At 8:00 a.m. on the dot, Joan unlocked the front door to True Colors. In rushed Miss Lulu and her Just Peachy bridesmaids. They filled up all five pedicure chairs plus manicure stations one through eight.

First Brooke did her usual job of offering people

cups of water. Then she positioned herself right next to the polish display.

Aly was already seated at the front desk with the telephone and the appointment book. She felt kind of silly just sitting there, looking around at the yellow walls and stacks of magazines, doing nothing except listening to Brooke ask Miss Lulu a gazillion questions about her wedding.

"What color are your shoes?"

"Is your veil long?"

"Do you like roses?"

"Is your wedding cake chocolate? That's my favorite flavor."

Aly opened the appointment book. It was pretty full already, but there were a few slots open for pedicures in the afternoon and even more for manicures.

The first time the phone rang, Aly froze. Brooke

raced over and poked her arm. "Aly! Pick up the phone!"

Aly swallowed hard. On the third ring she answered. "True Colors. May I help you?"

On the other end, a girl asked for a rainbow sparkle pedicure at two o'clock. "My friend Jenica got one yesterday. And, oh, and, um, can Aly do it?" she asked.

Aly wanted to say yes, but she knew the rules. She had to be eighteen. And there were still open spots for the regular manicurists, which had to get filled.

"Aly can't do it," Aly said, pretending she was someone else. "But we can fit you in at two twenty. Will that work?"

"I can come then. Are you sure Aly can't do it?"

Aly swallowed again. "I'm sure," she said. "What's your name?"

"Bethany," the girl answered.

"Okay, thanks, Bethany. We'll see you later," Aly said, and hung up.

She wanted to tell Mom about Bethany asking for her. But Mom was in the middle of painting Miss Lulu's nails—a French manicure, pink on the bottom with white tips, and a rhinestone on her wedding ring finger—and needed to concentrate.

The phone rang again: two mani appointments for a woman and her husband. Then it rang a third time: another one of Jenica's friends, Mia, also asking for a rainbow sparkle pedicure. From Aly. The phone kept ringing and ringing until almost all the empty spots were booked.

Just as it started to calm down, a few walk-ins arrived. As Aly was taking down their names on the waiting list, her mom came over.

"Thanks, sweetie," she said. "I'll take it from here. Your sister's in the back room with some lemonade."

Aly stood up. "We're all booked up for pedicures," she told her mom. "Oh, and two people called about getting the same rainbow sparkle pedicure I gave Brooke and Jenica yesterday."

"We're *all* booked up for pedicures?" her mother asked. "Already?"

Mom ran her fingers through her hair. Aly spotted Just Peachy polish splotched on her elbow.

"I hate turning customers away," Mom said. "This is great, but . . ."

Aly didn't like it when her mom frowned. "Maybe no one else will want a pedicure today," she offered.

"Maybe," Mom said, but she didn't seem like she really believed it.

On her way to the back room Aly straightened the frames of the flower pictures on the walls and stopped to say hi to Mrs. Franklin, one of her favorite regulars. She had a tiny dog named Sadie. Sadie was a professional dog model. Mrs. Franklin carried around pictures of her dressed in different costumes from her photo shoots. Aly especially liked the one of Sadie dressed in a tutu with a bright pink flower in her collar. It was for some sort of dog food commercial.

Once Aly was inside, Brooke handed her a cup of lemonade.

"It's crazy out there!" Brooke said. "We need more paper cups. We ran out of Raspberry Good. And Miss Lulu hates roses!" Both girls flopped into the pedicure chairs.

"Crazy is right," Aly said, enjoying the sweet-and-sour taste the lemonade left on her tongue. "The appointment book is almost filled too."

Brooke waited for Aly to finish her drink. "So," she said, "since it's Saturday . . ." She pulled a bottle of gold glitter polish out of her shorts pocket. Go for the Gold. It was from a shipment two weeks ago.

Aly took the bottle. She'd almost forgotten! It was like they were in a backward world, where Brooke remembered things and Aly didn't!

The girls were always allowed to wear *toe* polish, but they had permission to wear *nail* polish only on weekends. So every Saturday they painted each other's nails. Well, Aly painted both of Brooke's hands and one of her own. Then Brooke did Aly's other hand, even though her polishing was a little wobbly. There was no other choice, because Aly's left hand wasn't as good at polishing as her right hand was.

"Let's get started," Aly said.

She painted Brooke's fingers, then the fingers on her own left hand. While she polished, Brooke peeked into the main salon.

"No way are there open dryers out there," Brooke said. "We'll have to fan." She started waving her hands around so the air would speed up the drying.

Just as Aly was finishing up her left pinkie and about to give the polish brush to Brooke, their mother came in. Now she had a splotch of Plum Delicious on her chin!

"This has to be the busiest Saturday we've ever had. I'll need you both out front when you're done with your break," she said.

"Look!" Brooke said, wiggling her glimmering gold-tipped fingers.

"Beautiful!" Mom answered, and then she caught one of Brooke's hands in her own. "And great manicure, Aly. Oh, by the way, three more of your friends called for a rainbow sparkle pedicure. I had to tell them we were booked for today. They asked for you too. I guess you made a real impression."

The idea of people calling and asking for her made Aly a little breathless. "Too bad I'm not eighteen yet," she said. "Then I could've done their pedicures."

"Mom, why does Aly have to wait?" Brooke asked. "I *hate* that rule! She's so good."

Mom inspected Brooke's fingers a little more closely and gave Aly a funny look. But then Carla appeared at the door. "Your eleven o'clock is here, Karen."

Mom let go of Brooke's hand. "Thanks," she said. "I've got to get back to it, girls."

When Mom left, Brooke finished painting Aly's nails. Aly was surprised by how nice it looked.

"You're going to be just as good as me soon," Aly told her sister.

And somehow, saying that made an idea explode in Aly's brain.

"Brooke . . . what if we ask Mom about opening our own salon, here in the back room, just for kids? I know we're not eighteen, but she *did* let me polish Jenica's toes. So maybe if there's one exception, there could be more!"

As the words came out of her mouth, Aly couldn't tell if they were really smart or really silly. "We're both pretty good manicurists, and Mom wouldn't have to turn down customers who want rainbow sparkle pedicures!"

Brooke started tugging on her left braid like she might pull it out of her head. "Really?" she asked. "Do you really, *really* think we could?"

"I think so," Aly said. "But it'll probably take some convincing."

Brooke looked thoughtful. "What kind of convincing?" she asked.

"Well," Aly said, "first we'd probably need to write up a plan and give it to Mom. That way, she'll take us seriously, like she does when people come by selling nail dryers and clippers and stuff. They give her lots of papers with information on them."

Brooke pushed her glasses up, tight against her

face. "Okay. We can come up with a plan. But right now I need to neaten up the polish shelves. And I promised Mrs. Franklin I'd look at Sadie's new pictures. Also, Joan asked me to refill her box of rhinestones because she's running low."

Aly nodded. "Let's meet back here when Mom gives us another break," she said. But she had already started making a list in her head.

And as she did, she had the feeling that this was not just a good idea, but an awesome one. At least she hoped it was.

Aly just had to figure out how to make Mom break her own rules so it could happen.

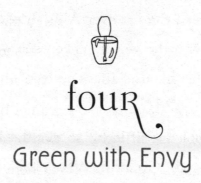

four

Green with Envy

True Colors Problems

1. Too crowded
2. Customers don't like waiting
3. Lots of kids want pedicures (not a
   problem, just a fact)

How OUR Salon Could Fix the Problems

1. Two more polishers, so more nails can
   get done
2. More spots for grown-ups in the main salon

Brooke read the list over Aly's shoulder, moving her mouth with the words. When she was finished, she clapped her hands. "That's perfect," she said. "But I have more to add."

Aly scribbled a little bit to get the ink flowing again, then said, "Go for it. What else?"

"Well," Brooke said, "we can experiment on the other kids to see how new colors look, so I don't have to be the only tester. And we can host polish parties, like the one for the Sweet Sixteen girl today, but for younger kids. And we could polish little kids' nails while their moms are getting manicures—kind of like babysitting—so they don't get bored from waiting."

Aly wrote very quickly. When she finished, she put down her pen. "Those are great ideas, Brooke. You should be a professional idea person."

Brooke smiled. "That would be a fun job. Except

I think I might want to be an organizer instead. And also a manicurist. And an artist."

Aly thought Brooke would be good at all those.

"Okay," Aly said, "I have our list. I think we should wait until we get home to give it to Mom, when she's more relaxed, you know?"

Brooke peeked out the door of the back room. There were tons of people in the salon. "I think so too," she said. "Come on. It looks like Carla and Joan could use our help."

Over the next two hours Aly cleaned up two broken bottles of nail polish (Green with Envy and Really Rosie), took out the trash three times (it was overflowing with the soft twisty paper that went between people's toes for pedicures), and went to the bank once to get one hundred dollars' worth of one-dollar bills so her mom could give people change.

In the meantime, Brooke ordered pizza for the

staff, fixed the nail polish display four times, and read *Big Dog, Little Dog* to Mrs. Fornari's two-year-old son. Three times in a row. Mrs. Fornari was a jewelry maker, and to thank Brooke, she gave her a box of extra beads and some leftover string that she had in her pocketbook.

"Aly!" Mom almost shouted when Aly came through the door with the money. "Thank goodness you're back! I need you to take over the phones."

Aly took her seat behind the desk and looked at the people still waiting. One was Jenica's friend Bethany, whom Aly recognized from school. Bethany walked over.

"Hello," Aly said, trying to be professional. "Do you want a magazine?"

"You're Aly, right?" Bethany said, ignoring the question.

Aly nodded. "Right."

"That's what I thought," Bethany said. "So instead of me waiting on this line, can you just give me a pedicure? At our game this morning Jenica said you're awesome at it, as long as your hair isn't in your eyes. And that you're really fast."

"I, um, I . . . ," Aly said, not really sure what to say. "You have to ask my mom?" is what she finally ended up with. It was kind of a babyish answer, but also a true one.

"Okay," Bethany said. "Which one's your mom?"

Whew. Bethany wasn't acting like Aly's answer was babyish.

"She's over there," Aly said, pointing. "The one with the same hair as me. In the blue shirt."

Bethany returned to the waiting area and spoke to a grown-up—probably her own mom. Then the woman went over to Aly's mom. And then Aly's mom got up from her station and walked over to Aly.

"Did you tell Bethany's mom to ask me if you could do her toes?" Mom asked. Aly could tell she wasn't happy.

"I didn't know what else to say," Aly answered, which was the total and complete truth. "She's a sixth grader," Aly added.

Aly's mom chewed on her lip for a moment, then sighed. "I know I keep breaking my own rules, but do you think you could give Bethany a pedicure? And Jenica's other friend should be here in fifteen minutes. Could you do her, too? Her name is Mia."

Aly couldn't believe it. She got to do two more pedicures and she hadn't gotten in trouble. Maybe it would be easier than she thought to convince Mom about the kid salon later.

Aly took Bethany to the back room, and Brooke followed with all the sparkle polishes.

"Thanks, Brooke," Aly said.

"Yeah, thanks," Bethany added.

Aly slipped a hair elastic off her wrist and pulled back the top half of her hair. She got down to cleaning and filing and polishing, and Brooke got down to chatting with Bethany. Aly was paying so much attention to Brooke's conversation about Sadie the dog and how famous she was that she almost spilled the bottle of Under Watermelon polish on Bethany's flip-flop. Luckily, she caught it just in time and Bethany didn't notice, and Aly quickly finished.

Brooke glanced into the main salon. "No free dryers," she reported. "But don't worry, I'll fan you."

She picked up two magazines and waved them back and forth over Bethany's toes.

"Thanks, you two," Bethany said. "Jenica was right—this was awesome."

Just then Mia appeared in the doorway.

"Hey," she said, cracking her gum. "Aly, right? Your mom said I should come back here."

"Mia!" Bethany squealed. "I didn't know you were coming too!"

Mia sat down next to Bethany. "Jenica's toes looked so cool. I think the whole soccer team should get them. Even though you can't see the sparkles with our socks and cleats on, we'll all know we have sparkle power underneath."

"Some other girls called today," Aly told them. "But we were booked."

"Overbooked is more like it," Mia said. "Did you see the crowd out there? I'm so glad I don't have to wait on that line."

Aly got to work while Mia and Bethany chatted. Brooke was still fanning, which made it hard for her to talk. Then Aly accidentally dipped the Orange You Pretty brush in the Strawberry Sunday bottle.

"Aly!" Brooke panted, her eyes huge. "Did you just . . ."

Aly blinked her eyes extremely hard, the Secret Sister Eye Message for *I know, but don't say it out loud!* Then she quickly wiped off the brush.

Brooke touched one of Bethany's toes carefully and pronounced her dry. Then she slid next to Aly. "Do you want me to open and close the polish bottles?" she whispered.

A polish assistant! Just what Aly needed. Sometimes having a sister really was the best thing in the world. Aly and Brooke worked together to finish the pedicure. Then both sisters took up fanning Mia's toes.

"We need some dryers back here," Brooke whispered. "My arms are getting tired."

Aly agreed. When Mia's nails were dry, both sixth graders stood up.

"Thanks so much," Bethany said as she was leaving.

"Yeah, thanks," Mia echoed. "This was a totally awesome pedicure. I'm going to tell the rest of the team that they *have* to come get some sparkle power."

"You're welcome," Aly and Brooke said together.

"And that would be great!" Brooke added.

Once they were alone, the sisters fell onto the small couch, exhausted but happy. "That was so much fun," Brooke said. "Even if my arms feel like noodles from all that fanning."

"You were right before," Aly said. "If Mom lets us have our own salon back here, we're going to need dryers—for fingers and for toes."

All of a sudden, Aly was extra worried about their salon. If Mom had to spend a lot of money to make it work, there was a big chance she'd turn them down.

That's why, a few hours later, after they'd closed

up the salon and were having dinner at Trattoria
Spaghetto, Aly found herself unable to swallow her
mouthful of meatball.

It didn't matter if Aly was able to talk or not,
though. As usual, Brooke's mouth didn't stop going.
While she was sucking down spaghetti, Brooke
blurted out, "Mom, Aly and I have something
important to ask you."

Aly managed to choke down her food. She pulled
the list she and Brooke had made earlier out of the
back pocket of her jean shorts.

"We, um," Aly said, unfolding the paper. "We,
um, think that we could really help out at the salon if
we, um . . ."

"We want to open our own kid salon!" Brooke
said, bouncing up and down in her seat. "In the back
room! And we'd do kids' nails and have parties and it
would be good for True Colors because, because . . ."

Aly handed the paper to her mom. "It would be good because we could handle all the kids so you could polish even more grown-ups."

Mom looked at the girls' proposal. She read it over once. Then twice. Maybe even three times.

Brooke grabbed Aly's hand under the table. Aly's legs were jiggling hard. She couldn't stop them. *Say yes, say yes,* she thought.

But Mom sighed.

"This is a terrific idea, girls," she said. "It would be a big help to me and to the salon. I know I've asked Aly to give a few pedicures these last two days, but I can't agree to this."

"Why not?" Brooke asked, tears already filling her eyes. Aly felt like she wanted to cry too.

"Because your father and I have spoken about this before. We both agreed that schoolwork and being a kid should always come first for you two. That's why we both work so hard, why he travels all the time—so you two can focus on being children."

"But we don't want to be children," Brooke cried. "We want a salon."

Aly bit her lip. "What if we could do both?" she asked. "What if we could be children *and* run a salon?"

"I don't think so," Mom said, finishing the last of her chicken parmesan.

Aly and Brooke looked at each other. They couldn't eat another bite.

"Okay, kids," Mom said, leaving some money on the table. "It's been a long day. Let's go home."

On the way home, though, Aly had another idea—one she wouldn't tell Brooke, in case her sister opened her mouth again. She wasn't about to give up on the salon just yet. But she would have to wait until tomorrow to put her plan into action.

five

So Berry Blue

B*eep, beep, beep.*

Aly opened her eyes to the sound of the alarm on her purple polka-dot watch. It beeped softly from its spot underneath her pillow. She pulled it out and clicked it off: 6:45 a.m., just like she'd planned.

Super quietly, Aly slid out of her bed. She turned the doorknob really slowly so it wouldn't make its normal loud click and tiptoed down the hallway to the kitchen. She wished her parents would let her have a cell phone so she could make calls whenever and wherever she wanted, but that was another Tanner rule: No cell until middle school.

Right next to the toaster oven was the phone. Aly picked up it up and walked over to the back door—as far away from Mom's bedroom as possible. She dialed.

Ring, ring, ring.

Answer already, Aly thought anxiously.

"Hello?" a deep voice answered. "Honey? Is everything okay?"

"It's me, Dad," Aly whispered. "Not Mom. And everything's okay. Except for not exactly everything."

Aly leaned against the door, resting her head against the pale gray window shade.

"What do you mean?" Dad said, sounding worried.

"I mean—" Aly took a deep breath, and when she let it out, all the words came with it. "I mean that when you get home, you have to talk to Mom because Brooke and I don't care about our childhoods, and the thing we want to do most is polish other kids' nails at True Colors in the back room, and even if you and Mom don't want us to work, we want to, and also it'll teach us a lot of responsibility for when we're older, plus it'll help Mom out a lot at the salon because it's mega-busy and it's making her tired and also it'll be fun."

There was a pause on the other end of the phone. "So, you girls asked Mom, and she said no?"

Now there was a pause on Aly's end. "Yes," she said, in her smallest voice.

Dad sighed. "Let's talk about this when I'm home tonight," he said. "Okay?"

All of a sudden, Aly got a little excited inside. "You mean there's still hope?"

"There's always hope, Alligator, but I've got a plane to catch. We'll all talk later."

Her father said, "I love you." Aly did the same and beeped off. Then she crept back to her room, got into her bed, and closed her eyes. But she was much too excited to sleep. So she got her favorite purple pen and a piece of frog-shaped paper and started a new list, writing down all the things that she and Brooke would learn from running a salon, like how to be responsible and organized and patient. When Aly heard Mom turning the doorknob, she stuffed the list underneath her pillow and pretended to snore.

"Move George over, Brookie," Mom said after she'd opened the blinds to let the sun in. Brooke put her stuffed monkey on the night table, and Mom lay down next to her.

"Uh-oh," Aly said. "What's the matter? Is Dad okay?" She started to worry, even though he had sounded fine when she'd spoken to him earlier.

"Everything is fine, girls," Mom said. "But how about you don't come with me to the salon today? Aly, why don't you go swimming at the Y with Lily? And,

Brooke, there's an art class there at the same time."

Aly felt like someone had punched her in the stomach. No salon? But that was her favorite place in the world. It was where she belonged. Plus, she *hated* swim class. Mean Suzy Davis was there.

Before Aly could say anything, Brooke took matters into her own hands: She started crying. Wailing, really.

Mom tried to put her arms around Brooke, but Brooke turned to face the wall.

"Why are you being so *me-ean*?" Brooke hiccuped, still not looking at Mom. "First no k-kid salon, a-and now no Tr-rue Colors?"

"Brooke," Mom said. "Enough."

"It's *n-not* enough," Brooke sobbed.

"Really, Mom," Aly said. "We don't want go to the Y today. Especially not to go swimming. Please let us come. *Please?*"

Mom looked at her watch. Then she looked at Aly

and Brooke. Finally, she shook her head. "Fine," she said. "But now we're running late. Let's get a move on."

It took only three seconds for Brooke to stop crying. Aly was impressed—she could never stop crying that quickly. Once she got started, tears kept coming.

Three green lights and two stop signs later, the Tanners pulled up in front of True Colors.

Aly and Brooke ran to the front door, but Mom got out of the car and stopped. In the middle of the sidewalk. Staring at a glittery banner on the empty store across the street—the one that used to be a candy shop: COMING SOON! PRINCESS POLISH! A NAIL SALON FOR THE WHOLE FAMILY! When did that sign show up? It wasn't there yesterday!

Mom stared at it for three minutes, according to Aly's watch. Then her mouth made a really straight line, and she marched into True Colors without looking at the girls. Clearly, Mom was not having a very good morning.

"Why is another salon coming across the street?" Brooke asked Aly.

Aly shrugged. "I don't know. I guess they want to polish people's nails too."

"But," Brooke said, her lower lip wobbling, "but what if people like that salon better than ours? What if Mrs. Franklin stops coming? And Miss Lulu? And all the other regulars?"

Aly figured that's just what Mom was worried about—why she had stood so long on the sidewalk.

"I think we just have to make sure they don't," Aly said. "Here's the plan. We're going to do our jobs today the very best we can. If something might possibly go wrong, we're going to stop it before it does. We've got to make sure everyone knows True Colors is the best salon ever."

six

Orange You Pretty

ater that afternoon, when the salon rush had slowed down a bit, Brooke, Aly, and Joan were having their traditional Sunday Pizza Picnic in the back room. The door to the main salon was open, and it was finally quiet enough to hear the background music over the hum of nail dryers and conversation. Aly couldn't help bopping her head a little while she chewed. When it was quiet like this, True Colors really felt like home.

"Want to trade your pepperoni for my mushrooms?" Brooke asked Joan.

"Sure thing," Joan answered, peeling three pieces of pepperoni off her pizza slice and handing them over.

Brooke popped them in her mouth and started laughing.

"What's so funny?" Joan asked. She looked over at Aly, but Aly shrugged. She had no idea why her nutball sister was having a fit about pepperoni.

"No pepperoni for Joanie!" Brooke laughed. "It rhymes!"

Joan smiled. "You mean like . . . no cookie for Brookie?"

Brooke stopped laughing immediately. "But . . . I get a cookie, right?"

Joan finished swallowing Brooke's mushrooms. "Of course you get a cookie. I'm testing out a new recipe. The rest of the manicurists are waiting for your verdict before they give it a go."

Aly loved Sunday Pizza Picnics. She loved that Joan brought them cookies to try. She even loved the way everyone else in the salon waited until Aly and Brooke gave a cookie two thumbs up before they ate it. Basically, Aly loved everything about True Colors.

"This is the best place in the world, isn't it?" Aly asked as Joan handed her a raspberry–peanut butter macaron.

"Absolutely!" Brooke said, snuggling next to Joan and taking a cookie from the tin.

Aly let her head rest against Joan's other shoulder.

"So what do you think?" Joan asked as the girls bit into the cookies.

"It tastes like you turned a peanut butter and jelly sandwich into a cookie." Brooke said, looking up at Joan. "How did you do that?"

"A baker never tells her secrets." Joan winked. "What do you think, Aly?"

Aly let the taste of the cookie settle on her tongue. "This is what I like about it," she said. "One, it's salty and sweet at the same time. Two, the peanut butter part is really creamy. Three, there's a little bit of crunch to the outside of the cookie. And four, it's big enough that you need four bites to finish it."

"Thank you for that wonderful list," Joan said. "I'll tell the rest of the ladies that these cookies have the Aly-and-Brooke Seal of Approval."

"Hey, Aly?" someone said from the doorway.

Aly looked up. It was Jenica! And Bethany and Mia. There were three more girls from the soccer team behind them.

"Any chance you can polish some more toes when you're done eating?" Jenica asked.

Aly stood up and swallowed her last bite of cookie. "We're all booked today," she said. She really wasn't sure if they were totally booked, but she didn't want to have to ask Mom to break her rules again . . . not yet, anyway.

Jenica put her hands on her hips. "You know, you and your mom always say that, but then you take people in here and give them pedicures. Can we just skip to that part?"

"Um . . ." Aly didn't have a choice—she looked into the main salon for her mom.

"How about if I go see if Karen is back?" Joan said, squeezing Aly's shoulder. "And if not, I'll come back here and we'll figure this out." Aly nodded, grateful, as always, for Joan.

"Mia and Bethany and I played awesome yesterday after you gave us the sparkle pedicures," Jenica said. "We have another game after school tomorrow. And we really need to win. So our starting forwards need pedicures too."

Jenica introduced the girls who had followed her

in: Giovanna, Maxie, and Joelle. They looked a little familiar to Aly from school, but she'd never spoken to any of them before.

Aly found it kind of amazing that the girls thought her sparkle pedicure made them play soccer better. She wondered if she'd be a soccer star if she painted her own toenails.

"Aly's not allowed to," Brooke said as she cleaned up the Pizza Picnic. "Really. Unless our mom says it's okay, and she's not here right now."

"There she is!" Mia said from behind Jenica.

Mom came walking toward the back room, carrying a bag from the grocery store. "Can I help you girls?" she asked as she slid the bag into the mini-fridge.

"Our friends need three rainbow sparkle pedicures," Jenica said. "Otherwise, we won't win our soccer game. But Aly said you're booked. Like she always does."

Bethany leaned in and whispered to Mia, "Maybe we should just go to another salon today." Even though she whispered, Aly could tell that Mom heard; her eyes darted toward the front window and the COMING SOON! PRINCESS POLISH! sign across the street.

"Aly," Mom said, "can I talk to you, please?"

Aly followed her mother into the corner near the two spare manicure stations stored in the back room.

"I'm *not* agreeing to your salon," Mom said. "But would you do three more pedicures? Or see if Brooke can do one? I want to make sure everyone is happy with our salon today."

Aly grinned. It wasn't a guarantee, but it seemed like the first step in making their own kid salon a reality. "Okay, Mom," she said.

After leading Maxie and Joelle to the pedicure chairs and turning on the water, Aly pulled Brooke over near the mini-fridge for a chat.

"I've never done a real customer before," Brooke said, tugging on her braid. "I don't even do both of your hands! Just one! Are you sure I'm ready for this?"

Lisa, another manicurist, walked into the back room to grab a bottle of water and heard the girls' conversation.

"You're going to be great," Lisa said. "Just take your time and go slow. Aly can do two of the girls. You only have to do one."

Brooke nodded, but she didn't seem convinced.

"Okay," Aly said, walking back to the pedicure chairs, "so, um, after you're done splashing, I'm going to do Maxie's toes, and Brooke will do Joelle's. Then I'll do Giovanna's. Sound good?"

Brooke smiled, but she wrapped her hand around the bottom of her braid so she could tug it if she had to.

"You're sure your sister can do it?" Jenica asked,

folding her arms across her chest. "She's just a little kid."

"We're all kids," Brooke told Jenica. "And I bet I can polish a million times better than you."

Aly swallowed hard. She couldn't believe Brooke. One of the main rules in a salon is never to be mean to the customers! Brooke was going to ruin this!

But instead of getting mad, Jenica laughed. So did Joelle. "I like her," she said.

"Why, thank you," Brooke answered, and even curtsied. Then she ducked outside to get the sparkle polishes. Jenica, Bethany, and Mia followed her out the door.

All three pedicures proceeded pretty much problem-free. Brooke was concentrating so hard on her work that she didn't say a word, but she still had to redo the Orange You Pretty on Joelle's pointer toe twice because it kept dripping. Once all the girls' toes were dry, though, they left with huge smiles on their faces.

Right before they walked out the door, Giovanna said, "If we win tomorrow, we're coming back every week. And we're bringing the rest of the team too."

"Sounds good," Aly said, smiling her biggest smile. But a list of worries started in her brain: How would True Colors handle the whole sixth-grade soccer team every week for pedicures? Would there be enough open spots? Maybe customers would actually want to go to Princess Polish across the street. Aly and Brooke couldn't let that happen.

Aly reached into her back pocket and pulled out the list she'd made on the frog paper that morning. She folded it in half and wrote *For Mom and Dad* on the front. Then she opened the closet in the back room where Mom kept her purse and taped the note to Mom's house key. That way, she wouldn't miss it.

✳ ✳ ✳ ✳ ✳

Later that night Aly and Brooke were sitting on the floor of their bedroom in their pj's, rubbing cotton balls dipped in polish remover across their Go for the Gold nails.

"It's a shame we have to take it off," Aly said. "Mine's barely chipped."

"I know," Brooke said, fluttering her fingers. "Look how it sparkles. I think our family has too many rules. Other kids are allowed to wear nail polish to school. And our mom has a nail salon! I mean, if *anyone* should get to wear polish, it's us, right?"

"Right." Aly was listening to Brooke, but she was also thinking about rules. And the piece of paper taped to Mom's key chain. Dad was due home any minute from the airport and Aly was hoping he and Mom would read the list together.

"Let's pretend . . . ," Brooke said, dipping her cotton ball in more polish remover. "Let's pretend that we have our own salon. What would we name it?"

There was a knock on their bedroom door, and both girls looked up.

"Daddy!" Brooke was on her feet and racing toward Dad's legs.

Aly stood up too, waiting her turn for a hug. But before she could even get her chance with Dad, Mom walked in behind him and started talking.

"So we've made a decision, girls," she said, slipping her arm around Dad's waist.

Aly's stomach did a cartwheel.

"We know how much it means to you two, and we know how responsible and helpful you both have been at True Colors, so, after a long, long talk, we've decided . . . that you can have your own salon!"

Brooke started screeching and jumping around the room. "We can do it! We can do it!" she yelled.

Aly was stunned. She just stood there, smiling.

Everything she'd been wishing for was going to come true! Mom and Dad had said yes!

Brooke jumped over and threw her arms around her sister. Finally, Aly jumped with her. "We can do it!" Aly whispered. "I can't believe we can do it!"

"Don't get too excited yet," Mom said. "There are lots of rules."

But Aly didn't care if there were a thousand million rules. She and Brooke were going to get their own salon!

seven
Red-Hot Pepper

Monday mornings were always a mad rush in the Tanner house—Dad usually had to leave on a new trip, the girls had school, Mom had the salon, and they all had to be out of the house much earlier than they would have liked. Plus, they couldn't forget backpacks or school lunches or briefcases or pocketbooks.

This Monday was no exception. Usually, Dad drove the girls to school on Mondays himself, but today Mom hopped into the car too. Once they pulled out of the driveway, Mom turned around and handed Aly and Brooke each an envelope. "These are the rules I was talking about," she said. "And there are a lot of them."

Aly looked at the list.

<u>Rules for Aly and Brooke's Salon</u>
- Aly and Brooke may polish only kids' nails.
- Aly and Brooke may polish nails only three days a week: two school days and one weekend day.
- All homework must be done before their salon can open for business.
- Aly and Brooke may not charge clients. Instead, there will be a donation jar. After the cost of supplies is covered, the rest of the money will be donated to any charity of Aly and Brooke's choice.
- Aly and Brooke will be on probation for one week before the salon becomes official.

Probation? That was one of Aly's spelling bee words. But she couldn't remember the definition.

"What's that word?" Brooke whispered.

Aly shook her head. "Mom," she asked, "what do you mean by 'probation,' and why do we have to be on it?"

Mom twisted around to face the girls. "It means we're going to use this week as a test run."

Aly took a deep breath. A test! This would be hard. But they had to try it.

"Okay," Aly said. "We're okay with your list."

Brooke nodded her agreement.

"Then look at the bottom of the papers," Mom said.

Aly saw a blank line with *Alyssa Tanner* printed beneath it. Brooke's paper had the same line, but with *Brooke Tanner* underneath.

"Here's a pen. I need you to sign these papers, to prove that you understand the rules."

Aly had never signed anything official other than the electronic package machine for Arnold. She took a pen and signed her name in her neatest handwriting. Then she handed the pen to Brooke, who did the same, drawing a flower next to it.

"Okay, done," Brooke said. "We're signed. What do we do now?"

"Congratulations, girls," Dad said, glancing at them in the rearview mirror. "You are now salon operators! But first you have school. Time to go."

Aly and Brooke got out of the car and ran in different directions toward their classes.

Aly couldn't believe it. Her biggest dream had just come true. Even with all the rules.

"Hey, Nail Polish Aly!" someone called from the other side of the hallway.

Aly looked up. It was Jenica, with a group of soccer girls. Jenica had never spoken to Aly at school before. Was she really talking to her now?

"Me?" Aly asked, immediately feeling silly for saying it. Of course Jenica meant her. What other Alys were there in school who polished nails?

"We had a scrimmage yesterday after the forwards got their pedicures," Jenica said, "just to see if the sparkle pedicure really worked. And every single person who had your rainbow polish either scored a goal or blocked a goal. We think we need you and your sister to do the rest of the team before our game next weekend."

Aly could barely answer, she was so excited. Today, she and Brooke wouldn't be at True Colors, so she told Jenica to call the salon tomorrow afternoon and she would make the team appointments. Maybe the soccer team would be the first real customers for the kid salon!

The bell rang, and Aly headed into her classroom. The morning was pretty regular: Aly sat between

Garrett and Cameron, who were pretty cool for boys. And during art class she got to work on a scratchboard art project with her best school friend, Lily. Her other best school friend, Charlotte, and Charlotte's twin brother, Caleb, were doing their own scratchboard project at the other end of the table.

Everything was going smoothly . . . until lunch.

Aly was sitting between Lily and Charlotte, about to take a bite of her peanut butter sandwich when Brooke came running over. Third-grade recess was just ending, so Brooke had only a few minutes to talk.

"Guess what! Guess what!" she said, her braid flying behind her.

"Are you okay?" Aly asked automatically.

"*More* than okay!" Brooke said. "I booked us a ton of appointments and also a birthday party!"

"You booked us a *what*?" Aly choked out.

"It's for this first grader, Heather, who I sometimes

jump rope with. Her birthday's tomorrow, and she wasn't going to have a party on the actual day. Her parents are doing one for her over the weekend, but her babysitter told her yesterday that she could have an actual day party too! She didn't know what kind of party to have, so I told her about our salon, and she's going to have her party there. Tomorrow!"

Aly was speechless for a second. Then she said, "We have to check with Mom. We're on probation, remember? What if Mom doesn't want us to do a party yet? We didn't even decide if we were working tomorrow!"

"Well, she'll have to say yes. I already booked it," Brooke answered, like it wasn't a big deal.

Aly closed her eyes to focus her thoughts. "*Whose* party did you say we were doing?"

"Heather," Brooke said. "Heather Davis. I think her sister's in your grade."

All of a sudden, Aly felt kind of pukey. "You agreed to do Suzy Davis's sister's party?"

Maybe she said it a little louder than she meant to, because Brooke's eyes started filling up with tears. "I thought it was a good thing to book a birthday party! It's only a few girls. Why are you getting so upset?"

"No, it's fine, it's fine," Aly said, giving her sister a hug. "I just . . . um . . . I'm not really friends with Suzy. Not that it matters. But it's fine. We'll give Heather a great birthday party."

Aly gave Brooke another hug, and then Brooke ran off toward the third-grade hallway. Once she was gone, Aly laid her head down on the lunch table.

Lily moved her chair closer to Aly's. "Did I hear that right? Are you going to be polishing Heather Davis's nails for her birthday?"

"Yes," Aly said into the table.

"You don't think Suzy will be there, do you?" Lily asked. "And will want her nails polished too?"

"Yes and yes," Aly said, still muttering into her lunch. "I can't believe Brooke did this."

"It sounds like she was just trying to help," Charlotte said.

"I know." Aly finally lifted her head. "But this is the worst kind of helping possible. And I have a feeling my mom's going to be mad. *Really* mad. And we don't even have a real salon set up yet. It's just a back room, with a refrigerator and lots of boxes in it. What kind of party will that be?"

Lily offered Aly a chocolate chip cookie. Aly took it and crammed the whole thing into her mouth at once. But it would take more than a chocolate chip cookie to make this day better. And tomorrow? "I think I need another cookie, Lily," Aly said. "Or six."

eight

Silver Celebration

On Tuesday afternoon at four o'clock, Heather Davis and her partyers appeared.

Heather's babysitter sat down for her manicure with Lisa, and the three party girls started dancing around the salon, talking and laughing and coming dangerously close to knocking things over. As Aly had suspected, her mom was already not very happy that they'd agreed to host a birthday party without talking to her first.

"You have to keep them under control," Mom said

quietly to Aly. "I said you could have your own salon, but you have to remember that this is a business. My business. And your salon can't cause problems for my customers."

Aly gulped. "I promise, Mom. Brooke and I can handle it." Really, they had no other choice. Otherwise, their salon was doomed.

"Okay, birthday-party people," Aly said. "If you want your nails polished, follow Brooke through that door!"

The three girls started marching behind Brooke. After grabbing a handful of nail polish colors, Aly joined them in the back room. Brooke was in front of the pedicure basins, turning on the water.

"Who wants to choose a polish color?" Aly asked.

The girls came running.

Aly held out the colors she'd grabbed: Red-Hot

Pepper, Silver Celebration, Orange You Pretty, and Pinkie Swear.

"I want the red!" the girl with the headband said.

"No, *I* want red!" the other girl said.

"You can both have the same color," Aly told them.

"But *I* want red! Just me," Heather said, her voice starting to wobble. "And I'm the birthday girl."

Brooke walked over to Heather's two guests. "You know what I think would be perfect on you guys?" She picked up the sparkly silver bottle. "Silver Celebration. Look how glittery it is! And today's Heather's birthday celebration, so even the name is perfect. What do you think, Tali?" she asked the girl with the headband.

Tali examined it. "I like sparkles," she said.

"Jayden?" Brooke asked the other girl.

"I like sparkles too," Jayden said.

"Great!" Brooke said. "And, Heather, you can have Red-Hot Pepper."

Heather smiled. It was the kind of smile that changed her whole face. "Me first."

Aly let out a breath she didn't know she'd been holding. Maybe they could do this after all. "Actually, I think we can do all three of you together. Tali and Jayden will just have to share a chair."

Aly led the three girls to the chairs and told them to climb on. But she forgot to tell them to take off their shoes first, and Heather's flip-flop fell right into the water.

"Oh no!" Heather said, and promptly jumped off the chair *into* the water to get it. Now both of her flip-flops were wet! It was a good thing she was wearing shorts or her pants would've gotten soaked.

Aly helped Heather back into the chair and wrapped her flip-flops in towels so they'd dry faster.

If she and Brooke had their own toe dryers back here, she would've stuck them in there. But for now, towels were the best she could manage.

"So I'll do you," Aly told Heather, "and Brooke will do Tali."

"Who's going to do me?" Jayden asked.

"Both of us," Brooke told her.

Jayden seemed intrigued by that.

Aly kneeled down next to the pedicure basin to get to work, but it turned out that first graders are much squirmier than sixth graders.

"That tickles!" Heather squealed when Aly rubbed soap on her feet. But she didn't just say it, she also kicked water on Aly's shirt.

Brooke took a break from working on Tali to explain the bite-your-tongue-so-you-won't-feel-the-tickle trick, which made things a little better, but Heather was still pretty wiggly. Aly had to hold on to her feet super tightly to keep the polish in the right place.

"Hey, you got it on my skin!" Aly heard Tali say to Brooke as she wiggled in the chair.

Brooke cleaned off the polish and told her, "You've got to try to stay still, or that's going to keep happening."

"I can't help it!" Tali said. "It's hard to sit still."

"Is it my turn yet?" Jayden asked.

Aly looked around to find something for Jayden to do. Her eyes fell on the box of beads and the string that Mrs. Fornari had given Brooke.

She quickly opened the box of beads and handed it to Jayden. "While you're waiting to get your nails done, you get to make a bracelet. You can use any color beads you want," she said.

"Wait!" said Brooke. "I just had a better idea. *Everyone* can make bracelets. Ankle bracelets, actually, since they're bigger. That way, you'll have something to do in the chair to help you stop jiggling."

Brooke quickly cut three lengths of string and gave one to each girl, telling them to knot one end so the beads wouldn't slip off. The girls all starting beading. And they finally sat still! And Heather bit her tongue so she wasn't ticklish. This party was turning out okay after all.

Aly finished up Heather's Red-Hot Pepper toes just as Brooke finished up Tali's Silver Celebration pedi. "One foot each?" Brooke said, handing a second bottle of Silver Celebration to Aly.

"Great idea." Aly smiled.

Working as a team, the sisters finished Jayden's toes in no time. All three girls worked on their bracelets as their nails dried.

"So," Aly asked, "how do you like your toes?"

"Mine are beautiful," Jayden said, wiggling them and watching them sparkle.

"Mine too," Tali agreed, glancing down at her feet.

"I"—Heather sniffled—"I hate mine! Red-Hot Pepper is the worst color ever!" And she burst into tears.

Aly looked at Brooke in a panic. Brooke was looking panicked too.

"Um," Aly said. "Wait—we can redo it. Do you want Silver Celebration like your friends?"

Heather shook her head. "I want a sp-special birthday c-color."

"How about . . . Under Watermelon? Or Strawberry Sunday? Those are both really sparkly," Brooke said.

"Not red or pink," Heather said, wiping her eyes. "Something even more special."

"My favorite's Purple People Eater," Aly offered. "How about that one?"

"That's a scary name," Heather said. "I don't want one with a scary name."

Brooke's favorite was Pinkie Swear, which didn't

have a scary name but wouldn't work anyway, because Heather didn't want pink.

Brooke's eyes opened wide. "Hold on," she said.

She ran out into the main salon and came back with two bottles of Lemon Aid, bright yellow *and* super sparkly.

Heather stopped crying.

Since teamwork had worked so well with Jayden, Aly and Brooke did it again.

"What do you think *now?*" Brooke asked when they'd finished.

"I think they're beautiful!" Heather couldn't stop staring at her feet. "They're the brightest, sparkliest toes I've ever seen."

Brooke gathered up the cotton balls and nail polish bottles. "We did it," she whispered to Aly.

Aly opened the pedicure basin drains. "Nice job," she whispered back.

Then there was a knock at the door. "Okay, girls, party's over," Aly said, heading over to let in Heather's babysitter.

But when she opened the door, it was Suzy Davis.

"You have a silver splotch on your leg," Suzy said.

Aly looked down. Sure enough, there was silver nail polish there, in the shape of a very small banana.

"Oh," she said. "Thanks."

"I came to get my sister and her friends," Suzy said. "But before we go, I want a pedicure too."

Was Aly really going to have to polish Suzy's toes? Heather's birthday party had been hard enough. And now this?

"I'd like a rainbow," Suzy said. "With . . . with hearts painted on each toe. In opposite colors."

Opposite colors? What did that even mean?

"It's the first day of our salon," Brooke said from behind Aly. "We're closed now. This was just a test run. Our grand opening is set for another day. You can come back then."

Sometimes Aly had no idea where Brooke came up with this stuff.

"Who are you?" Suzy said.

"Aly's sister Brooke," Brooke answered. "Who are you?"

Aly looked over at Heather and her friends. They were still admiring their feet.

"I'm Heather's sister, and I want a rainbow pedicure. Aly's going to give me one."

"No," said Brooke, "she isn't. If you want a rainbow pedicure, please make an appointment in the main salon with one of those manicurists. I said we're closed." Her hands were on her hips now.

Brooke looked at Aly and gave her a Secret Sister Eye Message. Aly gave her one back: *Thank you, thank you, thank you.*

"What if I tell your mom that you won't give me a pedicure?" Suzy's hands were on her hips now too.

"This is our salon," Aly said, finally finding her voice and stepping forward. "You can try telling our mom that, but it won't make a difference. We have our own rules here."

Suzy looked hard at Aly. She looked at Brooke. And back at Aly.

Then she looked around the back room. "Everyone at school was saying how great this place is. But it's kind of gross. I'm going to tell everyone it's a dump. And that they should go to the place across the street when it opens. This place is fine for first graders, but no one else would ever step foot in here." Suzy walked over to her sister and her sister's two friends. "Come on, let's go," she said.

Next thing Aly knew, Suzy, Heather, and the

rest of the girls were leaving the back room. As they walked out, Aly heard them talking.

"This was the coolest birthday party ever!" Tali said to Jayden. "I want it for my birthday. It's February first. Can you come?"

Aly smiled. Well, at least Tali had had a good time.

And then she heard Suzy say to Heather. "Hey, your toes look pretty. Nice color."

Well, that was interesting. Aly hadn't expected Suzy to say anything nice about the salon.

But then Aly remembered the other things Suzy had said. And as she looked around the back room, Aly realized Suzy was right. It *was* a bit of a dump, filled with boxes and water bottles and mismatched everything. If this place was going to be a hit, they'd need to do some redecorating. Otherwise, like Suzy said, their only customers would be first graders.

nine

Teal Me the Truth

Since Dad was back on the road, dinner was going to be just the girls. But Aly wasn't interested in food at all.

Besides worrying about how Mom was going to react to the unofficial first day of the salon before the grand opening, Aly also couldn't stop thinking about what Suzy had said. The back room really did look more like a huge storage closet than someplace special.

If they couldn't make it look really cool and

inviting, they wouldn't get any customers—well, except for maybe the sixth-grade soccer team. But they'd need more clients than that to make the salon real.

By the time they'd gotten home from True Colors, it was later than usual for a school night. So Mom made "breakfast for dinner." It was super fast to make—eggs, toast, tiny sausages, and sliced-up orange smiles. Aly and Brooke sat down at their usual spots at the kitchen table, next to each other. Aly pressed her left leg against Brooke's right one. For courage.

"Okay, girls," Mom said when she sat down.

Aly braced herself for trouble. Instead, Mom gave them a few more rules that were actually helpful: All appointments made at school had to be written down and then run by Mom before they were confirmed. No more parties until they got the salon up and running smoothly. And they couldn't forget about the charity donations. (Heather and her friends had not donated. But that might have been because Aly and Brooke had forgotten to ask them to donate.)

With their stomachs full of breakfast for dinner, Brooke and Aly went up to their room.

"Okay, so what can we do to make our salon look better?" Brooke asked. "I don't want our grand opening to wind up as our grand closing."

Other than the two teal pedicure chairs and the two blue manicure stations, everything in the back room was pretty much the same shade of Chocolate Brownies, which, even though it had a tasty-sounding name, was the girls' least favorite polish color ever.

"Let me get some paper," Aly said. "I think we're going to need a list."

The girls brainstormed:

- Curtains
- Paintings/pictures for the walls
- Cushions for the manicure and pedicure
  chairs
- Rugs
- Special floor pillows for when people
  make bracelets in the drying area
- A beautiful, fancy donation jar
- Signs that tell people about the donations
- A shelf to display nail polishes
- A sign for the door

Brooke looked at the list. "We're missing one thing," she said. "A name! Our salon needs a name!"

Brooke was right.

"Any ideas?" Aly asked.

Brooke shrugged. "Maybe . . . Twinkle Toes?"

Aly made a face. "We do manicures, too."

Brooke tucked one braid behind her ear. "I'll keep thinking."

The girls went downstairs to show Mom the list. She agreed to everything except the curtains and the rugs. And she offered to let the girls go on a treasure hunt in the attic for cushions and pillows and shelves.

Aly and Brooke hadn't been in the attic for ages. All they remembered was that it was kind of dark. And that whenever Mom or Dad wanted to store something there, they would usually just pull down the ladder and throw stuff up on the landing.

Aly grabbed Brooke's hand as Mom pulled the creaky ladder down from the ceiling. A duffel bag came tumbling out and landed on Mom's head.

Mom dropped it on the floor next to her. "Take that as a warning," she said. "It's going to be pretty messy."

Mom climbed up slowly until her head disappeared

from view. "Can one of you girls flick on the light?"

Brooke was right next to the light switch and turned it on. The attic looked like it was glowing.

"Come on up, girls!" Mom shouted down.

With the hand that wasn't holding Brooke's, Aly grabbed the railing tightly. The ladder creaked with each step.

Aly imagined finding mountains of colorful pillows and cushions and shiny new shelves. It was okay if the attic was a mess as long as it was filled with treasures.

But when she got to the top of the ladder, Aly was shocked. There wasn't anything new and shiny about the attic. Just dust and piles of junk all over the place.

From right behind her, Brooke whispered, "We'll never find anything cool up here."

But then Mom laughed. "Look at this!" she said. She had lifted a dusty flowered bedsheet off a table and picked up an old cookie jar shaped like a strawberry.

"That's perfect for the donation jar," Brooke said, getting excited.

"Where did you even get that, Mom?" Aly asked, taking a few steps closer to the craziest-looking cookie jar she'd ever seen. The strawberry was enormous enough for the giant in "Jack and the Beanstalk," and it was painted a sparkly teal.

Mom flipped the jar over. "See these initials?" she said, showing the girls the *KB* at the bottom of the jar. "They're mine. Karen Benson. I made it in art school. I remember this color—it was called Teal Me the Truth. I used it because I loved the name so much."

"*You* went to art school?" Brooke said. Her eyes were huge. "How come you never told us?"

Mom's cheeks turned pink. She hugged the sparkly

strawberry to her stomach. "I never finished."

She never finished? Aly couldn't believe it. Her mom *always* finished what she started. It made Aly think something bad had happened back then. "Why not?" she asked softly.

"There wasn't enough money. I needed to get a job and couldn't concentrate on my classes after that. So I left."

Wow. That was too bad. And sad. And maybe it was part of the reason why Mom was so serious about the girls paying attention to school and not working when they were kids.

"*I* want to go to art school," Brooke said. "And make strawberries like this."

"Maybe you can," Mom said, putting the cookie jar down in a safe corner of the attic. "But that's a long way away. Let's keep hunting. What else do you girls need?"

"Floor pillows," Aly said, remembering the list in her head. "And cushions. Oh, and paintings for the walls, too." As they started looking around some more, Aly realized that the attic wasn't as much of a mess as it first appeared. She got into the treasure-hunting spirit with Brooke, peeking underneath sheets and inside boxes.

After about twenty minutes, Aly, Brooke, and Mom had found four striped floor pillows, one set of shelves, two polka-dot seat cushions, and four paintings Mom had made in art school—two of the sun, one of the moon, and one of a rainbow.

"Mom, these are beautiful," Aly said. "Can we hang them in our salon?"

"They're one hundred percent perfect, Mom! Please?" Brooke pleaded.

Mom nodded. "Of course," she said, blushing. "I'm glad you like them."

"Maybe you should paint some more," Aly suggested. "It doesn't matter that you're not in art school."

Mom shrugged. "I don't know about that," she said. "I'm busy enough as it is."

Aly made a note in her brain that maybe she and Brooke should get Mom some paint and art canvases for her birthday.

As the Tanner women continued their hunt. Brooke kept coming up with salon names. Nonstop, as usual. Aly found some of Mom's old art supplies— some heavy sketch paper and pastels. They weren't in great shape anymore, but they'd do perfectly well for making signs.

"One more name," Brooke said. "How about the Glitter Girls' Salon?"

Even Mom wrinkled her nose at that one.

But everything else seemed like it was falling into

place. And Mom and the girls agreed that the grand opening would be this Saturday.

School moved slower than a baby snail on Wednesday, Thursday, and Friday. Even dodgeball, Aly's favorite gym game, seemed to take forever. And Brooke said that recess felt like it lasted a million hours.

But kids did keep coming up to Aly and Brooke, asking all about their salon and when it would be open for business.

Every afternoon for those three days, Brooke met Aly at 3:00 on the dot. They hurried over to True Colors, finished their homework, and then worked on the salon redecoration.

On Wednesday they hung Mom's four pictures on the walls—with some help from Joan and Carla. And they found ways to hide all the boxes of supplies as best they could, piled under tables and stacked in out-of-the-way corners of the room.

On Thursday they set up a drying area near the couch, with magazines stored in a crate they'd found and pillows and a table for a jewelry-making station. Then they created a polish display with the shelves from the attic.

On Friday they made a bunch of signs and taped them in all the right spots around them. Well, all the signs except for the one with the salon's name on it. They still hadn't settled on that. So while they worked, Brooke kept making suggestions, like Project Polish and Pretty Nails and Finger Fun. Also, Mermaid Manicures and Rainbow Polish and Tip-Top Nails. And Perfect Ten and Polish Palace and Happy Feet. Nothing seemed quite right, though.

As a finishing touch, they put the sparkly cookie jar on its own special table right next to the nail polish display. That way, no one would miss it.

"I can't believe how great this place looks," Brooke told Aly on Friday at closing time, as they stood in the doorframe admiring their work. "Now all we need to do is figure out a name!"

"And get some customers," Aly added.

And hope that know-it-all Suzy Davis wasn't right again.

ten

Power to the Sparkle

S hould we put out all the colors for the rainbow pedi-cures?" Brooke asked. She was pulling on her braid so hard that Aly wondered how it wasn't hurting her.

"Sure," Aly said. "Let's put out two sets."

It was Saturday morning, the day of their grand opening. Aly was nervous too—she kept checking her polka-dot watch over and over. Jenica's entire soccer team was supposed to be coming in three minutes so they could all get rainbow pedicures before their afternoon game.

"Do you think the jewelry station looks okay?" Brooke asked. She'd spent the last fifteen minutes moving things around, changing the angle of the table and which pillow went where.

"I think it looks fine," Aly told her, checking her watch again. One minute. She went through the salon's preparation list in her head one last time. Everything was all set and ready to go. Well, except for the name. Brooke had been mad when Aly rejected Glimmering Good Salon and Magical Manicures earlier that morning, but Mom said that they shouldn't rush it, that the perfect name would come to them in time. Aly really hoped it would come soon.

She was looking at her watch when there was a knock on the door. Aly opened it. Nine girls stood in front of her, with Jenica at the front of the pack.

"Welcome," Aly tried to say, but it came out more like a swallow. She tried again. "Welcome to our salon." Then she stepped aside to let everyone walk in.

"Looks nice in here," Jenica said. "Much better than last time."

"Totally better," said Bethany.

Brooke still had her hand wrapped tightly around her hair, but she wasn't too nervous to talk. "This is the jewelry-making station," she said. "While you're waiting for your pedicure or for your polish to dry, you can make an ankle bracelet."

"We can't wear those," one of the girls said. "Because of our soccer socks. And shin guards."

"We can wear jewelry on our wrists, though," Jenica said, rolling her eyes. "We'll just make regular bracelets. It'll be great."

"That's right. You can make regular bracelets there too," Brooke said, smiling a tiny bit.

Aly took a deep breath. It was time to take charge. "Okay," she said, "let's get started."

Aly put the girls in groups of two, giving everyone instructions.

"Anjuli can go alone," Jenica said, pointing to a girl with a French braid longer than Brooke's. "She's our goalie, so she needs to get her fingernails painted too."

"In a rainbow?" Aly asked. It wasn't a problem— she'd be happy to paint Anjuli's fingers, she just needed to know the plan.

"I think maybe I want something different for my fingers," Anjuli said.

Brooke was standing in front of the polish display. "Why don't you come over here and pick your favorite color?" she said to Anjuli. "Aly and I can paint any color you want."

Anjuli walked over and started examining the display, but then she pointed to the strawberry donation jar.

"What's this?" she asked.

"That's our donation jar," Aly said. "Since no one has to pay in our salon, we're asking for donations instead. Whatever you decide to give, we'll donate to a charity once we have"—Aly did some fast thinking—"one hundred dollars. Every time we get to one hundred, we'll give it to a different charity."

"That's really cool," Bethany said.

The other girls nodded and unzipped their backpacks, looking for dollar bills and coins.

"Okay," Jenica said, "let's get going. We have a game to play this afternoon. We don't want to be here all day."

But even as she said it, she was smiling at Aly. Like she probably wouldn't mind if they were.

Jenica sat down on the couch and picked up a string and some beads. The other girls followed her to the waiting area, except for Maxie and Joelle, who were going first. The two forwards sat down in the pedicure chairs, and Aly and Brooke got started.

"Did you know Cute Lucas has a crush on Maria?" Joelle asked Maxie.

"No way!" Maxie answered. "Is he going to ask her to the Halloween dance?"

"Why do you call him Cute Lucas?" Brooke asked.

"Because Maxie thinks he's really handsome," Joelle answered.

"I do not!" Maxie said. "Okay, fine, I do. But you do, too!"

Maxie and Joelle started laughing. So did Aly and Brooke.

The first two pedicures went pretty smoothly, though there were a few times when Brooke needed to use the wooden stick with polish remover on it.

When Joelle and Maxie moved over to the drying area, Bethany and a girl whose name Aly didn't know took their places in the chairs.

"Hi, I'm Aly," Aly said while she was filling the basin with fresh water.

"I'm Valentina," the girl answered.

Valentina, it turned out, was ticklish and needed to hear about the tongue trick.

"You really want me to bite my tongue?" she asked.

"Not hard," Aly told her.

"It works!" Jenica piped in.

Valentina bit her tongue, and everything went well from there.

As the other girls got polished, Aly and Brooke listened to them chat about their strategy for the soccer game, their Halloween dance costumes, and which teachers gave the hardest sixth-grade math tests. The girls seemed really comfortable, and Aly and Brooke started feeling comfortable too, just like they did when they were hanging out in Mom's salon.

Brooke had just done the first coat of rainbow

polish on Giovanna and was getting ready for round two when Giovanna looked down at her. "I love how this looks," she said. "Maybe I'll keep coming even after soccer season."

Brooke looked up. "I didn't even know soccer girls liked sparkles until Jenica came to the salon."

"Just because we're good athletes doesn't mean we don't like sparkles," Giovanna said.

"Exactly," said Jenica.

"Definitely," said Mia, who was in Aly's chair now. "Girls can be smart, strong, *and* sparkly."

Aly liked that idea. Smart. And strong. And sparkly. She made a brain note to work on that.

After Giovanna and Mia were done, it was finally Anjuli's turn.

"I can do hands while you do feet," Brooke said to Aly.

"Fine," Aly said.

"Which color did you pick for your manicure?" Brooke asked Anjuli.

"Power to the Sparkle," she said, handing over a bottle.

"The multicolor glitter is really cool," Aly commented from where she was crouched, painting Anjuli's big toe.

"So," Anjuli said, "are you guys going to do this for us each week, for luck?"

Aly stopped polishing. "Well, as long as you guys want to keep coming, sure."

"As long as we keep winning, we keep coming!" Jenica said from the couch.

"Totally!" Bethany said.

"Power to the Sparkle!" Anjuli shouted.

"Power to the Sparkle!" Mia repeated.

Then they all started chanting, "Power to the Sparkle! Power to the Sparkle!"

Aly looked at Brooke and smiled. Brooke was grinning too. They didn't need any Secret Sister Eye Messages to know that their salon was off to a spectacular start.

That night the girls sat in their bedroom, counting the money from the donation jar.

"Seven dollars and thirty-one—no, thirty-two—cents," Aly announced.

After the soccer team had left, Lily and Charlotte showed up for manicures *and* pedicures, and then Brooke's friend Sophie and a few other third graders had come in for just pedicures. And then a couple of people who saw the sign in the True Colors window for the grand opening of a kids' salon.

"Do you think we'll have regulars now?" Brooke asked, tucking the donation money into a glittery zippered pencil case.

"Well, the soccer team probably," Aly said. "Jenica invited us to watch them play sometime." She slid the elastic off Brooke's braid.

"Ooh, that would be fun," Brooke said, scooting closer so Aly could brush her hair out. "I hope they won today."

"They're really good. I bet they did," Aly said, reaching for the hairbrush that was on her bed. "But really, I bet they could win without our sparkles."

"Maybe 'sparkle' should be in the name of our salon," Brooke said, squirming. "Ouch, Aly. I think I have a knot over there."

"Sorry," Aly said, putting the brush down and working on the knot with her fingers.

"How about Power to the Sparkle?" Brooke suggested.

"That sounds like a nail polish color," Aly said, "not like a salon."

"The Sparkle Sisters' Salon?" Brooke asked. Then she shook her head a little, but not enough to mess up Aly's unknotting. "That's not right either."

"How about . . . how about . . . Sparkle Spa."

Sparkle Spa. Sparkle Spa. Actually, it sounded perfect. Just like she'd done by choosing Lemon Aid for Heather's nails and suggesting two-person polishing during busy times, Brooke had the right idea at the right time.

"I love it!" Aly said.

Brooke twisted around and gave Aly a huge hug. The grand opening had been a grand success. And with a name like Sparkle Spa, Aly hoped things would only get better.

The Tanner sisters were smart. And strong. And sparkly. And their spa was too.

How to Give Yourself (or a Friend!) a Rainbow Pedicure

By Aly (and Brooke!)

* . * * . . * . . * . . * . * *

What you need:

Paper towels   Orange polish

Polish remover   Yellow polish

Cotton balls   Purple polish

Clear polish   Pink polish

Red polish

What you do:

1. Put some paper towels on the floor so you don't have to worry about spilling polish. (Once, Aly spilled while she was painting my toes, and Mom got so, so mad and we still have a purple splotch on our carpet!)

2. Take one cotton ball and put some polish remover on it. If you have polish on your toes already, use enough to get it off. If you don't, just rub the remover over your nails to get off any dirt that might be on there. (Even if you can't see it very well, there still might be dirt!)

3. Rip off two paper towels. Twist the first one into a long tube and weave it back and forth between your toes to separate them a little bit more. Then do the same thing with the second paper towel for your other foot. You might need to tuck it in around your pinkie toe if it pops up and gets in your way while you polish.

4. Open up your clear polish and do a coat of clear on each nail. Then close the clear bottle up tight. (Aly usually starts with my big toes and works her way to my pinkies. You might want to do that too.)

5. Open up the red polish. Do a coat on each big toe. (When you're finished with each color, be sure to close the bottle up tight.) Open up the orange polish. Do a coat on each pointer toe. Open up the yellow polish. Do a coat on each middle toe. Open up the purple polish. Do a coat on each ring toe. Open up the pink polish. Do a coat on each pinkie toe.

6. Fan your toes a little to dry them a tiny bit, and then repeat step five. (This is when your colors start to look very bright—and sparkly if you have sparkle polish!)

7. Fan your toes a little again, and then open your clear polish. Do a top coat of clear polish on all your toes. Be sure to close the bottle up tight. (You can go in the same order you did last time!)

8. Now your toes have to dry. You can fan them for a long time, or sit and make a bracelet or read a book or watch TV or talk to your friend. Usually it takes about twenty minutes, but it could take longer. (After twenty minutes, you should check the polish really carefully by touching your big toe super lightly with your thumb. If it still feels sticky, keep waiting so you don't have to redo any nails!)

And now you should have a beautiful pedicure! Even after the polish is dry, you probably shouldn't wear socks and sneaker-type shoes for a while. Bare feet or sandals are better so all your hard work doesn't get smooshed. (And besides, then you can show people how fancy your toes look!)

Happy polishing!

✳ ⋅ ⋆ ✳ ⋅ ⋆ ✳ ⋅ ⋆ ✳ ⋅ ⋆ ✳ ⋅ ⋆ ✳

Purple Nails
and Puppy Tails

✳ ✳ ✳ ✳ ✳ ✳

For the real Mrs. Franklin—my Gram—

who is strong and sparkly, inside and out.

Special thanks to my glitter-tastic editor, Karen Nagel,

as well as to my super-shimmery writer friends

Marianna Baer, Betsy Bird, and Eliot Schrefer.

one

Shake It Up Silver

Aly Tanner leaned forward with the Shake It Up Silver brush in her hand. She was about to put the second coat of nail polish on her friend Charlotte Cane's pinkie.

"What do you think?" she asked. "Should Shake It Up Silver be our Color of the Week?"

It was a new idea Aly had—picking a Color of the Week so that everyone who came to the Sparkle Spa would get to know all the nail polish choices one by one.

"I like it," Charlotte said. "Nice and sparkly. My fingers look like little fairy wands."

Aly's younger sister, Brooke, put down the nail file she was using for her best friend Sophie Chu's pedicure. "I need to take a break, Sophie," she said. "Just for a second. This is Very Important Polish Business." Brooke walked over to look at Charlotte's nails.

"Oooh, it's so shiny! I love it, Aly," Brooke said. "Maybe we'll get to paint everyone's nails with silver glitter."

"Silver glitter? Let me see," Jenica Posner called from the sitting area. Jenica was the captain of the Auden Elementary girls' soccer team. She already had a special rainbow sparkle soccer team pedicure, which Aly had done three days ago.

Aly topped Charlotte's nails with clear polish to seal in the sparkles and sent her over to the waiting area to dry—and to show Jenica the color.

"Can you give me a quick manicure too, Aly?" Jenica asked after seeing Charlotte's nails. "Before my nana's done out there?"

Aly smiled to herself. She couldn't believe that Jenica Posner, the most popular sixth grader in their school, was begging *her* for a manicure.

Just a few weeks ago Aly and Brooke had given Jenica a rainbow sparkle pedicure, which was how the Sparkle Spa began in the first place. In her next soccer game Jenica scored five goals, and then the rest of the team wanted matching pedicures for good luck. It was pretty unbelievable, but ever since they started getting rainbow pedicures, the team hadn't lost one game. Now Jenica liked to visit and would stop in whenever her grandmother came to True Colors to get her nails done.

The Sparkle Spa was really just a back room of Aly

and Brooke's mom's nail salon. The sisters had opened it and decorated it with paintings and rainbow-colored pillows to sit on. There were some old pedicure chairs and manicure stations for them to use. And the best part was that their mom let them polish kids' nails there three days a week—two days after school and one day on the weekend.

Aly opened the door and looked into the True Colors salon, where all the grown-ups were having their nails done. It was Friday afternoon, *always* a busy time.

Joan—Aly and Brooke's favorite True Colors manicurist—was taking polish off Jenica's nana's nails. Aly figured she could do a manicure almost as fast as Joan could, so the timing might work out perfectly. She waved to Mrs. Franklin, a True Colors regular who had a tiny dog named Sadie that she sometimes brought to the salon with her. Sadie was sitting on Mrs. Franklin's lap, so Aly waved to her, too. Then she slipped back into the Sparkle Spa.

"Sure," Aly told Jenica. "I can do it."

As Aly started on Jenica and Brooke finished up Sophie, Lily Myers walked in the door. Lily was Aly's best school friend, along with Charlotte.

"Hey, guys," Lily said as she climbed into the second pedicure chair, next to Sophie. "Can someone do my toes?"

Brooke looked at Aly with a Secret Sister Eye Message that involved scrunched-up eyebrows. It meant: *Our friends need to start making appointments!* But she leaned over anyway and turned on the water in a pedicure basin for Lily.

"I'm almost done with Sophie. Then it's your turn," Brooke said. "Did you pick a color? If not, I think you might like Shake It Up Silver. It's on Charlotte's nails if you want to see. It's our Color of the Week."

It seemed like Brooke never stopped chattering. She could paint nails and talk, run water and talk, chew gum and talk—Aly was surprised she didn't talk in her sleep.

"Color of the Week?" Lily popped out of the pedicure chair to check out Charlotte's nails. But before she could take even one step, a barking and yapping ball of fur came racing through the door and ran right into Lily's legs.

Lily jumped up and toppled into the almost-full pedicure basin. The water splashed all over Brooke. And the yapping ball of fur—which was actually Mrs. Franklin's dog, Sadie—kept barking and running around the Sparkle Spa.

Jenica hopped up from the manicure chair to chase Sadie, waving her wet Shake It Up Silver nails. "Stop! Sit! Stay! Down! Heel!" she yelled.

"Help!" Lily shouted. She was stuck, sitting in the

pedicure basin, her knees folded up to her chest.

But Sadie wasn't paying attention to either girl. She darted by Aly's feet. Aly dove after her, but the dog got away. Then Sadie headed to the jewelry area and—bam!—knocked over an open box of beads.

"Don't let her eat those!" Jenica said, still running after Sadie.

Charlotte tried to grab Sadie with her elbows so she wouldn't mess up her manicure, but Sadie was faster and raced toward the table with the Sparkle Spa donation jar on it.

Brooke wiped her wet glasses on a dry part of her shirt and scooted across the room, catching the big teal, strawberry-shaped jar just before it fell.

"Help!" Lily yelled again. "I'm stuck!"

Sophie swung her legs back and forth, yelling, "Get her! Get her!"

Aly cornered Sadie between the mini-fridge and a stack of nail polish boxes, bent down, and swooped the panting dog into her arms.

Sadie squirmed and squiggled, but Aly wouldn't let her go. She tried to calm the dog by stroking her head, but Sadie just yapped and yipped and started whimpering.

Mrs. Franklin burst into the Sparkle Spa, with Jamie, the manicurist who usually did Mrs. Franklin's nails, behind her.

"Oh no," Mrs. Franklin said. "Oh dear."

Aly looked around. The place was a mess!

Pedicure water was everywhere. Bottles of Key Lime Pie, Reddy or Not, and Go for the Gold were all over the floor. Lily was still stuck in the pedicure basin, and multicolored beads were rolling across the carpet from the jewelry-making area.

"I don't know what got into her," Mrs. Franklin said, hurrying over to Aly to take the shaking Sadie from her. "A truck horn blared on Main Street, and she took off like a shot."

While Mrs. Franklin soothed Sadie, Jamie pulled Lily out of the pedicure basin. Brooke handed her a few washcloths from a pile she had grabbed to help dry her off.

"I think I need some new clothes," Lily said, trying to blot her shorts dry.

"I have an extra pair of soccer shorts in my duffel," Jenica volunteered, and went over to the couch to get her bag.

"Sadie girl," Mrs. Franklin said, shaking her head at the dog. "Just look at you! What are we going to do now?"

"She'll dry pretty soon," Brooke said. "Or do you

want some washcloths? They're kind of small, but they're probably about the right size for Sadie."

Mrs. Franklin shook her head again. "It's not that," she said. "Sadie was just groomed this morning. She has a dog-modeling job tomorrow at three o'clock. She's the new spokes-dog for the shelter on Taft Street, Paws for Love. They're planning to photograph her for a poster to promote pet adoption. And she's a mess! I'm even going to have to clean her toenails."

Sadie was finally quiet, happy to be in Mrs. Franklin's arms. It was funny how they kind of looked alike. They both had fluffy hair that was mostly white, and Sadie's red collar matched the red sweater Mrs. Franklin had draped over her shoulders.

"Hey, that's the shelter I volunteer at," Jenica said, still rifling through her duffel bag for shorts. "I didn't realize Sadie was the dog that was going to be on the Adoption Day posters."

"Mrs. Franklin? Are dog toenails like people toenails?" Brooke asked. She dropped the wet towels she was holding into the basin and walked over to inspect Sadie. Aly followed her. She'd never really looked closely at a dog's toenails before either.

Mrs. Franklin held up Sadie's paw. "Here they are," she said. "Different from ours."

Brooke took Sadie's paw in her hand. And then she looked at Aly. She was wearing a face that said: *I have an idea!*

"Do you think . . . ," Brooke began. "Do you think we could give Sadie a pedicure tomorrow?" Then she started laughing. "Not a pedicure . . . a pet-icure! Get it?"

Aly got it, and she giggled for a second too. But

then she stopped. She wasn't sure this was the best idea Brooke had ever had. Brooke had lots of ideas all the time. Some were really good, like the name Sparkle Spa. But a puppy pedicure? That sounded like trouble.

two

Purple Paws

Aly bit her lip. She looked at the mess around her. "I, um, I think we have to talk this over, Brooke," she said. "We've never even done a pet-icure."

From her perch on the pedicure chair, Sophie said, "I'll help!"

"Me too!" said Charlotte.

"And me," said Lily, who was behind a closet door, changing into Jenica's shorts.

"I wish I could," Jenica said. "But we have a soccer game."

Aly knew they would have to check with Mom first, but she figured that five of them would hopefully be enough to handle Sadie.

Mrs. Franklin smiled. "Thank you, girls. I'm—or rather, Sadie is—willing to give it a try. Why don't you ask your mother and let me know. Here's my phone number," said Mrs. Franklin, handing them a business card with Sadie's picture on it. "Now say good-bye, Sadie."

Sadie wagged her tail and yipped twice.

Mrs. Franklin, Sadie, and Jamie returned to True Colors. "Would you still like your manicure?" Jamie asked as they walked out the door.

Mrs. Franklin looked down at her nails and sighed. "I think I'll reschedule for early next week and come *without* Sadie."

Aly thought that was a very good idea. Maybe there should be a rule about no pets in the salon. In fact, Aly was surprised her mother hadn't come up with that rule already, since Mom was kind of the queen of rules—there was even a No Dogs Allowed rule in their house. Would she make a rule about pet-icures?

Aly woke up Saturday morning with a knot in her stomach. She couldn't believe Mom had actually said yes to Sadie's pet-icure, that "one little dog, one time, would be fine."

Brooke, still asleep, rolled over in her bed across the room. She squeezed her stuffed monkey, George.

Aly loved Brooke—more than anyone else on the planet, really—but lately it seemed like Brooke was coming up with one crazy plan after another, and then it was Aly's job to make sure that they didn't turn into total disasters.

There was Heather Davis's birthday party, which

Brooke agreed to before the Sparkle Spa was even open for business. And then there was last week's fiasco, when Brooke added Red-Hot Pepper polish to the hand lotion so it would turn pink. The problem was that it also turned people's hands pink. And their arms. And feet, too. It took a lot of polish remover to get their skin back to normal.

The best way Aly knew to try to avoid disasters was to prepare herself as much as possible. So she got up super quietly from her bed and tiptoed over to her desk. She pulled out a piece of paper and a sparkly gel pen—her favorite kind—and started a list:

Perfect Pet-icure Rules
1. No running in Sparkle Spa (people or dogs)
2. No fur polishing (people)
3. No biting (dogs)
4. No chewing chairs, pillows, flip-flops (dogs)

Aly chewed on the cap of the pen. Writing the list had made her a little less worried. As long as she had a plan, she was pretty sure she could handle anything. Even polishing a puppy's nails.

A few hours later Aly and Brooke were in True Colors with their mom. Luckily, they didn't have any appointments at the Sparkle Spa until eleven o'clock, so they'd told Mrs. Franklin to bring Sadie early.

"Girls," Mom said, "please be extra, extra careful today. I don't want either of you to get hurt, and I don't want the back room destroyed."

"We will," Brooke said. "We promise. We'll be the carefullest we've ever been."

Aly nodded. "Charlotte, Lily, and Sophie are coming to help. Plus Mrs. Franklin. Sadie won't be able to run around. We'll make sure she behaves."

The front door jangled, and in walked Miss Lulu,

one of the salon regulars. Every Saturday at 9:30 on the dot, she got a pedicure. But for the past two weeks she'd been away on her honeymoon.

"You're back!" Brooke screeched. "Do you have pictures? What color dresses did the flower girls wear? How was Maine? Did you see a moose?" Brooke ran over to Miss Lulu and hugged her.

Mom took her seat at pedicure station number one, tucking a strand of hair behind her ear. "Slow down, Brooke," she said with a laugh. "I have to do Lulu's toes. You can visit with her while she's drying."

Brooke gave Miss Lulu a final hug and then headed to the Sparkle Spa with Aly. As they opened the door, Mom called, "Remember what I said. I don't want any surprises next time I come back there!"

✳ ✳ ✳ ✳ ✳

But from the minute Mrs. Franklin and Sadie showed up, it was one surprise after another.

First, Mrs. Franklin was late. She came rushing into the spa with Sadie, a little bit out of breath. Sadie had purple bows clipped on top of her ears with rhinestones in the center of each bow. She was also brushed and washed and much fluffier than she'd looked yesterday.

"She's sooo cute!" Sophie said, running over to pet her.

"Do you think I can get bows like that for Minerva?" Charlotte asked. Minerva was Charlotte's poodle and was also the cuddliest dog Aly had ever met. She loved going to Charlotte's house so she could squeeze in as many puppy cuddles as possible.

Back in first grade, when she first started playing with Charlotte and Minerva, Aly asked if the

Tanners could get a dog, but Mom and Dad had said no. That was when the No Dogs Allowed rule was established, and it had been a rule at the Tanner house ever since.

The second surprise was that a man with a camera rushed into the salon after Mrs. Franklin.

"Great news, girls!" Mrs. Franklin said. "Isaac's the photographer who's doing Sadie's photo shoot later. He wanted to take pictures of her getting ready so that Paws for Love can post an Internet feature. Isn't that wonderful?"

Aly started to panic. Wait a minute. This wasn't part of the plan! *They* were going to be in a photo shoot too? Aly checked to make sure she didn't have any nail polish on her clothes. Brooke straightened her glasses. And Charlotte said, "I'm so glad I had my nails done yesterday!"

Aly looked at her own fingers. No polish. She kind

of wished she had time to do her own nails before the photo shoot like she and Brooke did on Saturdays. Or that she was wearing a different shirt—her favorite one with the purple and green stripes.

Finally, Mrs. Franklin handed Aly two tubes filled with Purple Paws puppy polish. It wasn't what Aly expected—the polish wasn't in a bottle like people polish—it looked more like a marker, the kind Aly drew with in art.

Aly uncapped one tube and tried it on her own left thumb just to check it out. It dried in about two seconds.

"You should need only one coat for Sadie's nails," Mrs. Franklin said. "Or at least that's what Nina at the pet store told me." Mrs. Franklin handed Sadie to Brooke, who took her to the area they had set up for the pet-icure. Aly followed. She figured they could trust Miss Nina and her polish information because she was a True Colors regular too.

Sophie sat down, and Brooke put Sadie in her lap.

Charlotte held on tight to her leash.

Lily stood nearby with a just-in-case doggie treat.

Isaac took what seemed like a gazillion photographs.

And Sadie was happy as could be, soaking up all the attention.

Aly pushed the fur out of her way so she could see Sadie's nails better. They were skinny and black and kind of long. The purple color was bright and sparkly, and Miss Nina was definitely right: no second coat needed. It was actually almost easier than doing a pedicure on some people Aly knew—especially ticklish ones.

"This is usually what Sadie's like," Mrs. Franklin said. "It's why the shelter chose her for the Adoption Day campaign."

"What is that about, anyway?" Brooke asked. While she was waiting for her turn to polish Sadie's back nails, Brooke was busy making a string of beads—purple, silver, and pink—to wrap around Sadie's collar.

"The shelter is trying to get the ten dogs that have been there the longest adopted," Mrs. Franklin explained. "And they think that with an adorable spokes-dog like Sadie, people will come running to the shelter. These puppies really need homes, girls. If you met the dogs, you'd understand."

Aly finished Sadie's left paw just as Brooke finished beading. She sat next to Sadie, took the "paw-lish" from Aly, and started painting.

Sadie's tail was wagging so hard, Brooke almost got a splotch of paw-lish on Sadie's fur.

"Stop moving!" Brooke laughed. "You'll ruin your pet-icure!"

Lily gave Sadie her treat and then said, "Maybe we can visit the shelter tomorrow. My brother's allergic, but, Charlotte, maybe you could adopt another dog to be friends with Minerva."

"Maybe," Charlotte said. "Sometimes I worry that she gets lonely when Caleb and I are at school."

"That's such a great idea," Brooke said. "Can we go too?"

Aly nodded. "We're open today, so closed tomorrow. Let's do it."

"That would be lovely, ladies," Mrs. Franklin said. "And thank you all so much for making Sadie a star."

Just before they left, Isaac had Aly, Brooke, Sophie, Lily, and Charlotte pose around Sadie for one last photo. "Say 'puppies'!" he said.

All the girls said "PUPPIES"—Brooke the loudest.

What a fun morning! Aly thought. But now she

and Brooke had to get ready for some human customers. Two new girls from school—twins—who had asked for matching Blueberry Blue birthday pedicures. Aly hoped the two-legged customers were as well-behaved as the four-legged one!

three

Tickled Pink

I s it just me, or does this place smell a little?" Lily asked the next day, when Aly, Brooke, Lily, Charlotte, and Sophie were dropped off at Paws for Love.

Brooke sniffed loudly.

"Ewww. It does smell," Brooke said.

Aly looked around, trying to figure out where they should go, when she saw a very familiar ponytail.

"Jenica?" she said.

Jenica put a bag of dog food she was carrying down on the tile floor. "Hi," she said. "What are you all doing here? How did Sadie's pedicure go?"

"The pet-icure," Brooke corrected her. "And it was awesome!"

Jenica raised an eyebrow.

"It was," Aly said. "Sadie was really well-behaved. And Mrs. Franklin told us all about Adoption Day. She said we should come meet the dogs that need to get adopted."

Jenica picked up the bag of dog food again. "Come with me. I was just bringing this food over to that part of the shelter. Are you guys thinking of adopting a dog?"

"Maybe," Brooke said.

Aly shot her a look. "We're not allowed," Aly said. "But Charlotte might."

"If I can get my parents to agree that two dogs are better than one," Charlotte added. "I mean, *I* think that's true."

"Me too," Jenica said. "I have two dogs. And two cats—all from here."

"I wish I could have that many pets," Sophie said. "All I have is a gerbil."

Jenica dropped off the dog food and led the girls into a room with ten cages. "These are our old-timers," she said. "They're not really old, but they've been here so long we gave them temporary shelter names. They all answer to them now."

Brooke raced over to a cage with a sign that said MELVIN. Inside was a super-slobbery-looking dog.

"Look at this one," she said. "Hi, Melvin. Don't you wish we could have him, Aly?"

Aly looked at the dog. He had soft brown eyes and a wagging tail, but his slobber would be everywhere! No wonder he was an old-timer. She didn't want him.

Then Aly spotted a teeny-tiny dog curled up in the back corner of a cage. He was all eyes and ears with a curly little tail, and he was shaking. Shivering, really. The sign on his cage read SPARKY. He was the cutest dog Aly had ever seen. And clearly, he needed someone to love him.

"Actually," Aly said, "this is the one I wish we could have." She kneeled down next to Sparky's cage and put her fingertips near the bars. Sparky sniffed her fingers with the tiniest nose ever—one that was cold and just a tiny bit wet—and then licked the tip of Aly's pinkie. Aly melted. How could she leave this dog here? She hated the No Dogs Allowed rule more than ever!

"That one?" Brooke made a face. "He looks like a rat."

"A what?" Aly wanted to yell at Brooke, but instead all she said was, "I think he's cute."

And for the rest of the shelter visit, Aly ignored Brooke. She ignored her while they met the other old-timers: Laces and Sneaker and Bob and Murphy and Reginald and Penny and Marjorie and Frida. She even ignored Brooke when she started telling Sophie how she was going to get her mom to change the rule so they could adopt Melvin. Aly knew the rule couldn't be changed. And she knew that even if it could, Mom would never agree to disgusting, slobbery Melvin.

Jenica came into the room with a tall lady who had long braids with beads on the ends that clicked together when she moved. "Everyone, this is Irena. I told her you were the ones who painted Sadie's nails, and she wanted me to introduce her to you."

"It's so nice to meet you girls," Irena said. "Sadie looked beautiful with her nails polished."

"I loved her bows, too," Charlotte said.

"Me too." Irena looked at the cages around her. "It's too bad these puppies can't all get pampered like

Sadie. It might improve their chances of finding a home."

Aly looked around the room. Irena was right. These dogs really could use some spiffing up.

"Ah, well," Irena continued. "Let's hope the Adoption Day campaign will bring in so many people that each dog will find its perfect match."

Aly hoped so. She really hoped so for Sparky. He needed an owner to love him. Aly kind of thought he needed *her* to love him, but that wasn't even worth thinking about. She looked at her purple polka-dot watch. Almost two o'clock. Time to head back to True Colors for the weekly Sunday Pizza Picnic with Joan.

"That would be great," Aly told Irena. "It was really nice to meet you and the dogs."

"Especially Melvin," Brooke said. "I love Melvin."

Irena's eyes lit up. "Would you like to adopt him?"

Before Brooke could answer, Aly said, "Our parents won't let us have a dog. Even though we wish they would."

"I'm going to talk to my parents about this one, though," Charlotte said, pointing to Bob, a black poodle. "I think he and my dog Minerva might get along. She's a poodle too, but a brown one."

"Bob is a sweetheart. I'll keep my fingers crossed," Irena said.

As the girls made their way back through the shelter, they ran into Miss Nina, Mrs. Franklin, and Isaac, who were choosing which pictures of Sadie to use for the Adoption Day advertising.

Aly never thought that today would end with *both* sisters wanting to adopt old-timers. It turned out there were a lot of nice surprises in a smelly shelter.

four

Up the Lavender to the Roof

On Tuesday, after school, Brooke and Aly were in the Sparkle Spa, finishing up their homework—Sparkle Spa Rule Number 1—before opening for business.

Brooke hadn't mentioned Melvin all day, so Aly didn't say anything about Sparky. Aly hated being mad at her sister, and she figured that as long as they didn't talk about dogs, she wouldn't have to be. But that didn't mean she'd stopped thinking about shelter pups, especially Sparky. It made it kind of hard to concentrate on homework.

"Aly?" Brooke asked, looking up from her worksheet. "Did you have to do decimals in third grade?"

Aly stuck her finger on the word "secret" in her copy of *Bridge to Terabithia* to save her place. Chapter four was her fifth-grade assigned reading homework, and she was almost finished.

"Everyone at Auden Elementary has to do decimals in third grade," she said. "How come?"

Brooke pushed her glasses up to the top of her nose. "Decimals go with money, right? That's how you add up all the donations in our jar?"

Aly nodded. "Uh-huh. We studied money in third grade too. Like, how many nickels are in a dollar and all that. . . . The answer is twenty, in case you're wondering."

"How many nickels are in ten dollars?" Brooke asked.

Aly looked down at her finger, which was still resting on the word "secret." Then she looked at her watch. "How about I tell you after we finish our homework? We need to open the Sparkle Spa in five minutes—Tuesday is Soccer Team Rainbow Pedicure Day."

"Oops," said Brooke, looking back at her worksheet. "I forgot. I'd better finish this math sheet."

Aly closed her eyes for a long second and opened them again. Sometimes it seemed like there were so many ideas whirling around in Brooke's brain that she forgot regular stuff that had to happen. But today she really couldn't blame her sister. She wondered if Brooke was thinking about the shelter dogs too.

A few minutes later, just when the girls had finished their homework and started setting up for the soccer team's pedicures, Joan stuck her head into the Sparkle Spa.

"Joanie Macaroni!" Brooke said, smiling. "You weren't here when we came in after school."

"Brookie Cookie!" Joan laughed. "I was delivering brownies for a party tonight at the Paws for Love animal shelter."

Aly finished the last word of chapter four and looked up. Joan was the best baker she and Brooke knew. Sometimes Joan baked cookies and brownies for special events like birthday parties and anniversaries. But Joan baking brownies for the Paws for Love was something new. "That's the same shelter that Sadie's the spokes-dog for!" Aly said.

"I know," Joan said. "It's all Mrs. Franklin has been talking about." She handed Aly a small plastic bag with two brownies inside. "Here's one for each of you. I have to do Mrs. Howard's nails now. See you both later."

By the time Joan was out the door, Brooke was

already standing next to Aly, waiting for her brownie.

"This is soooo good," Brooke said after she swallowed her first bite. "It's really chocolatey, but I think there's also something a little salty in there."

"And maybe some caramel? I like the crunch." Aly examined the size of the brownie. "It could be a little bigger, though."

"Do you think people would pay money for Joan's brownies?" Brooke asked through her second mouthful.

Aly swallowed. "They already do," she told her sister. "I bet Paws for Love paid a lot to have her brownies at their party."

Brooke shook her head. "I mean regular people. What if Joan made brownies and we sold them in True Colors? Then maybe we could give the money to Paws for Love to get bows and pretty collars for the old-timer dogs."

Aly stopped mid-chew. She didn't want to talk

about dogs with Brooke, but this was an awesome idea. "I wonder . . . ," Aly said. "I wonder if Joan can make cookies for dogs, too, and their owners could buy them. And maybe if we raise enough money, we could get puppy polish and give all the dogs pedicures."

"You mean 'paw-lish' and 'pet-icures,'" Brooke said with a smile. "Awesome!"

"Hi, guys."

The sisters turned around. They'd been so excited that they hadn't noticed that Jenica and Bethany, the first two soccer players with appointments, had arrived.

"What's up?" Jenica asked. She and Bethany climbed up into the pedicure chairs and Aly filled them in. Brooke interrupted every five seconds with "It was my idea."

Aly would have to tell Brooke later that it wasn't

really polite to brag. "We also thought we could give them all pet-icures," she said.

"I love that idea!" Jenica said. "The dogs need baths, too."

"And maybe little sweaters," Bethany added. "I mean, if you want them to look their best, they need cute outfits."

Brooke clapped her hands. "They totally need outfits!"

Aly thought about bows and outfits and fancy new collars, maybe even bandanas for the boy dogs, then all the paw-lish they'd need for ten dogs. "I'm not sure if Joan's brownies or doggie treats will make us enough money for all that," she said.

Brooke ran over to the sparkly teal strawberry that served as the Sparkle Spa's donation jar and lifted it up. "We can donate all the money that people give us for polishing nails," she said.

Aly was pretty certain it still wouldn't be enough.

"What else can we do to make money?" Jenica asked as Aly polished her pinkie with Under Watermelon.

Aly asked, "What else are we good at?"

Bethany thought for a minute and said, "We can wash cars. Or walk dogs. I can feed my neighbor Mrs. Berman's cat."

Brooke was starting on Bethany's right foot when she said, "We're good at polishing nails."

Aly stopped Jenica's pedicure in the middle of her big toe. That was it! A polish-a-thon!

"Remember when we did that math-a-thon at school?" she said, and started to polish again. Auden had held an event where people donated money for every math problem the students finished, and then all the funds were given to a hospital that treated kids with cancer.

"Sure," Jenica said.

"Well, what if we had a polish-a-thon and people donated money each time we polished someone's nails?"

"You can do that, but wouldn't it be easier if you just asked for a donation from the person who was getting their nails done instead?" Bethany asked.

That was a lot like charging money, it seemed to Aly, and Mom had said no charges for Sparkle Spa services. Just donations. But maybe this would be different, if it was just for one day.

Aly knew she'd have to compose a list to convince Mom. She'd come up with the list later. Right now they had the rest of the soccer team to do.

But then Bethany said, "I've been thinking about a manicure, too. But maybe not the same one Jenica has."

"Hey! I like my color," Jenica said.

Bethany shrugged. "It's nice, but I want something different."

Brooke jumped up. "I know—Up the Lavender to the Roof." She ran over to the polish display and pulled down a bottle of a really light lavender shade, with dark lavender sparkles. "Cool, right?" she said, handing it to Bethany.

"Actually, it *is* pretty awesome. Can you do it?"

Aly looked at her purple polka-dot watch again. Adding this manicure would mess up their schedule a bit, but if she finished up Jenica's toes especially quickly and then started on Bethany's hands while Brooke was finishing up her feet, it just might work.

"Okay. We can do it," she said.

Jenica leaned back in her pedicure chair and pressed the little button that activated the back massage built into the chair. Bethany did the same. "So, do you think Woodrow Wilson is going to be a tough school to beat?" Bethany asked Jenica.

Jenica shrugged. "As long as Maxie and Joelle keep assisting each other up near the goal, I think we can handle it. Plus, remember, we have sparkle power," she said, wiggling her toes.

"What do you think?" Aly began. "Would the soccer team and their sparkle power want to help out if we get my mom to agree to the polish-a-thon?"

"Let's find out when the rest of the team gets here," Jenica said.

Just then Brooke and Aly's mom came into the Sparkle Spa to refill the mini-fridge with water. "Find out what?" she asked.

Aly sighed. She wasn't ready to ask Mom about the polish-a-thon. But Brooke started talking immediately.

"We want to hold a bake sale and polish-a-thon

to raise money for Paws for Love," she said. And then she blurted out the whole plan. It wasn't the way Aly would have explained it, but Brooke got the point across.

When Brooke finished, Aly held her breath.

Mom pressed her lips together for a second. It was one of the things she did when she was trying to make a decision. She loaded the mini-fridge and didn't say anything for a while. "You know," she finally said, "I think that would be great for True Colors to do too. Why don't we have a polish-a-thon for kids in the Sparkle Spa and one for adults in True Colors? Then we'd raise even more money, and maybe get newspaper coverage too.

"We can put flyers up all over town. It would give us a leg up over that Princess Polish shop that's supposed to open across the street next month." Mom barely took a break before continuing: "As far as the bake sale and the doggie treats are concerned, you're going to have to ask Joan. That's up to her. Let's discuss this more later. Right now I have to go paint Miss Nina's nails. I'll talk to her about this plan too—I know she's very involved in the shelter."

Mom headed back into the main salon.

The girls were speechless. That was the quickest Mom had ever agreed to *anything*. Aly didn't even have to make a list! And Mom wanted True Colors to get involved too! And be in the newspaper! And put posters up all over town!

They'd have to check with Paws for Love and get two "paws-up"—but once they did, the old-timers would be on their way to new homes. Or at least Aly hoped they would.

five

Reddy or Not

On Thursday night boxes of green- and red-pepper pizza were on the welcome desk. Lemonade and apple juice cartons sat on the windowsill. People sat in pedicure chairs, at manicure stations, some even on the floor. True Colors had never looked quite this way before.

It was the first meeting of the polish-a-thon planning committee, and the salon was packed. All the manicurists from True Colors were there, along with the Auden Elementary soccer team. Charlotte, Lily,

Sophie, and even Mrs. Franklin showed up. She'd left Sadie at home.

Joan and Aly were the "captains," while Mrs. Tanner was on the phone being interviewed by the local paper, *The Auden Herald*.

"It's great having you all here," Joan said. "We have a lot to figure out tonight. Anyone who wants to bake or be involved with selling the cookies and brownies and dog treats, come with me. Anyone who's going to help out with the polishing, you can talk to Aly."

Aly walked to the front door, a clipboard in her hands. Brooke, Lily, Sophie, Jenica, Mia, Giovanna, Joelle, Anjuli, and almost all the manicurists from True Colors followed. She was kind of nervous, looking at the group in front of her.

"First, thank you, everyone, for volunteering your time," she said quietly. Joan had helped her make a list of what to say, and it started with saying thank you.

"Speak louder!" Jenica said.

Aly turned bright red.

"I'm happy to do whatever it takes to get the dogs adopted," Jenica added.

"Me too," Mia agreed.

"Second, we have to go over the rules. Grown-up manicurists, an adult manicure is ten dollars. Sparkle Spa manicures are five dollars. If too many kids show up, we might have to send them to True Colors, since it's just Brooke and me polishing. My mom said that's okay—their manicures will still be five dollars."

Lisa, one of the salon's manicurists, nodded. "Sounds good," she said.

Aly smiled. She felt a bit more relaxed. "For the polish-a-thon, people can get only one color—not fancy stuff."

"That's too bad," Joelle said.

"It would take too long," Brooke told her, answering for Aly. "We have to go as fast as we can to raise enough money for all the puppies."

"What about featuring one special manicure for the day, an easy one—like a sparkle top coat or a rhinestoned pinkie?" Giovanna suggested.

Aly thought about that. If it was something easy, they could probably pull it off. Plus, people might be disappointed with just regular polish.

"A paw print!" Brooke said excitedly. "We could do a paw print on people's thumbs!"

"In a different color," Sophie added.

Aly nodded her head. "Okay, we'll do special paw print manicures and pedicures for anyone who wants them. I like it."

"It makes sense because of the dogs," Jenica said. "But what do we do? The people who aren't polishing?"

"You'll be assisting," Aly said. "The kind of stuff Brooke and I do for True Colors all the time."

"Like keeping the polish wall organized?" Joelle asked.

"Exactly," Aly said. "Joelle, do you want to be in charge of the polish display in the Sparkle Spa, and, Mia, you can be in charge of the wall in True Colors?"

Mia nodded.

Brooke's friend Sophie raised her hand. "I want a job," she said.

"We really need a polish checker, Sophie—someone who can make sure the bottles don't run too low and can replace them when they do. We also need someone to collect the donations."

"I can do that," Jenica said. "I'll do it in the main salon."

"And I'll do it in the Sparkle Spa," Lily said. "That's an easy job."

Aly wrote down everyone's roles. She said, "We also need two general helpers to empty trash cans, stack magazines, get customers coffee and water, and keep the jewelry station in the Sparkle Spa stocked with supplies."

"I'll do it for the Sparkle Spa," Anjuli said.

"And I'll do it in True Colors," Giovanna added.

Then she, Jenica, and Mia did a three-way high five. "Go Team True Colors!" Jenica cheered. "We'll make sure things run really smoothly," she assured the manicurists.

Lisa and Jamie smiled at her. Then Jamie turned to Aly. "Do you need us for anything else? We know the prices, we know the rules, and we know who's going to be helping us out."

Aly scanned the list on her clipboard. "I think that's it," she said. "Except—don't forget to get here extra, extra early on Sunday. The polish-a-thon starts at nine a.m. on the dot. Thanks again, everyone."

Aly glanced over at Joan's group. It looked like they, too, were wrapping up their discussion.

"Is it time for posters yet, Aly?" Brooke asked. Aly was amazed at how patient Brooke had been, quietly waiting.

Aly nodded. "Yep. Grown-ups can go grab some pizza. Girls, it's time to make some posters."

Brooke stood up and announced loudly, "Listen everyone. We need to make a ton of posters to hang all over town. I've got lots of markers and paper in the Sparkle Spa. You can draw wherever you want. I like the floor best."

Everyone pitched in, even Mom, who was an awesome artist. She drew pictures of puppies—some on posters, but some on smaller flyers, too, so she could photocopy them and hand them out around town.

Above, below, and all around the drawings, Aly

and some of the other girls filled in the space with all
kinds of banners:

POLISH-A-THON FUND-RAISER FOR
PAWS FOR LOVE ADOPTION DAY!

#5 Manicures for Kids!
#10 Manicures for Adults!

Baked Treats for Humans & Dogs: $2/each!

THIS SUNDAY, 9:00 A.M.-2:00 P.M.
AT TRUE COLORS NAIL SALON
ON MAIN STREET.

Then Brooke told the rest of the helpers to use real
polish to color in the dogs' nails on the posters—she'd
picked Reddy or Not. Aly thought the posters looked
fantastic, especially Mom's. She had even drawn a
dog that looked kind of like Sparky!

* * * * *

Later that night Aly was brushing out Brooke's hair and weaving it into a French braid. It was the best way to sleep when you had long hair, Brooke had decided. That way, it didn't get too knotted up, and she didn't have a hard ponytail holder pushing into her head when she rolled over in her sleep.

"I can't believe the polish-a-thon is only three days away," Brooke said as Aly's fingers danced through her hair, making a neat and even braid.

"I know. It's fast," Aly said. She sometimes wondered if they should add French braiding to the services they offered at the Sparkle Spa. "But Adoption Day is a week from Sunday, and we need to make sure we have time to buy all the bows and sweaters and collars and bandanas and—"

"And paw-lish!" Brooke said, turning her head so fast that the braid slipped out of Aly's hands. "Don't forget the pet-icures."

Aly *had* almost forgotten the pet-icures. With all the polish-a-thon planning, she wasn't even thinking about next weekend.

"Are you worried about doing them?" Aly asked.

Brooke shook her head, and her braid started unraveling. "Nope. I think they're going to be the best part. I'm going to make Melvin look so nice that Mom's going to let us adopt him."

Ugh. Dumb, drooly Melvin. "Mom is never going to let us adopt Melvin," Aly said. "If she lets us adopt any dog, it would be Sparky. Sparky is the abso- lute cutest. Plus, he's little and doesn't drool all over everything."

"Melvin can't help it if he drools!" Brooke said. "That's so mean of you not to like him just because he drools. Would you hate *me* if I drooled?"

Aly could not believe they were having this argu- ment. "Of course not," she said. "You're my sister. I'd

love you no matter what. Even if you drooled everywhere. And besides, it's not just the drooling. Melvin
is huge."

"Would you hate me if *I* were huge?" Brooke
asked, crossing her arms over her chest.

"Brooke!" Aly couldn't help yelling a little. "What
I think about you is different from what I think about
a big, drooly dog!"

Brooke's voice grew louder and louder. "I'm going
to make sure that Melvin gets the best sweater and the
best collar and the best pet-icure of all the old-timers.
And then Mom and Dad will love him, and it won't
even matter what you think."

"Just you wait." Aly could not stand the idea of
Melvin being the best-looking dog on Adoption Day.
"I'm going to make sure Sparky is the handsomest
dog there. And Mom and Dad will love *him*, and
then Melvin will go home with another family."

Brooke stood up. "Take that back!"

"I will not," Aly said, getting up herself and grabbing her pajamas out of her dresser.

Brooke stormed across the room to her own dresser and took out her pajamas, too. "And one more thing," she said, pushing her now-unraveled hair back over her shoulder. "You did the worst braid tonight. It already fell out." She started crying.

Aly couldn't believe it. Brooke had turned her head before Aly had been able to put an elastic at the bottom. She marched over to where she'd left Brooke's brush on the floor and threw it on Brooke's bed. "Maybe you should brush your hair yourself from now on."

Brooke glared at her. "Okay!" she shouted. "I will."

Aly climbed into bed and grabbed a book off her night table. At times like these, she wished she had her own room.

Six
Golden Delicious

For the next two days Brooke and Aly spoke to each other only when they had to discuss the polish-a-thon. They each led different teams of friends around to hang up posters in town, and even though they still had to share their bedroom, Brooke brushed her own hair and did her own braid at night. It wasn't as good as the ones Aly did for her, but at least it kept her hair out of her face when she slept.

Before the girls knew it, it was Sunday morning. Mom marched into their bedroom, pulled up the shades, and announced, "Happy Polish-a-Thon Day! Rise and shine!"

Aly rubbed the sleep out of her eyes. "Happy Polish-a-Thon Day," she grumbled.

"I just got an e-mail saying that the *Auden Herald* is sending a reporter to the salon today, and the local TV channel might even have cameras there. This is going to be great for business. Thanks for coming up with this idea, girls."

"TV!" Brooke said, jumping out of bed, her hair flying behind her. "We're going to be on TV?"

"Maybe," Mom said. "It's not definite."

But Brooke didn't seem to be listening anymore. "I'm going to wear a dress! The one with the ruffled skirt that's the same color as Magical Mystery Tour. And maybe Aly can fishbone-braid—" Brooke looked at her sister. "Never mind. I'll just wear it in one long ponytail."

Aly thought about offering to braid Brooke's hair
for the polish-a-thon, but then she changed her mind.
Brooke still hadn't apologized. Aly hadn't apologized
either, but Brooke was the one who had started the
Melvin vs. Sparky fight.

As Brooke got dressed, Aly pulled on her favorite
long purple T-shirt and paired it with green leggings
and high-tops.

Then both girls grabbed a piece of cinnamon toast
their dad had made them, kissed him good-bye, and
jumped into the car.

From the moment they got to the salon, everything was crazy!

"Girls!" Joan said. "I need help setting up the bake
sale!"

"What do you need us to do?" Aly asked.

Joan handed one tray of bone-shaped dog treats
to Aly and one tray of puppy-faced treats to Brooke.

The girls took them to Maxie and Bethany, who were waiting outside.

"These are for you," Aly said, putting her tray in the center of the table.

"Awesome. Joan told us that even though these are for dogs, they're safe for people to eat too," Bethany said. "I kind of wonder what they taste like."

"I'll try!" Brooke said. She picked up a bone-shaped treat and took a bite.

"Ew!" Maxie said. "I can't believe you ate that!"

Brooke shrugged. "It tastes kind of like peanut butter and oatmeal."

"Brooke! Aly!" Mom yelled out the door of the salon. "I need you!"

Aly and Brooke had been at True Colors for Perfectly Peach weddings, Silver Celebration birthday parties, and Sunday Pizza Picnics. But nothing could have prepared them for the polish-a-thon.

At nine o'clock, people started streaming in, and they didn't stop.

At eleven, the TV cameras and the newspaper showed up.

At noon, after Aly and Brooke had already done six manicures and two pedicures, Charlotte came in with her twin brother, Caleb.

"They're giving me a break from the bake sale table, so I'm here for a manicure," Charlotte said. "And Caleb, too! I told him it was okay for boys."

"No polish," Caleb said. "But Charlotte said you could get all the dirt out from under my nails. And, well, whatever. I like dogs."

Charlotte gave Lily a ten-dollar bill. "That's for both of us," she said.

"Thanks," Lily answered. "You can choose your color. And you can choose a separate color if you want a paw print on your thumb."

"A paw print—that's so cool." Charlotte smiled.

As soon as they finished one customer, another would sit down. The girls barely had a moment to breathe. Just when Aly thought it couldn't get any busier, a girl from Brooke's class named Tuesday came in.

She was carrying a rabbit! "Can you polish Fluffy's nails?" she asked. Then she looked around. "I thought this was for *animals*. On the posters the dogs were wearing polish."

As the Sparkle Spa's general helper, Anjuli should have handled this, but she was too busy talking to people in the waiting area. So Aly stopped her manicure and went over to talk to Tuesday.

"You'll have to take your rabbit home. But you can come back later or even another day to get your nails done. Okay?" Aly explained.

Disaster averted, Aly thought. But two more third

graders arrived with pets—a dog and a cat. Then a girl with a hamster showed up. And another one with a guinea pig.

Aly pulled Brooke behind the closet door. "What's going on?" she said. "Why are all these third graders coming with pets?"

Brooke's eyes started to get watery. "Maybe it's because I told them that we polished Sadie's paws."

"Did you tell them that we would polish their pets' paws too?" Aly hissed.

"Maybe," Brooke said, a tear rolling down her cheek. "I'm really sorry!"

Aly took a deep breath. She stood on a chair and made an announcement: "We can't do your pets' nails. You'll have to take them home. Please come back later or another day."

The girl with the hamster said, "But, Brooke, I thought you said—"

"I'm sorry," Aly said, still standing on her chair. "This polish-a-thon is for people only!"

The kids paraded out with their pets, and Aly and Brooke got back to three girls waiting.

"Next customer, please," Aly said. Then she turned to her sister. "Only fifteen more minutes, Brooke. Let's do these last ones quickly."

When two o'clock came and the last customer had left the salon, everyone cheered. Both True Colors and Sparkle Spa were total and complete messes: Bottles of polish, packages of nail files, stacks of washcloths, and piles of magazines covered every surface.

Aly took Charlotte's hand and said, "Come on, let's go outside just for a sec."

They sat on the Blue Skies bench in front of the store. Aly looked down at her hands, which were covered in what looked like a million shades of

Raspberry Rainbow, Cocoa Cupcake, and Cheer Up Buttercup.

Charlotte said, "Let's play Good, Better, Best. We haven't done that in forever!"

Aly grinned at her best friend. They had made the game up in third grade. It *did* seem like forever since the last time they had played.

Charlotte began. "Good was watching Joan do two manicures at once. Better was when Caleb stepped in that rabbit's poop. And best was . . ." She paused. "Best was having the reporter ask me about Paws for Love and me maybe being on TV. Your turn."

Aly thought for a moment and then said, "Good was that tons of people now know about Sparkle Spa. Better was watching Brooke eat about five of Joan's doggie treats. Yuck! And best was the best of all—making more than one thousand four hundred dollars for the puppies!"

seven
Hound Dog Blues

Immediately after school on Wednesday, Aly and Brooke raced to True Colors, picked up the polish-a-thon and bake sale money, and headed straight to Pups 'n' Stuff, the pet store where Miss Nina worked. It was one block plus two stores away from True Colors.

"How much did we make again?" Brooke asked, tugging on her braid, which Brooke did whenever she was nervous or excited. Aly knew that this time, it was because she was excited.

"One thousand four hundred and fifty-six dollars," Aly said, holding on to the pouch tightly. All the money wasn't in there, but a lot of it was. Mom had already given most of it to Mrs. Franklin so that the shelter could pay for baths and special groomers for all ten of the old-timers. They'd raised so much money, in fact, that the shelter was going to offer a free year's worth of dog food to any family who adopted one of the dogs on Sunday. "And we have six hundred and fifty-six dollars to spend on collars and sweaters and bows and bandanas and stuff."

Brooke nodded. "That's, um, six, um . . . how much money is that for each dog?"

Aly did the math in her head: *Six hundred and fifty-six divided by ten* . . . "Sixty-five dollars and sixty cents each. But it doesn't have to be exactly even." She thought maybe they could spend more money on Sparky and less on slobbery Melvin.

Brooke, of course, had other ideas. "You mean we can spend more on Melvin? I want to get him the best sweater in the store!"

Aly bit her tongue—hard enough that it even hurt a little. Both sisters seemed to have moved past the Melvin vs. Sparky fight, and Aly really didn't want to get into another one.

"Maybe," she said, stopping right in front of Pups 'n' Stuff.

Miss Nina was standing behind the counter as they walked in.

"Are you girls ready for Doggie Makeover Day on Saturday?" she asked. "My friends and I are going to bathe and groom all ten of the pooches."

Aly wasn't sure they were completely ready. Ten sets of four dog paws each was an awful lot of puppy nails to paint, even with their friends helping.

"I'm *so* ready!" Brooke said. "And we're here to

buy collars and bows and sweaters and bandanas and jackets."

"And paw-lish," Aly added. They couldn't forget that.

"Why don't we pick out the paw-lish first?" Miss Nina said, pushing up her sleeves.

She walked the girls over to the paw-lish bin and pulled out a few colors. "We have Bone White, Red Rover, Grass Green, Purple Paws, and Hound Dog Blues," she said.

"I think we need two of each," Aly said.

"Maybe not white," Brooke said. "That one's so boring."

"I thought maybe some of the boys could get white," Aly answered, picking up a tube of paw-lish. "You know, just in case red or purple doesn't go with their fur or their sweater or something."

Brooke scratched her head. "I think the boy dogs

won't mind. There are boys in my class who like red and purple."

Aly thought about that. Brooke was actually right—there were boys in her class who liked red and purple too.

"So just the four colors?" Miss Nina said.

Aly nodded.

"You know," Miss Nina added as she placed the paw-lish tubes on the counter, "my boyfriend wears nail polish. He's a rock musician. Lots of guys who play rock music wear nail polish."

"Maybe our dogs will be rock stars! Maybe *Melvin* will be a rock star!" Brooke said. She was looking at the different outfits and pulled out a leather vest. "This looks like Melvin," she said, bringing it to the counter.

Aly picked it up. It was pretty cool. But it was also $175. "Brooke," she said, "this is a little too expensive.

If we get him this, we won't have enough money to spend on the other dogs."

Brooke crossed her arms in front of her. "It's just because you hate Melvin. If you loved him like I did, you would get this vest. If it were for Sparky, you'd get it."

Aly sighed. "It's not that, Brooke. I don't hate Melvin. I just want to give all the dogs a fair chance. They all have to look good so they'll all get adopted."

Miss Nina walked over to a different wall and pulled down a black vest decorated with sparkly gold lightning bolts. "Here," she said, giving it to Brooke. "I think this will look neat on Melvin, just like a rock star. And it's much less expensive."

Brooke gave Aly one last glare and then inspected the vest. "Well, it *is* cool," she said.

"My boyfriend would love it." Miss Nina grabbed

a sparkly gold collar and leash, too. "And I think these match perfectly."

Brooke's face lit up. "Let's get those," she chirped.

Aly let out a big breath. At least Melvin was taken care of.

The girls split up the rest of the list, and with Miss Nina's help, they picked outfits for each dog.

For Bob, the one Charlotte liked: a plaid sweater with a green collar and leash.

For Marjorie: a pink T-shirt with a silver heart on the back, a silver collar and leash, and pink bows for her ears.

For Laces: a denim vest, a yellow collar and leash, and a yellow bandana for her neck.

For Reginald: a neon-green T-shirt with a fluorescent yellow leash and collar.

For Penny: a gold-and-silver-striped sweater, a silver leash and collar, and one gold bow.

For Frida: a dark-purple beret, a plum-colored bow, and a lavender collar and leash.

For Murphy: a black T-shirt with a silver star on the back and a matching silver leash and collar.

For Sneaker: a hot-pink warm-up jacket, a rhinestone collar and leash, and a hot-pink bow.

Slowly but surely, the pile on the counter got taller until only one dog was left: Sparky. What would make Sparky look his very best?

Aly looked at the clothing racks and shelves, and then she saw it: a little blue T-shirt with a sparkly rainbow on the back and a sparkly rainbow-colored collar and leash to match. He'd look like a walking version of their rainbow sparkle pedicure, and considering how magical that pedicure was for the soccer players, Aly figured it would be even more magical if it was all over Sparky's body.

Miss Nina rang up all the puppy outfits. "Six hundred and twenty-five dollars."

The girls were shocked—the clothing was so tiny; how could it cost so much?

"We have more than that," Brooke told her.

Aly unzipped the pouch and counted out the money, handing Miss Nina the exact amount.

"How much do we have left?" Brooke asked.

"Thirty-one dollars," Aly answered, and then she saw Brooke's eyes move around the store and zero in on a sign: FOR SALE: PUPPY PERFUME! $30!

Brooke made a beeline for the display. "This!" she said. "We need this so that they all smell good!"

She brought the bottle to Aly. Aly spritzed it in the air and sniffed. It smelled like fresh grass and clean laundry. Not bad. And they did have some money left.

"Okay," she said, handing Miss Nina another thirty dollars. "We can put this last dollar in the donation jar back at the Sparkle Spa," she told Brooke. "For whatever charity we decide to donate to next."

"It was so nice of you to raise the money for these dogs. There are so many dogs that need to be adopted and not enough people who get involved," Miss Nina said.

Aly watched Miss Nina's fingers as she started bagging all their merchandise and noticed the cool polish job. She felt kind of proud that it was her mom who did Miss Nina's manicure and applied the rhinestones to her pinkies.

"Did you two ever think about adopting a dog?" she asked.

"I looooove Melvin," Brooke said, pulling on her braid with one hand and holding one of the clothing bags with the other.

Aly picked up the second bag. "I like Sparky," Aly said. "But we're not allowed to have a dog. Our parents said."

Miss Nina nodded sympathetically. "Well, maybe you can get them to reconsider."

"I doubt it," Aly said. "They seem pretty serious about it."

As Brooke and Aly walked back to the salon, Aly thought it would be hard enough convincing her parents to adopt one dog. But two? No way. Especially if one of them was Melvin.

eight

Grass Green

All week long Aly had been thinking about Doggie Makeover Day. She hoped the old-timers would like their outfits and wouldn't squirm or chew or cry once they were dressed. She hoped all the groomers would show up. She hoped the pet-icures would go well.

She also hoped, deep down in the bottom of her heart, that somehow, magically, Mom and Dad would fall in love with Sparky and let her adopt him. And that bottom-of-her-heart hope was what

Aly was thinking about when she and Brooke were in the backseat of their dad's car on the way to the shelter on Saturday morning, with their bags of outfits and paw-lish and puppy perfume for the makeover event.

"You know, I had a dog when I was growing up," Dad told them from the front seat. "His name was Mouse, because he was huge. A sheepdog."

"That doesn't make sense, Daddy," Brooke said. "If he was so big, you should've named him Elephant or something."

"It was a joke, Brookie," Dad said. "Anyway, he was a great dog. If I were home more to help take care of it, I'd get you girls a dog, but it doesn't seem fair to leave all that work to your mother."

Aly thought about this for a moment. Was this good news in terms of possibly getting Sparky, or bad news? She wasn't quite sure.

"What was the best part about having a dog?" Brooke asked.

"Oh, I don't know if I could pick one thing," Dad said. "Dogs are good company, and they're fun to play with in the yard, and once Mouse even scared away a burglar."

"A burglar?" Brooke gasped. "Really, Daddy?"

"Yes. He was a special dog," Dad said, pulling up in front of the shelter. "You know, I'm proud of you girls for helping out the community like this, even though we're not getting a dog."

"Thanks, Dad," Aly said, her heart dropping into her stomach.

"Yeah, thanks," Brooke said, looking just as sad as Aly felt.

When the girls got out of the car, Mrs. Franklin and Sadie were waiting for them just inside the door—

dressed, as usual, like twins: Sadie wore yellow and pink bows on her ears. Mrs. Franklin had on a yellow-and-pink-striped hat.

"I'm so glad you're here," Mrs. Franklin said. "Your friends are already inside."

Charlotte, Lily, and Sophie were planning to help. And Jenica was going to be around, volunteering.

Aly and Brooke followed Mrs. Franklin through the shelter and waved at Irena, who was in the middle of a cat adoption. They finally reached the old-timers' room. "I'll be right back, girls," Mrs. Franklin said as she headed back down the hallway. "I have to let Isaac know you're here."

Miss Nina was already in the room, with Bob walking behind her on a leash. Lily, Sophie, and Charlotte were there too.

"Oooh, he looks so fluffy!" Charlotte squealed, kneeling down next to Bob. Miss Nina handed her

Bob's leash and went to get Marjorie out of her cage.

"Hi, Bob," Charlotte said. "Do you like it when people call you Bobby?"

Bob licked Charlotte's hand, and she laughed.

"Are you going to adopt him tomorrow?" Aly asked, putting her bag of dog accessories on the floor.

"I think so," Charlotte said. "My dad wants us to come here with Minerva to make sure they like each other. If they do, Bob's coming home with me."

"I'm getting Melvin," Brooke said.

Aly closed her eyes and started counting Mississippis so she wouldn't scream at her sister. "Stop it, Brooke," she whispered.

"The slobbery one?" Lily asked. "Ick. I didn't think anyone was going to take him. Are you sure that's the one you want?"

"We're not getting a dog," Aly said. "Brooke's just pretending. Right, Brooke?"

Brooke looked like she was about to cry. "I guess." She frowned.

"I'd pretend to get Sparky," Sophie said. "He's so cute, with those comic-book eyes. But I'm not allowed to have another pet—just my gerbil."

"I'd pretend to get Sparky too," Aly said. Then she walked over to his cage. "Hey, where is he?"

"He's in the back, waiting for his bath," Sophie said. "Miss Nina and the other groomers just started. They've got Bob, Laces, and Murphy done. And Marjorie's back there now, along with Frida and Sparky."

Bob started barking when Irena walked into the room with Isaac, Mrs. Franklin, and Sadie.

"Let's set you up in that corner over there," Irena said. "Isaac's going to be taking pictures. And don't worry if things get a little messy with the dogs."

Aly looked down at her T-shirt and jeans. She was glad she wasn't wearing any of her favorite clothes.

Irena continued, "There are towels and treats for the dogs, and a basket for all your dog polish."

"It's called paw-lish," Brooke told her. "And Hound Dog Blues is going to be the doggy Color of the Week." She giggled. "I mean, the Color of the Day."

Irena laughed. "Excuse me," she said. "Paw-lish. Anyway, I'll be coming in and out, but Nina said she'll keep an eye on you and the dogs. Isaac will be here too, if you need anything."

"Okay," Aly said, glancing up at Isaac. He smiled and gave her a thumbs-up.

"And," Irena said, leaning against one of the empty cages, "on behalf of the whole shelter: Thank you."

The girls polished the old-timers' nails, and the pups were yappy and didn't know if they wanted to sit, stand, or—in the case of Laces—roll over. But for the most part, they liked the attention and the treats, which Joan had made just for today and Aly had brought with her to the shelter.

As Aly was putting the finishing touches of Red Rover on Marjorie's back paw, she heard "Ew!" from the other side of the room, and "Ack!" She turned her head to see Lily holding her left hand with her right one. "I think Melvin tried to bite me!" she said. "I got my hand away in time, but that's so not cool."

Charlotte went racing to Lily. "Are you sure you're okay?" she asked, taking Lily's left hand in her own.

"Let me see," Miss Nina said, running at Charlotte's heels. She bent down and took Lily's hand from Charlotte. "No broken skin. Not even a mark," she said. "I think he was just trying to give you a kiss. He's a licker, not a biter."

"Well, I don't want to take him out of his cage," Lily said. "Either way, he's kind of gross."

Charlotte looked at the drool hanging down from his lips. "I don't think I want to either."

Brooke was tugging on her braid, clearly worried. She asked, "Can we polish Melvin's nails last? When all the other dogs are done?"

"Good idea, Brooke," said Miss Nina. "Let's finish up the others and then tackle Melvin."

Just then Jenica brought Sparky in from the back. "Hey, guys," she said. "One of the groomers asked if I could deliver this furball to you. He's such a sweetheart. I hope he goes to a great home."

Aly felt her heart tug. She hoped whoever got Sparky would love him as much as she would if he were her dog.

They had picked Purple Paws for Sparky, which went nicely with his rainbow collar and leash. But as cute and cuddly as Sparky looked . . .

He absolutely *hated* getting his pet-icure.

"Please don't take any pictures, Isaac," Aly pleaded. "I think the camera is making Sparky more nervous." Even though Aly was holding him steady, he shivered, whimpered, cried . . . and then peed on the floor.

"Yuck! It that what I think it is?" Lily squealed. The girls moved to the opposite side of the room, away from Aly and Sparky.

Luckily, Irena had come back into the room and took charge. "No worries. I'll take Sparky to the back and clean him up. But I don't think he's a candidate for nail polish," she said, and whisked him away.

Aly felt terrible. Without a pet-icure and with all his shivering, would anyone want Sparky?

She didn't have more than a second to worry, because it was finally time to do Melvin's paws. Miss Nina went to get him, since no one else would.

"He's so slobbery," Sophie said quietly. "I hope he doesn't bite anyone."

Aly knew Melvin was slobbery, but she was pretty sure he wasn't dangerous. If Miss Nina said he was nice, then Aly trusted her. But she understood if the other girls didn't.

"Brooke?" she asked, sending her a Secret Sister Eye Message by raising one eyebrow twice: *Can we do this—just us?*

Brooke smiled at Aly. "Teamwork," she answered.

Aly looked up at the rest of the girls from where she was sitting on the floor. "If you guys don't want to do Melvin, Brooke and I can do him, with Miss Nina's help." She knew Melvin was important to Brooke. And the Melvin versus Sparky fight didn't seem to matter as much as making sure he got a great pet-icure.

"You really wouldn't mind?" Charlotte asked.

"Nope," Aly said. "It's totally okay."

"It's okay," Brooke said. "Aly and I can do it." She walked over to Aly and grabbed her hand. The sisters knew that as a team they could do almost anything. Other people helping made things easier, but as long as they had each other, Aly and Brooke would be fine.

Miss Nina rubbed Melvin's head. "He's a good guy, I promise," she said, giving him a treat.

Aly and Brooke got to work, and were done pretty quickly, even with his drool. But maybe Brooke tickled Melvin, because he dropped his treat out of his mouth and licked her cheek, slobbering all over her face, the drool dripping down her neck.

"Ewwww!" Brooke said, but she was laughing. "Melvin, that's gross! There's spit all over me!"

While Brooke cleaned herself up, Aly tidied the pet-icure area, then stepped back to take in all the dogs at once. With their baths and new haircuts and colorful paws and sparkly collars, they looked like the most adoptable bunch of dogs ever. And once they had their new outfits on tomorrow, they'd look even more spectacular.

Sparky may not have had Purple Paws paw-lish on, but he still looked super adorable. What was most important, Aly realized, was that they were nice dogs on the inside too, even Melvin.

"You know what?" Brooke said, walking over to Aly. She was still scrubbing her neck with antibacterial wipes that Miss Nina had found for her. "I think you're right about Sparky."

"What do you mean?" Aly asked.

"I think," Brooke said, "he's the best dog for us. Better than Melvin after all."

Aly turned to her sister to see if she was kidding, but Brooke looked one hundred percent serious. "You think so?" she asked.

"Actually, I more than think so," Brooke said. "I know so." She stopped wiping her face long enough to tug on her braid. "Do you think we can make a list to convince Mom and Dad to let us adopt him tomorrow?"

Aly walked over to Sparky. "Hi, buddy," she said to the dog. His little nub of a tail wagged like crazy. Very slowly, Aly put her hand out and touched the dog's head. He licked her. And then licked her again and again. Brooke came over and petted him too, and he started licking her fingers.

"I think," Aly said, "that we should definitely try."

nine

Red Rover

After Mom had tucked the girls into bed that night, Aly reached into the crack between her bed and the wall and pulled out a small pad, an astronaut pen her dad had brought her back from New York City, and a miniature flashlight.

"Brooke," Aly whispered, pointing the flashlight beam at her sister, "are you ready to make our dog list?"

Brooke sat up in her bed with a stuffed animal in each arm and nodded.

"Okay, let's go," Aly said.

It wasn't a very long list. . . .

Why We Should Be Allowed to Get a Dog
1. Sparky needs a home.
2. Sparky is well-behaved. He doesn't bite
   or drool.

(Aly left out the part about him peeing during the
pet-icure.)

3. Dad had a dog named Mouse that
   saved the house from a burglar, and
   Sparky's bark could save us from a
   burglar one day.
4. Sparky is the perfect size to take
   anywhere, so when we go visit Grammy
   and Papa, he can come too.

Aly and Brooke hoped it would do the trick. Tomorrow was not only Adoption Day—hopefully, it would also be Sparky Day.

When the Tanners drove over to Paws for Love, Dad couldn't stop saying how proud he was of Aly and Brooke.

"Did I mention how terrific you are?" he said.

Brooke laughed. "You *did*, Dad. You did yesterday."

"But you can say it again," Aly added. "We don't mind."

"It's true, we don't." Brooke was looking at Aly and raising her eyebrows high. *Now?* she mouthed about the Sparky list.

Aly shook her head again. She really hoped Brooke didn't jump the gun on this one.

"I'm looking forward to seeing what you did with these dogs," Mom said. "I'm impressed you were able to polish ten sets of dogs' nails yesterday."

"Nine," Aly said, and grinned at her sister.

"It wasn't that hard," Brooke said. "They're like people, but with funnier-shaped nails. Plus, our friends were there to help."

Mrs. Franklin and Sadie were in the front of the shelter. Sadie was wearing her best sweater—gray, woven through with silver sparkle thread—and a silver bow in her hair. Mrs. Franklin was holding an armful of flyers.

"Hi, Sadie!" Brooke said, getting out of the car.

"Hi, Mrs. Franklin," Aly said. "Were any old-timers adopted yet?"

"Yes," she answered. "Your friend Charlotte is inside, completing the paperwork for Bob. And Marjorie went first thing this morning. Nina is thinking about adopting Melvin, but I don't know if she's decided for sure yet."

Brooke looked up from petting Sadie. "I think Melvin and Miss Nina would make a great family. Especially because her boyfriend is a rock star and so is Melvin."

Mrs. Franklin looked confused, but Aly laughed. "Come on," she said, holding her hand out to her sister. "Let's go check out how the rest of them look."

But the girls didn't get too far. Joan was in the lobby with her dog treats, which she had named Joan's Bones. Each bone-shaped cookie was wrapped in plastic with a sticker on the front.

"Those look so good," Aly said. "Like they belong in a store."

Brooke and Aly saw Charlotte and her family leaving with Bob. He looked fabulous in his plaid sweater and green collar. As the Cane family waited to get their free-year's-supply-of-dog-food coupon, Caleb came over to Aly.

"I have a question for you," he said.

"What is it?" she asked. What could he want to ask her?

"Um, if I came to your, um, your room at the back of where your mom works, do you think you could make my thumbnails match Bob's? I like the green. There's, um, something cool about it."

Aly was surprised. A boy had never asked her for a manicure before. At least not one with polish—for his thumbs. She shrugged. "I guess," she said.

"Um, cool," Caleb said. And then he went back to his family.

Brooke was looking at Aly with her hands on her hips. "Are we doing *boys* now?"

"We were never *not* doing boys. Just none of them wanted to come," Aly said.

"I don't know about boys," Brooke said.

"Hey, Brooke! Hey, Aly!" A little girl with a

butterfly clip in her hair came running over to the sisters. It was Heather Davis, Suzy Davis's little sister, whose birthday party had been the very first Sparkle Spa event, when the girls opened their salon. "We just got a dog!"

Suzy came into the room next, with Sneaker on a leash. She was the dog that Aly and Brooke had dressed like a sparkly athlete, in a hot-pink warm-up jacket and a rhinestone collar and leash, with a hot-pink bow in her hair. Her nails were painted Red Rover.

"Why haven't you adopted a dog yet?" Suzy asked Aly. "Is it because your parents won't let you? Like how they won't let you wear nail polish during the school week?" Suzy rolled her eyes.

Aly ignored Suzy's questions. All she said was, "I hope you like Sneaker."

But then she turned to her parents. "Mom! Dad!"

she said. "We have to go look at the dogs."

"We have to! Now!" Brooke added.

The Tanners made their way into the old-timers' room. There were so many people there, and so many of the dogs were out of their cages. Aly tried to get through to Sparky's cage, but first she and Brooke were stopped by Anjuli, the goalie from the soccer team, who was adopting the tiny Yorkie named Reginald, and then Mrs. Bass, a True Colors customer, who seemed to be considering adopting Murphy, the bulldog.

Mom started talking to Mrs. Bass.

"I'm going to die of slowness!" Brooke whispered to Aly.

But Aly was thinking that she might die of worry. All around her, dogs seemed to be getting adopted. Lucas, whom half the sixth-grade soccer team had a crush on, was playing with Laces, the big golden retriever. Heather Davis's friend Jayden and a girl in Aly's grade named Annie were petting Penny the poodle.

Aly started to feel a little panicky. What if Sparky had been adopted? What if someone was playing with him right now and thinking about taking him home? What if he already found another family, before Brooke and Aly got to make their case for the dog? Aly checked her pocket for the list, just to make sure it was still there.

"Let's hold hands and push through the crowd," Aly told her sister. "We need to see if Sparky's still here. And if he is, then we can show him to Mom and Dad."

Brooke looked at Aly with terror in her eyes. "Do you think he could be gone?"

Aly took a deep breath. "I don't know, Brookster. I just don't know."

But just before they could start pushing their way to Sparky's cage, Irena saw them.

"Girls," she called "I'm so glad you made it! Look at what you've done. All these dogs are going to have homes because of you and your friends."

Aly and Brooke smiled and thanked her, but Aly couldn't stop her leg from bouncing with impatience. They *had* to find Sparky.

"You know, I think this is a record. All the dogs but one have been spoken for, and it's not even noon yet," Irena said.

Aly felt her heart start to race. "All but one have been adopted?"

Irena nodded, the beads on her braids clicking. "Isn't that wonderful?"

Brooke grabbed Aly's hand and squeezed it hard.

Aly swallowed.

"Which one—" she started to say, but the words

got caught in her throat, so she tried again. "Which one is left?"

Irena looked down at her clipboard.

Aly held her breath. *Please don't be adopted, please don't be adopted, please don't be adopted*, she wished.

ten

Call Me Sparkly

et's see," Irena said. "It looks like the only one left is . . . Sparky." She smiled at the girls. "Maybe he's just a little too small for most people. It's a shame, though, because he's such a sweet dog."

Aly let out her breath in a whoosh. Thank goodness.

"Wewanthim!" Brooke blurted out so fast that her words ran together. "Please don't let anyone take him. We want him."

"Oh!" Irena looked surprised. "I thought you girls weren't allowed to have a dog."

"Would we be able to see him?" Aly asked. "So we can show him to our parents?"

"Of course," Irena said. "I'll go get him myself, for our star fund-raisers."

Irena left, and Aly pulled the list out of her pocket. "Okay, Brooke," she said. "I'm going to go get Mom and Dad away from Mrs. Bass. You wait here and hold Sparky when Irena comes back. Got it?"

"Got it," Brooke answered.

Weaving through the crowd, Aly made her way over to her parents. Mom was still in deep conversation with Mrs. Bass, but Dad was kneeling on the floor, petting Murphy, while Mrs. Bass's sons filled out the adoption papers. Aly kneeled down next to him and gave Murphy a pat. He was a really sweet dog and hadn't minded at all when his nails were painted.

"Hey, Dad," Aly said. "Brooke and I want you to meet someone."

"Hey, Alligator," he said. "This guy looks great." He gave Murphy another scratch behind his ears. "Who do you want me to meet?"

"It's a surprise," Aly told him. "Come with me."

Dad followed, and Aly threaded through the crowd of people and dogs and cages back to where Brooke was standing. She was holding Sparky, who kept trying to lick her face. His rainbow collar shone.

"You want me to meet Brooke?" Dad asked.

Aly started laughing. "No, Dad! We want you to meet Sparky."

"That little guy? Is he actually a dog?" Dad was joking, but Brooke didn't like it.

"Of course he's a dog!" she said, and handed Sparky over to her father. Dad was so much bigger than the tiny dog that Sparky fit right in the crook of his elbow. Sparky wasn't anything like Dad's dog

Mouse, but when he turned his head and licked Dad's fingers, Dad smiled.

"He's really sweet," Dad said. "Was he your favorite?"

Aly nodded.

Brooke said, "Well, not at first, but at second, yeah. And now I love him the most."

Dad looked down at Sparky. "So is one of your friends adopting him?" he asked.

Brooke looked at Aly. Aly cleared her throat. "We thought maybe we could adopt him," she said.

"There you are, girls. I thought I'd lost you," Mom said, walking over to Aly and Brooke. Then she saw the dog in Dad's arms. "Who's that?" she asked.

"It's Sparky," Brooke said. "He's the last dog left that doesn't have a family."

Aly handed Mom her list. "These are all the reasons why we think he'd be the perfect dog for us," she said.

Mom looked at the paper, then stepped closer to Dad so he could read it too. "You girls must've been thinking about this for a while," she said.

Brooke pushed her glasses up on her nose. "We have. For a very long time. At first I wanted Melvin, but he's really slobbery and too big, and Aly knew all along that Sparky would be the best one."

"He really is, Mom," Aly added. "And we think he'd be a great puppy for our family."

Mom looked down at the paper in her hand again and started reading it over carefully.

"Hi, everyone," Joan said, walking over to the Tanners. "Guess what? I just sold out of all the Joan's Bones." She was smiling.

"That's great news," Mom said.

Brooke couldn't wait another second. "Mom! We want a dog," she said. "The one Dad's holding."

Mom gave Dad and Joan a look. "I'm not sure if our

house can handle a dog. And he'd be home alone all day. That's not a very nice way for a dog to spend his time."

Aly hadn't thought of that. That was a problem. She didn't want Sparky to be alone all day. There had to be a way to make this work. She had to think fast.

"How about the Sparkle Spa?" Aly said. "What if he lives at the Sparkle Spa during the day? We could get him a bed and toys, and he could live in the corner next to the pedicure chairs. We could even get him an enclosure gate so he won't be able to go into the main salon and wander around."

Mom tilted her head sideways. She raised her eyebrows at Dad. Brooke started bouncing on her toes.

"Who would walk him?" Mom said. "While you girls are at school?"

"Um . . . ," Aly began.

Joan raised her hand. "I could do it," she said.

"Really?" Brooke asked, throwing her arms around Joan. "You'd do that?"

"Sure," Joan answered. "I love dogs. It would be fun to have one at the salon."

Dad cleared his throat. "You girls have been so responsible with the fund-raiser and the shelter dogs, I bet you'd do a great job with Sparky. But you know I'm not around very much, so this decision is really up to your mom."

"I promise we'll take such good care of him," Aly said. "You won't have to do a thing!"

Brooke nodded. Then she took Sparky out of Dad's arms and handed him over to their mom.

Mom's face looked soft and sweet. The girls knew they had her—it was love at first sight. Or first cuddle.

"Well . . ." Mom looked at Joan again. "You're sure you want to take on the dog-walking responsibility?"

Joan ruffled Aly's hair. "Absolutely," she said.

"You girls *have* been very responsible," Mom said. "And since Joan is willing to help, I say okay."

Brooke screamed and threw her arms around Mom and Sparky. "Thank you, Mommy!" Then she hugged her dad.

But Aly turned and hugged Joan. "Thank *you*," she said quietly. "Mom never would've agreed otherwise."

"My pleasure," Joan said as she gave Aly a squeeze. Then Aly went to hug her parents, too. She was smiling so wide, her cheeks were hurting a bit, but she couldn't stop. Other than the day she and Brooke got Mom to agree to the Sparkle Spa, this was one of the happiest days of Aly's life.

When they had all the adoption papers signed and the coupon for a free year of dog food from Pups 'n' Stuff in hand, the Tanners—along with Joan and, of course, Sparky—walked over to True Colors. Dad had already taken the car and would meet up with them at the salon.

Aly was holding Sparky's leash, the sparkly rainbow one that she'd picked out herself, and Brooke was telling Sparky all about the salon.

"There's lots of nail polish there," she was saying, "but it's not the kind for you. You have special nail polish. This kind at the Sparkle Spa is just for people."

Sparky twitched his ears. Aly started laughing.

When they reached True Colors, Aly and Brooke sat outside on the Blue Skies bench. Aly held Sparky on her lap, and while she rubbed his belly, she couldn't help but come up with a good, better, and best for today:

Good was that she and Brooke were friends again, no matter what.

Better was that all the old-timers were adopted into loving homes.

And best was that the cutest old-timer of all was their brand-new dog.

Brooke interrupted her thoughts. "Aly? Let's take Sparky into the Sparkle Spa so he can see how cool it is." The sisters walked into True Colors and headed for the back room. They watched Sparky sniff around, getting to know his new home.

"Can you believe Mom really agreed?" Brooke asked.

Aly shook her head. "It's kind of a miracle."

"There's one thing," Brooke said.

"What's that?" Aly asked.

"I think we have to change his name."

"Change his name?" Aly asked. "Won't that be confusing for him?"

"Not change it *too* much," Brooke said. She was

over near the polish display, grabbing a bottle out of the silver section. "Here!" she said. She ran over and gave the polish to Aly.

"Call Me Sparkly," Aly read. "I forgot about this color."

"See?" Brooke said. "His name *should* be Sparkly."

Aly smiled. As usual, Brooke's ideas turned out perfectly in the end. Sparkly it would be.

How to Give Yourself (or a Friend!) a Puppy Paw Pedicure
By Aly (and Brooke!)

* . * * . . * . . * . . * . . * . . * . . * . . * . . * . . * . . * . . *

What you need:

Paper towels

Polish remover

Cotton balls

Clear polish

One color polish for the base (we suggest yellow)

One color polish for the paw prints (we suggest pink)

Watercolor paintbrush

What you do:

1. Put some paper towels down on the floor so you don't have to worry about what will happen if you spill some polish. (Seriously. This is important. Polish stains badly. We know from experience.)

2. Take one cotton ball and put some polish remover on it. If you have polish on your toes already, use enough to get it off. If you don't, just rub the remover over your nails once to get off any dirt that might be on there. (If there's dirt, it'll make your polish look lumpy. And lumpy polish is the absolute pits!)

3. Rip off two paper towels. Twist the first one into a long tube and weave it back and forth between your toes to separate them a little bit more. Then do the same thing with the second paper towel for your other foot. You might need to tuck it in around your pinkie toe if it pops up and gets in your way while you polish.

4. Open up your clear polish, and do a coat of clear on each nail. Then close the clear bottle up tight. (You can go in whatever order you want, but our favorite is big toe to pinkie on your

right foot, then big toe to pinkie on your left foot. Just make sure you get them all!)

5. Open up the yellow polish. (Or whichever color you chose for your base. Just make sure it's a color that will make it so you can see the paw print! For example, orange on red might be a little hard to see.) Do a coat on each toe. Close the bottle up tight.

6. Fan your toes a little to dry them a tiny bit, and then repeat step five. (If you don't do a second coat, the polish won't look as beautiful and bright.)

7. Fan your toes again. (You should fan them for a while. We recommend singing the whole alphabet song three times through. Aly likes to show off and sing it backward, but I do forward and that's just fine.)

8. Open up your pink polish (or whatever accent color you chose). Don't use the regular polish brush. Take the watercolor paintbrush, which has thinner and pointier hairs, and dip it into the pink polish. Then touch the paintbrush to the middle of your big toenail to make a medium-sized dot. After that, touch it above the medium-sized dot three times to make three smaller dots in a row. It'll look just like a paw print! (If it doesn't, you can just get nail polish remover and start over.) Then do it on the other big toenail. (You could do it on every nail, but we think it looks cooler on the big toes. Also, the rest of the toenails are pretty tiny, so it's hard to make the dots small enough to make the paws.) When you're done, close the bottle up tight.

9. Fan your toes a little bit (one alphabet song should do the trick) and then open your clear

polish. Do a top coat of clear polish on all your toes. Close the bottle up tight.

10. Now your toes have to dry. You can fan them for a long time (like at least fifteen alphabet songs), or sit and make a bracelet or read a book or watch TV or talk to your friend. Usually it takes about twenty minutes, but it could take longer. (After twenty minutes, you should check the polish really carefully by touching your big toe super lightly with your thumb. If it still feels sticky, keep waiting! Patience is the most important part, otherwise you might smudge it and you'll have to take it off and do it all over again, which, let me tell you, is a very grumpy-making thing.)

And now you should have a beautiful puppy paw pedicure! Even after the polish is dry, you probably shouldn't wear socks and sneaker-type shoes for a while. Bare feet or sandals are better so all your hard work doesn't get smooshed. (And besides, then you can show people your puppy paw toes!)

Happy polishing!

∗ ⸱ ⸱ ∗ ⸱ ⸱ ∗ ⸱ ⸱ ∗ ⸱ ∗ ⸱ ⸱ ∗ ⸱ ⸱ ∗

Makeover Magic

* . * * . * * . *

For my community of friends and family.

I'd love to give each and every one of you an On the Ball trophy.

And extra-special thanks to Karen Nagel,

Marianna Baer, Betsy Bird, and Eliot Schrefer,

who help Aly and Brooke (and me!) to sparkle.

one

I'm So Grapeful

Aly Tanner glanced at her purple polka-dot watch. *Uh-oh.* She and her sister, Brooke, had only four minutes to unpack the new polish colors before their first appointments showed up at Sparkle Spa.

"Brooke," Aly said, looking to where her sister was carefully reorganizing the bottles at the polish display, "we've got to go a little faster. Jenica and Bethany are going to be here for their pedicures soon. And then the rest of the soccer team will be coming in all afternoon."

Sparkly, the girls' tiny dog, who lived in Sparkle Spa during the day and at home with them at night, barked in agreement.

"I know, I know," Brooke said. "But I just can't decide if I'm So Grapeful should go before Plum Delicious or after We the Purple. It's hard to tell how the color's going to come out on people's nails. And I want the display to be absolutely right so that no one thinks they're getting one color and ends up getting another."

Aly smiled. Brooke's attention to detail was partially what made Sparkle Spa look so beautiful— she'd been in charge of picking the paintings on the walls, the colorful pillows in the nail-drying and bracelet-making area, and the huge rainbow display of polish. Aly quickly opened up a bottle of I'm So Grapeful and brushed it onto her thumbnail. Then she blew on it and added a second coat.

"Does this help?" she asked. "Can you tell better now?"

Brooke's eyes lit up. "Yes. Now I know exactly where it should go." She slid the bottle in right next to Purple People Eater and went on to the next color.

"You know," Aly said, handing Brooke Cider Donuts, which was a very light orange, and Apple Crispy, which was a bright red, "I think later we should pull out all the colors that have to do with fall stuff. You know, for the Sixth-Grade Fall Ball."

"Okay," said Brooke. "And maybe we can come up with some special Fall Ball combinations."

"Maybe tomorrow?" Aly asked. "When Sparkle Spa is closed?"

Brooke nodded as she put a bright yellowish-gold polish called Candy Corn on the Cob next to Lemon Aid. Sparkle Spa, which was really just the back room of True Colors, Aly and Brooke's mom's nail salon, had a lot of rules. One of them was that the girls could be open only two days after school and one day during the weekend. That was so they could still do homework and hang out with their friends.

"I can't wait until I'm in sixth grade and can go to the Fall Ball," Brooke said, reaching for a silvery Very Ice Try. "Only three more years."

Aly closed the box and put it in the corner with the rest of the extra polish bottles. "And only two more years until you get to decorate. I can't believe I get to be a decorator this year."

The Sixth-Grade Fall Ball was one of the biggest events of the school year at Auden Elementary. The fifth graders always decorated the gym for the dance. It was tradition. It was also tradition that two sixth graders, one girl and one boy, got trophies for being "On the Ball." They were chosen by teachers and always had to be kids who were good students and good friends and gave back to the school community. Aly wondered who was going to get the trophies this year.

"Are you guys open yet?" a voice called from the Sparkle Spa doorway. It was Jenica Posner:

- sixth-grade captain of the girls' soccer team
- the most popular girl at Auden Elementary
- and Sparkle Spa's very first customer, back when Aly and Brooke started the salon a little more than a month ago.

Jenica was also the person Aly would vote for to win one of the On the Ball trophies if winners were chosen by students instead of teachers.

Jenica was more than just a great soccer player. She had also created an after-school program called

Superstar Sports. Two days a week, she and a group of volunteers helped the younger kids at school learn how to play soccer and kickball and practice things like teamwork and good sportsmanship.

"We're open!" Brooke said. "And we have lots of new colors. The polish company is really pushing a fall theme this year."

"We thought some of these would be perfect for the ball," Aly added, securing her chin-length hair in a half-up so it wouldn't fall in her face while she was polishing.

"Sounds cool—can I see?" Jenica asked.

"But you're still going to get the rainbow sparkle pedicure today, right?" Brooke said, handing over a bottle of Cider Donuts.

"Absolutely," Jenica answered, slipping off her sneakers and socks. "Otherwise, we might kill our winning streak." Ever since Jenica and the other soccer players had started getting rainbow sparkle pedicures, they'd won every single soccer game they'd played. The girls said it was because their feet had sparkle power, but Aly was pretty sure it was just because they were really good soccer players.

Still, she liked having so many regular customers at Sparkle Spa and especially liked hanging out with Jenica Posner. Sometimes she still couldn't believe that the two of them were friends.

"But," Jenica continued, jumping up into a pedicure chair, "I'm thinking I might get something different for the Fall Ball. Because I just bought my shoes—silver sandals with little heels. It's the first time I'm allowed to wear heels."

"Really?" Bethany asked, walking into Sparkle Spa. "My glamma got me my first pair of high heels when I was six. But they were for dress-up only."

"Your glamma?" Brooke asked.

"Yeah, 'glamorous' plus 'grandma' equals 'glamma,'" Bethany said. She sat down in the chair next to Jenica and unbuckled her sandals, and Aly and Brooke started the sparkle pedicures. "My glamma is super-glamorous. She was even in a television commercial once."

Aly thought about her own grandma, who wore jeans and sweatshirts and was not very glamorous at all. She'd never been on TV, either. Aly decided she liked it that way.

"Which boy do you think is going to get the On the Ball trophy?" Bethany asked.

"Everyone thinks it's going to be Lucas," Jenica answered. Aly had never spoken to Lucas Grant, but she knew who he was. He played basketball and the trumpet, and all the girls called him "Cute Lucas" because, well, he was really handsome. He'd also started a program called Reading Buddies, where sixth graders went into the kindergarten classes to read to the kids. It was a pretty cool program, and Aly hoped it would still be going next year so she could volunteer for it.

"I think it's going to be Oliver," Bethany replied, looking at her toes.

"That's just because you like him," Jenica said, rolling her eyes.

"Well, he's very likeable!" Bethany answered. Aly was pretty sure she was blushing. "But still, I think he has a good chance. He was the one who got the cafeteria to donate its extra food to homeless shelters, after all. That does more for the community than reading to little kids."

Just as Aly and Brooke were applying the top coat of clear polish to the rainbow sparkle pedicures, Mia, their next appointment, ran into the spa. Anjuli, the team's goalie, was right behind her.

"Guys," Mia said dramatically, standing in the

middle of the doorframe, "I have crazy news."

"What?" Brooke asked, whipping around to face Mia.

Aly twisted her head to look at Mia too.

From his fenced-in corner, Sparkly even turned to see what was happening.

"Princess Polish just opened!" Mia said. "Can you believe it?"

Sparkly whimpered and turned back around.

Aly and Brooke exchanged a Secret Sister Eye Message that meant: *Oh no!*

Princess Polish was a new nail salon across the street that'd had a COMING SOON sign in the window for the last month or so. It had worried Aly and Brooke's mom for a while, but then it seemed like it might never open. Now it had. This was not good news for Sparkle Spa. Or for Mom's salon, True Colors.

"Does it look any good?" Bethany asked. "My cousin told me there's a Princess Polish in her town and it's really awesome."

"Bethany!" Jenica elbowed her. "It won't be any better than Sparkle Spa."

"Sheesh," Bethany said, rubbing her arm. "I was just asking."

Aly had to bite her cheek not to smile. She loved how loyal a customer Jenica was.

"But I didn't even tell you the craziest part yet!" Mia still hadn't moved from the doorframe, and Anjuli was still behind her. "They're offering a *free* Princess Pedicure to anyone under thirteen who goes into the salon! And a manicure, too, if you're going to Auden's Fall Ball. How did they even know about our school's dance?"

Aly gulped. This was even worse news. It wasn't like they charged a lot at Sparkle Spa; in fact, that was one of Mom's rules—there was no set price, just a donation jar for customers to pay whatever they could afford. Then, each time the jar reached $100, Aly and Brooke gave the money to a worthy cause. So far, they'd donated money to Paws for Love, an animal shelter on Taft Street. The jar was getting kind of full again. They'd have to pick another charity soon.

"Wow," Bethany said. "That's a really nice offer."

"Right?" Mia said.

Jenica glared at them. Then she cleared her throat. "Aly, Brooke, I'd like to book my appointment for a manicure and pedicure for the Fall Ball. Here at Sparkle Spa. Can I book it now?"

Aly smiled at Jenica. She let out a breath she didn't know she was holding. "You definitely can," she said, pulling out the new appointment book Mom had gotten them just for Sparkle Spa. Mom reviewed it every week to make sure there weren't too many appointments for the girls to handle. "When would you like to come?"

"Next Saturday morning at eleven," Jenica answered, after thinking for a bit. "We have an early soccer game, but I'll be free after that."

"You got it," Aly said, writing her into the book.

"Me too," Anjuli said from where she stood behind Mia. "I'll come at eleven thirty."

"And me," Mia said after Aly had finished writing. "I'll come at the same time as Anjuli."

Bethany didn't say anything, though, no matter how hard Jenica glared at her. And if Bethany, one of their regulars, wanted to check out Princess Polish, Aly knew they had a problem brewing. A big one.

two

Kiss and Tell

The problem followed the Tanners home. That night, Mom was not in the very best mood. The minute she and the girls and Sparkly arrived home, she grabbed the cordless phone, went into her bedroom, and called Aly and Brooke's dad. He was away on a business trip and wouldn't be back until the weekend.

Brooke and Aly stayed in the living room, playing fetch with Sparkly. They'd trained him so that when Brooke threw a tiny ball, Sparkly would get it and bring it to Aly. And then when Aly threw it, he'd bring the ball to Brooke. It had taken ages for Sparkly to learn that.

"You think Mom is talking to Dad about Princess Polish?" Brooke asked as she threw the ball.

"Probably," Aly said, taking it from Sparkly's mouth and throwing it again.

"Do you think—" Brooke held on to the ball until Sparkly barked, and then she threw it. "Do you think Princess Polish could ever be more popular than True Colors? And if that happened, would True Colors close? And then Sparkle Spa? And then would the soccer team lose all their games because they couldn't get rainbow sparkle pedicures? And then would everyone be sad and mad, especially us?"

Aly rubbed Sparkly's head, thinking about it for a while. "Well," she said, "True Colors is older than you and it's older than me. No other salon has put it out of business yet, so I think it'll be okay."

"But Mom's still worried?" Brooke asked.

"Yeah," Aly said. "But Mom's still worried."

After Mom got off the phone, she, Aly, and Brooke made a dinner of macaroni and cheese—the kind that came from a box—and steamed broccoli. Then the three Tanner girls sat down to eat, and Sparkly lay down underneath the table to chew on a bone. Mom was very quiet and didn't even notice when Brooke took a second helping of macaroni before finishing her broccoli. That worried Aly.

"Mom," she said, after swallowing a broccoli stem, "you know True Colors is the best salon, right? And you have so many regulars who come every week and would never go anywhere else. You don't have to be nervous about Princess Polish or anything."

Mom put her fork down and sighed. "Thanks, Al," she said. "But I don't know if everyone would agree with you. I think I might start offering deals or special pedicures like Princess Polish."

Brooke reached for a third helping of macaroni. But this time, Mom raised an eyebrow at her, so Brooke sat back in her seat and dipped her broccoli in the leftover cheese instead. "What if you offer the same specials they do?" she asked. "Then it would be equal, so no one would have a reason to choose Princess Polish instead of True Colors."

Mom shook her head. "I don't want to start that kind of thing, because then I'm stuck offering whatever Princess Polish does. I want to come up with different promotions. Ideas that will make True Colors stand out."

Brooke chewed her cheesy broccoli. "What if you had a special deal for bridesmaids, like when Miss Lulu got married? Remember how many she had?"

"I do remember, Brookie," Mom said. "But I don't think enough people get married in our town each week to make that idea work."

Aly had slipped off her flip-flop and was petting Sparkly under the table with her toes. "The Sixth-Grade Fall Ball is a big deal," she said. "And we have some manicures and pedicures booked already. True Colors could have all Sparkle Spa's customers for the ball, if you want."

"That's a wonderful offer, sweetie," Mom answered, "but I think you should keep those customers. You've been working hard to build up your business. Just like I'm going to work hard to keep building mine. Don't worry, I'll think of something."

Everyone ate quietly for a little while.

Finally, Brooke asked, "What was it like at your Sixth-Grade Fall Ball, Mom?"

Mom took a sip of her water and smiled. "I didn't have a Sixth-Grade Fall Ball," she said. "But I did go to a Valentine's Day dance in sixth grade."

Aly tried to imagine what Mom looked like in sixth grade. She wondered if maybe Mom looked kind of like her. They did have the same hair, after all. And the same green eyes.

"What was it like?" Brooke asked, wiping another tree of broccoli through the last of the cheese on her plate. "Did you wear high heels? And have a sparkly pedicure?"

Putting her glass down and leaning back in her chair, Mom said, "It was a magical night. The gym was decorated with pink and red streamers, and there were hearts on all the walls. There was music, too, and candy and fruit punch."

"And you had high heels?" Brooke asked.

Mom shook her head. "No high heels. You know

how when we visit Grandma and Grandpa in the winter, there's always snow on the ground?"

Aly nodded. They usually visited their mother's parents in the summer, but the three times they'd gone in the winter, it was cold and snowy and Aly had to borrow Grandma's friend's daughter's old winter jacket.

"Well, it was snowing during the dance," Mom said, "and it was really cold. So we all had on boots. And tights and thick skirts and sweaters. I did have nail polish on, though. It was light pink, kind of like Kiss and Tell."

Brooke made a face. "Kiss and Tell is so light, it's barely even nail polish! And I can't believe you had to wear boots. I'm glad we live here, where we can wear flip-flops all the time. And no tights."

Aly laughed, but she wanted to hear the rest of Mom's story. "Why was it so magical?" she asked.

Mom smiled. "Do you know who I met at that sixth-grade dance?"

Aly shook her head, but Brooke said, "Joan?"

Joan was Mom's best friend and Aly and Brooke's very favorite True Colors manicurist, but Aly was pretty sure that Mom hadn't met her in sixth grade.

"Not Joan," Mom said with a laugh.

Aly wondered who it could be. "Was it a boy?" she asked.

Brooke's eyes popped open behind the bright blue frames of her glasses.

"I'll give you a clue," Mom said, smiling again. "He was tall and had wavy blond hair, and he was the smartest boy I'd ever met."

Aly felt like lightning had struck her brain. Their dad was tall and had wavy blond hair and was really, really smart. "Was his name Mark?" she asked excitedly.

Mom nodded her head, a grin on her face. "How'd you guess?"

"Wait," Brooke said. "Dad's name is Mark."

"It is," Mom said. "And I met him at a sixth-grade dance. He wasn't my boyfriend until much later, though."

Aly thought about the boys in her class. Was it possible that one day she'd marry one of them and have two daughters and her own nail salon? And was it possible that she'd meet him at the Fall Ball next year? So many cool things happened once you were a sixth grader. But first, she had to focus on getting through fifth grade and helping everyone going to this year's Fall Ball look their best. As long as her customers didn't decide to go to Princess Polish instead!

thRee

Candy Corn on the Cob

After school on Friday, Sparkle Spa wasn't that busy. It was so quiet that Aly's two best friends, Charlotte and Lily, and Brooke's best friend, Sophie, stayed there after their pedicures, flip-flops off, feet all pedicured.

"Thanks for suggesting Candy Corn on the Cob, Brooke," Sophie said, wiggling her toes in the drying area. "The gold sparkles make the yellow extra glittery."

"Can I keep experimenting on your toes, then?"

Brooke asked. "Because I have a new idea for the Fall Ball. We can do special pedicures with a stripe of a different sparkly color on the top part of the big toe. You know, like the toe is dipped in caramel or chocolate or something."

"Just the big toes?" Aly asked. "Not all of them?"

"Trust me," Brooke said, pulling I'm So Grapeful off the shelf.

"I trust you, Brooke," Sophie said.

Aly trusted her too. Brooke was a really talented artist, and somehow she seemed to know exactly which colors would look best together. Brooke was the one who had invented the soccer team's rainbow sparkle pedicure.

Brooke painted a medium-size stripe of glittery purple on top of the glittery yellow. The purple made the yellow look even brighter. It would've looked too wild if this combination was on every toe.

"You were right, Brookster," Aly said, inspecting Sophie's feet. "We should make that design the Fall Ball special pedicure."

"And you should make Candy Corn on the Cob the Color of the Week!" Lily was looking at last week's color, a glittery green called Hoppy Birthday.

"We do need a new one," Brooke said. "But maybe we should pick this coppery Autumn Princess instead."

"Nothing with the word 'princess'!" Aly groaned. "Princess Polish is already annoying enough!"

The phone rang in the main salon, and a few seconds later one of the manicurists, Jamie, came into Sparkle Spa. "Phone's for you, girls," she said, holding the cordless out toward Aly.

"Thanks, Jamie," Aly said, taking the phone. "Sparkle Spa," she said into the receiver. "How may I help you?"

The girl on the other end was talking really quickly.

"You want to *what?*" Aly asked—she hadn't quite heard the first time.

"Cancel," the girl said, more clearly now. "Cancel my appointment before the Fall Ball. I had it for noon next Saturday. I'm Uma."

Aly felt the blood drain from her face. She knew Uma from school, but not very well, and Uma had booked her appointment only yesterday.

"Can I ask why?" Aly said, even though the polite thing to do would've been just to say okay, remove her name from the appointment book, and forget about it.

"I changed my mind," Uma answered.

Aly imagined her shrugging on the other side of the phone.

"Okay," Aly said. "Thanks for letting us know."

She beeped off on the phone and erased Uma's name from the book.

"Did we lose a customer?" Brooke asked.

Aly nodded. "Not a regular. A sixth grader named Uma. I bet she's going to Princess Polish. She didn't say so, but still."

Brooke balled her hands into fists. "What are they doing to us? I *hate* Princess Polish."

"I'm not a fan either, Brookster," Aly said. "I think they may be taking some of our walk-ins, too."

Usually, by this point on a Friday afternoon, Aly and Brooke had customers who walked by, saw their sign, and came in for a pedicure or a manicure or both. But today Sparkle Spa was quiet. Aly guessed people saw the FREE PRINCESS PEDICURE! sign across the street and went there instead. She figured if she were someone who didn't know how cool Sparkle Spa was and she saw that sign, she might check out the new place too.

Brooke was tugging on her fishtail braid. Aly knew that meant her sister was nervous about Princess Polish and the missing customers.

"Hey, Aly, did you braid Brooke's hair today?" Lily asked. She was stringing beads at Sparkle Spa's jewelry-making area.

Aly nodded.

"Could you braid my hair like that? And maybe weave these beads into it?" She held up the thread she'd been stringing in a pattern of alternating silver, gold, and orange beads.

"Sure," Aly said. "Why not?" It wasn't like they had nails to polish.

"I like that style too," Sophie said. "Can you do that for me, Brooke?"

Brooke shook her head. "I can't do that kind of braid."

"I can!" Charlotte said. She got up from petting

Sparkly, who was asleep in his corner of the spa, behind a little gate.

"I'll string some beads," Brooke volunteered.

Aly and Charlotte began weaving the strings of beads into their friends' hair. Brooke found some ribbons to add as well. When the braids were finished, they looked beautiful.

"I just thought of something!" Brooke was so excited, she couldn't stand still. "Sparkle Spa can do sparkly braids. And we can do them for the Fall Ball! Princess Polish doesn't do hair. We'll get all our customers back!"

Sometimes Aly couldn't believe how smart Brooke was.

"I can be a braider," Charlotte offered. "I don't mind working for Sparkle Spa."

Aly thought this was a very good idea—the kind of idea they probably didn't even have to run past Mom.

Brooke ran to the supply closet near the back of the room and grabbed paper and a handful of markers. "Time to make a sign," she said.

While Lily kept stringing beads, Aly, Sophie, and Charlotte watched as Brooke drew the back of a girl's head, with a beautiful, sparkly beaded braid cascading down. Then she handed the marker to Aly. "You write the words," she said.

Aly thought for a moment and then wrote:

Sparkle Braids at Sparkle Spa!
Perfect for Auden's Sixth-Grade Fall Ball!
Call for an appointment!

She added the phone number for True Colors underneath.

Lily inspected the sign. "I think you should add 'Free' on there," she said. "People like free."

Aly looked at Brooke. Brooke looked back at Aly.

"We don't want to copy what Princess Polish does," Aly said. Actually, she kind of wished they could charge real money for this special service, like five or even ten dollars. Then they could give the money to True Colors.

Just then Aly had an idea—a Brooke sort of idea, but it was all her own. "Do you think," Aly started, "that maybe we could give the money in the donation jar to True Colors this time?"

"Yes, Aly," Brooke said. "That's the best idea!"

"But . . ." Sophie scratched her head. "But True Colors isn't a charity."

"But it *is* a place we love, and if Mom is losing business, it's a place that could use some help," Brooke reasoned. "Come on, let's write that on the poster!"

Aly wondered if Sophie was right, if maybe this wasn't her best idea ever and was something that would make Mom mad. But she picked up a marker and added to the bottom of the poster, in much smaller lettering:

All donations will go to True Colors.

Hopefully, Mom wouldn't mind. But just in case, Aly didn't push down very hard on the marker, so the writing wasn't very easy to see.

four

Apple Crispy

"What are you girls doing?" Joan asked. She walked over to where Brooke was holding the poster to the window as Aly was taping it to the glass. Sophie, Charlotte, and Lily were outside, giving instructions on where to place the poster so that it would be most visible.

"Joanie Rigatoni Noodles!" Brooke said, turning her head. "We came up with a way to compete with Princess Polish. Aly and Charlotte are going to do beaded braids for the dance. Like mine. Look!"

She shook her head so Joan couldn't miss her sparkly braid.

"That's not a bad idea," Joan said, sitting down in an empty manicure chair. "We could use some more foot traffic in here. What did your mother think?"

Aly and Brooke gave each other a Secret Sister Eye Message: *Uh-oh, caught.*

"We haven't actually asked her yet," Aly said. "We looked for Mom before, while you were polishing Mrs. Bass's nails, but we didn't see her. And we figured this wasn't the kind of thing that needed her permission anyway. You know, it's a Sparkle Spa promotion."

Joan looked around the salon herself then, as though she doubted what Aly had said. But sure enough, only Lisa and Jamie were at the manicure stations, with Carla behind the welcome desk. And Emma was sitting all by herself in the waiting area, reading a magazine.

"Carla, do you know where Karen is?" Joan asked.

Carla stopped flipping through the appointment book to look up at Joan. "She said something about going to the print shop. To make coupons, I think."

Joan nodded. "I forgot she was doing that today." Then she turned to Brooke and Aly. "Well, I guess it's fine for you to braid hair in Sparkle Spa. I think I'm going to grab a coffee from Beans and Leaves. Carla can help you girls out if you need anything."

Only half an hour after the girls had hung their poster, Aly was braiding a customer's hair as quickly as she could—Charlotte, too—and there was a line of girls waiting to get their hair done. Not just sixth graders, either, and not just for a special occasion. Evidently, people liked getting their hair braided almost as much as they liked getting manicures and pedicures, for no particular reason at all!

Luckily, when Mom found out about the hair idea, she didn't argue. In fact, she thought it was a super plan.

Aly twisted a hair band around the bottom of a braid and sent her customer over to Sophie, who had gotten two mirrors—one from Carla and the other from Jamie—to show the girls what they looked like from behind once the style was completed. Sparkly was sitting next to Sophie and barked his approval every now and then.

The next girl in line sat down in front of Aly. Aly thought she recognized her from school.

"Hi," Aly said. "What color beads would you like in your braid?"

"Do you have red?" the girl asked.

"Brooke!" Aly called across the room. "Do we have red?"

Brooke inspected the strands of beads she and Lily had already made. "Red and gold!" she called back. "Kind of like Apple Crispy!"

"I like that," the girl in Aly's chair said. "I'm Daisy, by the way."

"Nice to meet you, Daisy. I'm Aly," Aly said. "And that's my sister, Brooke."

"I know who you guys are," Daisy said. "*Everyone* at school does."

This information was news to Aly. "Really?" she asked.

Daisy laughed. "How often do kids start a sparkly spa? You guys are famous."

Aly felt her face turn pink. "Um, anyway," she said, smiling, "do you want a French braid, Dutch braid, fishtail braid, backward braid, or regular braid?"

"Which one is the Dutch?" Daisy asked.

Aly pointed to one of the girls sitting in front of

Charlotte. "It's that one, where the braid kind of sits on top of your head."

"Okay, I'll go with that one," Daisy said. "I think it'll be a trial run for the Fall Ball."

Aly nodded and started the braiding, making sure every strand was even and straight as she wove in the beads. Aly thought it was the best braid she'd done so far. Braiding hair was kind of like polishing nails, she realized. The more you did it, the better you got.

Once Aly finished Daisy's hair and Daisy had checked herself out in the mirror, she asked to book an appointment before next weekend's ball. Within the hour, four other girls made Fall Ball appointments too—for braids *and* manicures and pedicures. They wanted the whole Sparkle Spa treatment!

Lily stood up and held the donation jar high in the air. It was a sparkly teal color, in the shape of a strawberry. Aly and Brooke's mom had made it back when she was in art school, before she owned a nail salon and became a mom.

"Don't forget to donate to the jar," Lily said. "We're giving all the money to True Colors!"

"Yay, True Colors!" Brooke cheered while stringing beads.

A few of the customers smiled, and Aly did too. Wait until Mom found out!

five

Pickle Me

Two days later, on Sunday morning, Dad was driving Aly and Brooke to the salon. Mom had gone in earlier to open up. Sparkly, who loved riding in the car, was standing on Brooke's lap with his nose out the window, sniffing the fresh air.

"So, Alligator," Dad said, looking in the rearview mirror at Aly. "Mom tells me this is the week you and your friends are decorating for the sixth-grade dance."

Aly nodded. With all the trouble because of Princess Polish, it had almost slipped her mind. "We are," she said. "Even though Brooke and I usually open Sparkle Spa on Fridays, we can't this week because that's the day the fifth graders are decorating the gym. The ball's on Saturday night."

"I wish I were a fifth grader," Brooke said, sighing. "Do you think I could pretend?"

Aly smiled at her sister. "I think people might notice that you're a little short for a fifth grader."

"What if I wore high heels?" Brooke asked hopefully. "Just a few inches?"

Dad shook his head. "You know the rules," he said quickly over his shoulder.

Brooke did know the rules. And Aly figured her sister didn't *really* believe that high heels would make her look that much older. But that was Brooke—she would try anything.

"Girls, I'll come get you around four," Dad said as he slowed to a stop in front of True Colors. "Mom's going to work late today. Maybe we can go to the movies tonight?"

"Can we get popcorn for dinner?" Brooke asked. "And Sno-Caps?"

Aly stopped herself from laughing out loud. She knew there was *no* way their dad was going to go for popcorn and chocolate as dinner.

"How about for dessert?" Dad said.

"Deal!" Brooke said. She popped the lock on her door, opened it right onto the sidewalk, and scooted out, with Aly and Sparkly following.

Aly couldn't help but steal a glance across the street at Princess Polish. She so wished they would just disappear into thin air. And she couldn't believe what she saw—a *new* sign was in their window: PRINCESS HAIR DESIGN! BRAIDS! CURLS! UPDOS! BEADS! FEATHERS! SPARKLES! TIARAS! WE HAVE IT ALL!

Under the words was a huge photograph of a girl

wearing a glittery crown with braids decorated with beads and feathers.

Aly felt like someone had kicked a soccer ball into her stomach. After Dad drove away, she quickly crossed the street so she could look inside the salon. She saw a few manicurists with high ponytails and matching pink aprons.

"What are you doing?" Brooke called out. "You know I can't cross without you!"

"Sorry, Brookie," Aly said, running back across the street to her sister. Then she pointed out the sign to Brooke.

"I can't even stand it!" Brooke shouted. "They copied our idea and made it even better. That's not fair."

Brooke stomped into True Colors and straight into Sparkle Spa without saying a word to anyone. Mom looked up at Aly and Sparkly, who were trailing behind.

"She saw the sign?" Mom asked from behind the welcome desk.

"We both did," Aly answered. "And we don't want to feel better about it. We just want to be mad for a while."

Mom nodded. "Okay. But just so you know, I'm mad too. You girls came up with a wonderful idea. I'm sorry they one-upped it."

"Me too," Aly said. And then she went into Sparkle Spa to be mad along with her sister.

When Clementine and Tuesday, two third graders who first came into Sparkle Spa during the pet adoption polish-a-thon Aly and Brooke had held, showed up for their manicures, Brooke was on the verge of tears. And when three different sixth graders called to cancel their Fall Ball hair-braiding appointments for next Saturday, she started crying.

After that, luckily (or unluckily), the salon was empty. Aly didn't think it would be great for business for customers to see one of the owners weeping.

"Don't worry, Brooke. We'll fix this," Aly assured her, and handed Brooke a cup of water. She wasn't really certain they could, but she wanted to make her sister feel better.

Aly realized she didn't feel sad, she felt mad. But she knew from dealing with mean Suzy Davis ever since kindergarten that being mad wouldn't change anything. It was time to do something to make the situation better. Anything at all.

"What if we make a list of ways to get more customers?" Aly said. "If we keep coming up with new ideas, maybe we can eventually wear Princess Polish down."

"But that's the *problem*," Brooke moaned. "They're idea stealers. Every idea we come up with, they'll just steal it and make it better. If they keep doing that, we might not even *have* Sparkle Spa for much longer."

"Then it's a good thing we're creative thinkers," Aly said. "Because we'll have to come up with *lots* of ideas. And maybe we'll come up with some they *can't* steal."

Aly went to the back of Sparkle Spa to get some pens and paper. She chose a blue pen for Brooke and a purple one for herself—one of her two favorite colors (the other was green), so maybe it would be lucky. She picked Sparkly up and put him on her lap. She thought that might be lucky too.

"Brooke, you face the door and I'll look at the wall. That way we don't distract each other. I'll set my watch and we'll brainstorm for five minutes. Okay?" Aly asked.

"Okay," Brooke answered, her blue marker uncapped and ready to write.

"Three, two, one, go," Aly said.

But just like the wall she was staring at, Aly's mind was blank. She kept hoping ideas would some-

how magically appear. But when five minutes passed,
Sparkly was asleep, Aly's paper was covered in purple
hearts, and Brooke had drawn a picture of a puppy.

Later there was a knock at the door. As Sparkly barked, Aly turned to see Charlotte with her twin brother, Caleb.

"Hi," Aly said. "Is your mom getting her nails done in True Colors?"

Charlotte nodded. "I figured maybe you could give me a new manicure? My polish from last time is starting to chip."

"Sure," Brooke said, standing up. "What color do you want?"

"I'll take a look," Charlotte said. "And Caleb wants his nails done too."

"No problem," Aly said, standing up next to Brooke. "Just cleaning and filing, like we did at the polish-a-thon?" she asked him.

Caleb stared at his shoes. Charlotte elbowed him. "Tell her!" she prodded.

Caleb kept staring at his shoes, but he said quietly, "Charlotte was telling me how rock stars get nail polish . . . and when we adopted Bob from Paws for Love, he had cool green nail polish. So, um, I was thinking maybe green?"

Brooke looked at Aly with raised eyebrows. Aly

returned the look and shrugged. "Sure, okay," she said to Caleb. "Why don't you pick out which green you want."

When Caleb and Charlotte walked over to the polish display, Brooke whispered to Aly, "I don't want to do a boy."

Aly sighed. "Boy hands are just the same as girl hands. And Mom and Joan and all the manicurists do men sometimes. But it's fine. I'll take Caleb. You do Charlotte."

Brooke nodded and walked over to one of the manicure stations to set up.

"Um, Aly?" Caleb asked. "Do you think Oscar the Green is a good one? Is that close to what you used on Bob?"

Aly joined Caleb at the display. "We used a different kind of polish on Bob, special for dogs," she said. "But that color's pretty close. So is this one." She picked up a bottle of Pickle Me and handed it to him.

"I like this one better," Caleb said. "Thanks, Aly."

He smiled at her, and then he looked down at his shoes again. Aly looked at his shoes too, to see what was so interesting down there, but all she saw were dirty sneakers with double-knotted laces.

Aly sat down across from Caleb and started cleaning his nails.

Charlotte had chosen Strawberry Sunday and was sitting across from Brooke, who was taking off Charlotte's old polish.

"Aly," Charlotte said, "did you sign up for a job on the decorating committee yet? Caleb and I signed up for balloons."

Aly had been in such a hurry to get to Sparkle Spa after school on Friday, she'd forgotten to sign up. She shook her head. "I didn't. But I can see if there's still an opening for balloons tomorrow."

"I think balloons is the best job," Caleb said, "because you get to use the helium tank."

"When I'm a fifth grader, I'm going to sign up

for posters," Brooke said. She was filing Charlotte's right-hand nails while Charlotte's left hand was soaking in warm, sudsy water.

"Who do you think is going to get the On the Ball trophies?" Charlotte asked.

"Well, Jenica started the after-school sports program, and Lucas Grant made up that kindergarten reading program, so I think it should be the two of them," Aly said. "Or I hope so, at least. What about you, Caleb?"

Caleb shrugged but managed to keep his left hand steady. Aly was impressed. "I don't really know many of the sixth graders," he said. "But next year I bet it'll be you. For doing things like the polish-a-thon to help raise money for dog adoptions and stuff."

Aly felt her face turning really hot, and she knew her cheeks must be the color of Pink Lemonade Float. "Thanks," she said.

"Aly?" Caleb said once she was finished cleaning his nails. "I think I want Pickle Me only on my thumbs. I think it'll look cooler that way."

"What a cool idea, Caleb," Brooke said. "We can call it the 'thumbs-up manicure'!"

Caleb grinned at Brooke. After a few more minutes Charlotte's and Caleb's nails were done and dry, and their mom poked her head into Sparkle Spa to get them.

"See you at school tomorrow," Charlotte said, dropping some money in the donation jar.

"Yeah, see you," Caleb said. "And thanks for my rock star nails—I mean thumbs." He scratched Sparkly behind the ears and gave a thumbs-up sign to Brooke and Aly.

"You're welcome," Aly said. "Come back whenever you want."

Brooke pulled out the girls' doodle-covered lists from before. "Okay," she said, "let's start thinking about how to get more customers. For real this time."

Aly stared at the paper and then said, "Before we start again, I'm going to take Sparkly for a walk."

Aly and Sparkly walked past Beans and Leaves and A Taste of Chocolate. She stopped in front of John's Sport Shop, looking at the soccer balls, baseball bats, and lacrosse sticks. And just like that, she got an idea.

"Come on, puppy. Let's run back to the salon." The two of them raced down the sidewalk.

"Boys!" Aly said when she rushed through the Sparkle Spa door. "We need to get more boys!"

Brooke wrinkled her nose. "But boys mostly don't like sparkles."

"But Caleb liked Pickle Me," Aly reminded her. "And we can tell them that even if they don't want rock star thumbs like his, they should still have clean nails for the Fall Ball! I mean, if dogs can get their nails done, so can boys."

* . * Makeover Magic * . *

Brooke pushed her glasses up higher on her nose. "I guess it's not the worst idea. But I'm still going to think of some more."

Just then Sparkly started whining as Joan walked into the back room carrying a large flat box and a brown paper bag. "Pizza Picnic time!" she announced to the girls. "I made some cookies for you to try, too."

Aly smiled. She loved Sunday Pizza Picnics with Joan. Her cookies were the best anywhere. Sometimes people even paid her to make cookies for weddings, birthdays, or fancy parties. "Great," Aly said, getting up to go grab their picnic blanket.

"We're trying to make another list of ways to get more customers," Brooke told Joan once the blanket was on the floor and they were eating. "But we only came up with one idea so far. Actually, it's Aly's idea. It's to get more boys to come."

Joan stopped eating mid-bite. Then she swallowed.

"That's actually an excellent idea, Aly." Joan got up from her spot and stuck her head into True Colors. "Karen, come in here for a sec," she called.

"What is it?" Mom asked. She took a seat next to Aly on the blanket.

"Aly has an idea for a special promotion for boys in Sparkle Spa. I think it might work in True Colors, too."

"Even if they don't want their nails polished, we can try to get them to have clean fingers," Aly explained.

"We can call them *man*-icures!" Brooke said with a laugh.

Mom smiled. A genuine big smile. "Fantastic!" she said. "Joan, when you and the girls are done with your pizza, let's figure out a plan. Princess Polish won't know what hit 'em."

Six

Midnight Blues

On Monday, Aly made sure to find Jenica before the first bell. She told her the boy plan for Sparkle Spa. Jenica loved it. "I'll spread the word," she said. "Don't worry, we'll have your salon filled with guys in no time. Man-icures it is."

By recess, Aly couldn't believe how quickly Jenica and her friends had relayed the message. Everyone at Auden Elementary knew about the man-icures. Some sixth-grade boys wouldn't set foot in anything that had the word "sparkle" in it, but three of them came up to Aly at recess, asking for appointments. They started with "Jenica told me . . ." or "Mia told me . . ." or "Anjuli told me . . . ," and they finished by asking about a "thumbs-up man-icure," stressing the "man" part.

Aly was standing against the fence that surrounded the soccer field, talking to Charlotte and Lily, when Lucas walked up to her.

"You're Aly, right?" he said.

Aly nodded. But she couldn't squeak out any words.

"So Jenica told me," he said, "that all guys should get man-icures for the ball. So I was thinking maybe I should book one."

Aly nodded again.

Then Lily elbowed her, which seemed to fix whatever had happened to her mouth.

"Okay," Aly said. "That'd be great." She pulled

the little Sparkle Spa appointment book out of the pocket of her jean shorts—the one that she brought to school so she could transfer appointments into the bigger one later—and opened it up. "Do you want the special thumbs-up man-icure or just a regular man-icure?"

"Thumbs-up means a color?" Lucas asked.

"Yes," Aly said. "Like black or green or gold or blue or really anything you want. Just on your thumbs, though."

Lucas looked down at his fingers, then back up at Aly. "I think just regular," he said. "No offense, I've just never had polish on my fingernails, you know?"

"Sure," Aly said, even though she wanted to explain to him that Caleb had looked really cool with his thumbs-up man-icure. "How's Saturday at one thirty?"

"That works for me." Lucas put his hand out to

shake Aly's. She stuck her pen in her pocket and stuck her hand out too. She couldn't believe she was actually touching Cute Lucas's skin.

"See you Saturday," Lucas said. And then he left to go join a soccer game on the field.

"Oh my gosh, Cute Lucas is coming!" Charlotte said. "I'm so glad I'm braiding hair so I can see him there."

"I think maybe I have to come in and string some more beads," Lily said. "You need more, right?"

Aly laughed. "Absolutely," she said.

After Lucas made his appointment, two more sixth-grade boys came by asking about man-icures, followed by a couple of fifth graders.

"I know I'm not going to the dance," said Garrett, who sat next to Aly in class, "but I want a man-icure anyway—one like Caleb's."

Cameron, who was also in Aly's class, made a face, but Caleb high-fived Garrett while Aly opened her appointment book again. "No problem," she said. "Let's pick a time."

By the end of the school day, Aly was thrilled with the success of the man-icure promotion—at least seven boys were coming. A few girls had booked nail appointments too, along with sparkle braids. Even though Sparkle Spa was closed on Mondays, Aly asked Brooke if she wanted to stop by True Colors to tell Mom about all the appointments and new customers.

"Definitely," Brooke said. "And then we can get Sparkly from the salon and take him to the park."

The two girls took their usual route from school to True Colors, walking slowly, not worrying about how long it took them to get there. The sun was shining, they had tons of customers, and nothing could ruin their happy mood. Not even Princess Polish.

When they got to the salon, they saw a couple of

new signs in the window. One was for man-icures. In midnight blue lettering, the sign read:

> A man's hands work hard all day.
> Take care of them with a man-icure
> engineered especially for men,
> offered at a discount!

Mom had added a hand-drawn illustration to the poster. The girls had only recently learned how good an artist their mother was, and Aly was amazed by how realistic the hands looked.

Next to the man-icure poster was another one that Aly and Brooke weren't expecting:

> After a long day at school,
> your feet need a break!
> Special half-price pedicures
> for teachers!

On this poster, Mom had drawn feet at the bottom and decorated the border with images of math equations, alphabet letters, an apple, a ruler, and various other school supplies.

Aly stopped in her tracks. "Brooke, do you see what I see?" she asked.

"The half-price offer for teachers?" Brooke asked back.

"Yes," Aly said, looking away from the sign and over at her sister.

"Does that mean . . . Mrs. Fishman?" Brooke asked in horror. Mrs. Fishman was Brooke's third-grade teacher. She and Brooke didn't get along very well. Well, they got along fine when Brooke stopped jabbering all day long, but that didn't happen too often.

Aly nodded. "I think it could. And Mrs. Glass and Mrs. Roberts."

Brooke's eyes were enormous behind her glasses.

"If all those teachers come in and we have to see their bare feet . . . I don't think I can do this."

Aly felt the same way as Brooke—teachers should stay in school. They shouldn't become customers of your mother's nail salon. But then Aly glanced back across the street at Princess Polish.

"It's for business, I guess," Aly said.

Brooke shook her head. "Teacher feet! What's next?"

Aly laughed. "I don't know, Brookster. Principal Rogers's toes?"

Princess Polish was making their lives more interesting, that was for sure.

seven

Plum Delicious

The girls opened Sparkle Spa on Tuesday and Thursday that week—taking care of as many advance Fall Ball appointments as they could before Saturday's rush—so on Friday afternoon, Aly was free to focus on decorating the school gym for the dance.

"I'm *soooo* excited," Charlotte said as she and Lily walked down the hall with Aly. "Did you sign up for balloons, Lily?"

"I did," Lily said.

When the girls got to the gym, they checked in

with Miss Gonzales, who was the newest sixth-grade teacher and was in charge of the dance. "Balloons are in the back corner, girls," she said, looking at the list on her clipboard. Then she added, "Can you please tie the ribbons on for the boys? They're over by the helium tank."

"But—" Lily began.

Aly gave her a look that said, *Shush.* "No problem," she told Miss Gonzales.

"We'll ask the boys to switch later," she whispered to Lily. "Don't worry."

As the girls walked through the gym, they couldn't believe how busy it was everywhere.

One group of fifth graders was coloring posters with glitter markers. Another was laying out tablecloths on the folding tables and sprinkling glitter on top. There were kids twisting purple and gold streamers—Auden's colors—and handing them to teachers who were up on ladders, attaching them to walls and rafters. The gym was definitely starting to look less like a place for PE and more like a place where people would wear fancy clothes and beads in their hair.

Caleb and Garrett were filling balloons with helium, then handing them to Daniel and Bennett, who knotted them closed.

Aly, Charlotte, and Lily took the balloons and tied long purple and gold ribbons to each one. They started chatting as they worked.

"Are we all set with customers tomorrow?" Charlotte asked. "I'm still doing braids, right?"

Aly nodded. "Absolutely. I think it will be crowded . . . though the schedule isn't completely filled yet."

Aly was disappointed that some of the girls from the soccer team—Bethany, Maxie, Valentina, and Joelle—hadn't signed up for appointments. It could mean that they weren't going to the ball or that they just didn't want to get their hair or nails done, but Aly suspected it meant they'd chosen to go to Princess Polish instead. It wouldn't be so bad if sixth graders Aly didn't know very well did that, but it upset her to think some of her regulars might.

"It's okay, Aly," Charlotte said, seeming to read her thoughts. "We don't need *all* the sixth-grade girls who are going to the ball there. We just need enough of them to keep us busy all day."

"And enough so that we make money to help out True Colors," Aly said, because that was really the point of this. "As long as my mom agrees to take it, that is. It's going to be a big surprise."

"We're going to make so much money," Lily said as she tied a golden string tightly to the bottom of a balloon. "I can help too, right?"

"You can be the organizer and donations collector," Aly said. During the polish-a-thon that raised

money for Paws for Love, Aly and Brooke had orga-
nizers, and it had really helped the day go smoothly.
"You can make sure everyone knows when their
appointments are and remind them to make a donation before they leave. And you can keep an eye on
the boys so they don't get too . . . boyish."

Lily laughed. "I'll make sure to tell them about
the suggested donation of three dollars. I'll keep saying it, so everyone really understands." She and Aly
had come up with the idea of suggested donation
amounts during lunch that day, figuring it would be
a good way to guide customers toward fair donations
for True Colors.

Lily tied another ribbon to another balloon and
then let it float up to join all the others they'd already
finished. The ceiling was starting to look really cool,
with the lights shining through the balloons casting
purple and gold spots all over the gym floor. "Do you

think we can trade places with the boys at the helium tank now?"

Charlotte nodded. Lily went to talk to Caleb and the rest of the boys, who had started playing keep-away with a purple balloon. Mr. Mehta, the music teacher, who was in charge of the helium tank, didn't look too happy.

But the person walking toward them looked *really* happy. It was Aly's least favorite person in the whole school: Suzy Davis. She'd been mean for as long as Aly could remember, and she'd been especially mean to Aly since Sparkle Spa had opened.

"Hey, Aly," Suzy said, holding a box of markers and smiling the biggest smile Aly had ever seen on her. "So I heard Princess Polish is taking all your customers. I mean, I understand why. Who would want to come to your silly little back room when they can go to a real, grown-up spa and be treated like a princess? For free."

Aly swallowed. Whenever Suzy said something like that to her, Aly didn't know how to respond. Mostly because what Suzy said always sounded like it might be true. Who *would* want to come to Sparkle Spa when there was a real spa that welcomed kids right across the street?

Charlotte walked a few steps closer to Aly and snapped a knot in a Plum Delicious–colored balloon. "For your information," she said to Suzy, "Sparkle Spa has a packed schedule tomorrow. And *I'm* braiding hair."

"Well, Heather and I," Suzy said, "are going to Princess Polish to get ready for our parents' anniversary party. I'm sure that their braiders are better than you."

Aly clenched her fists. Insulting Sparkle Spa was one thing, but insulting Charlotte was something else altogether. "Charlotte is the best hair braider around,"

Aly said. "I bet she could braid circles around any of the grown-ups at Princess Polish."

Charlotte and Aly were standing shoulder to shoulder now, staring at Suzy.

"Whatever," Suzy said. "Sparkle Spa will always be for babies." Then she marched off in the direction of the poster team.

"She is the pits," Charlotte said, rubbing the balloon she was holding across her head to make her hair all staticky.

"The absolute pits," Aly agreed, even though she couldn't help feeling that Suzy was a little bit right.

Aly looked around at the transformed gym. Tomorrow night the sixth graders would be having the best time ever, and hopefully Sparkle Spa would have something to do with that—no matter what Suzy Davis thought.

eight
Very Ice Try

Aly felt a thud on her chest and then a lick on her cheek.

"Stop, Sparkly," she giggled. But Sparkly kept licking until Aly got out of bed.

It was just as well that Sparkly woke Aly up early, though, because today was the day of the Fall Ball.

Aly got dressed quickly and took Sparkly out for a walk. By the time they got back, Brooke was sitting at the kitchen table, ready to go.

"I'm so excited, it's almost like we're going to the ball ourselves," Brooke said on the drive to True Colors.

But Aly shook her head. "I think it's more like we're the fairy godmothers and all our customers are Cinderella."

Brooke laughed. But then she got serious. "Remember, I'm not doing boy feet."

"I don't think we have any boys scheduled for pedicures," Aly said after swallowing a bite of her granola bar. "Just for cleanings and thumbs-up man-icures."

"Ew," Brooke said. "That means their feet will be even grosser. It's a good thing fancy boy shoes cover up their toes."

Aly and Mom laughed. "Brooke, I don't know where you come up with that stuff," Mom said. Brooke just shrugged and laughed a little herself.

* * * * *

Once they got to Sparkle Spa, the sisters set out all the fall-themed polishes on a special table. Brooke also drew the shape of a foot on a piece of paper. Then Aly polished the toenails with Brooke's special "caramel-dipped pedicure" so everyone could see what it would look like. And she pulled out the strands of multicolored beads Brooke and Sophie had strung all week. There were dozens of them in at least eight different colors, and Brooke had organized them in rainbow order. They looked beautiful all by themselves, but they were going to look even nicer in people's hair.

By ten thirty, the girls were ready for the big day ahead, and Jenica was the first customer to arrive. She was carrying a royal-blue dress with spaghetti straps and ruffles. "I brought my dress to make sure the polish matched," she said. "I'd hate to get home and find that the polish clashed with this color."

Brooke had a very serious expression on her face. "You'd never want that," she said, tugging on her braid. "What color are your sandals again?"

"Silver," Jenica answered.

Brooke nodded. "Aly can start on your hair. I'll bring you different color choices for your nails."

Once Jenica sat down, Aly asked, "Silver beads to go with your shoes? Or blue?"

"Silver!" Brooke called from the polish display.

Aly smiled and raised an eyebrow at Jenica.

"Silver," Jenica confirmed. "And can you do that kind of braid that goes across my head? Like a crown?"

"Sure," she said, picking up a strand of silver beads to start.

Meanwhile, Brooke came back holding a bottle of silvery Very Ice Try and a bottle of hot-pink I Like to Mauve It Mauve It. "Here's what I'm thinking," she said. "Pink looks really good with bright blue, so I can use mauve on your toenails and then a stripe of silver on your big toes. And then we could do the opposite for your fingernails—silver with a stripe of pink."

"Will that be too much silver on her toes, since her sandals are silver?" Aly asked as Jenica's silky hair slid through her fingers.

Brooke ran back over to the display. She returned with Good Knight, which was almost the exact color of Jenica's blue dress. "Pink with a blue stripe on her toes. Then silver polish with a pink stripe on her fingers."

"Love it," Jenica said, and gave Brooke a high five.

Aly tucked the ends of Jenica's braid underneath the braid itself and lifted up a hand mirror. "What do you think?" she asked.

Jenica breathed out slowly. "Wow, Aly, I hardly

recognize myself. Thank you." She gave Aly a big smile before she followed Brooke to a pedicure chair.

As soon as Brooke began working on Jenica's toes, the rest of the Auden Angels soccer players started flowing in for their appointments. Just like Jenica, a lot of the sixth graders had brought along their dresses to make sure the polish they picked would look good with their outfits.

- Anjuli's dress was bright purple.
- Giovanna's was light pink.
- Mia was wearing orange.
- Avery, emerald green.
- Aubrey, mint green.

It was so busy for the next few hours that Aly really didn't have time to think about Princess Polish once. Okay, maybe once. All but four of the sixth-grade team members were there—Bethany, Joelle, Maxie, and Valentina—and Aly tried not to let that bother her, but it was kind of hard.

"My mom is letting me wear lip gloss," she heard Mia tell Giovanna. "Actually, it's more like tinted ChapStick. But it makes my lips a little pink."

Giovanna sighed. "I'm not even allowed to wear that. Just clear ChapStick. It's so not fair."

"But do you get to wear heels?" Brooke asked.

"Little ones," Giovanna said, showing Brooke the height with her thumb and pointer finger—about half an inch, Aly figured.

Aly had just finished painting Aubrey's fingers Candy Corn on the Cob with a crown of Very Ice Try on the thumbs when she looked up and saw Lucas Grant standing in the doorway, right on time. Her breath caught in her throat.

Cute Lucas! At Sparkle Spa! And she was going

to do his nails! She'd known it was going to happen, but it still caught her off guard. She had to remind herself to breathe. And to talk.

"Come on in, Lucas," she said. Only her voice sounded more like a croak than real words. His friend Oliver was behind him. "You too, Oliver," Aly added. They were the first two boys scheduled.

They walked in slowly—like they weren't sure they really wanted to do this—and the minute they entered, all the girls stopped chattering.

It was the quietest Sparkle Spa had ever been.

"Um, hi," Lucas said.

Every one of the girls—in the manicure chairs, in the pedicure chairs, and at the braiding stations— stared at the boys.

Was this a mistake? Aly wondered. Were the man-icures a bad idea?

The air seemed so thick that Aly felt like she would

need nail clippers to cut it. She took a deep breath.

"I think it's so neat that you guys are here," Mia finally said from where Charlotte was braiding her hair. "Right, Giovanna?" she asked.

Giovanna nodded. "Definitely," she said. "Extra cool."

Aly saw Oliver smile. Maybe this was going to be okay after all.

Lily looked at the appointment book. "Lucas, you're first," she said. "You can go over there with Aly. Oliver, you're welcome to wait in the corner on the pillows until he's done. Then Aly will do your nails."

Oliver plopped himself down next to Aubrey, whose nails were drying. Lucas sat across from Aly.

"Hey," he said.

"Hey," Aly said back, suddenly very aware that she was touching a boy's fingers. A really cute boy's fingers.

But Lucas didn't seem to notice how awkward she felt. He just smiled so that a dimple appeared on his left cheek.

Aly smiled too. When she was done with his nails, Lucas looked at his fingers and grinned. "My hands look like my dad's now," he said. "Like, important. Nice job."

Then he jammed his hands in his jeans pockets and traded seats with Oliver.

As Aly started cleaning Oliver's nails, some more girls came in, and then Garrett and Caleb, even though they weren't going to the dance.

Mom poked her head in and winked at Aly. Aly winked back. It was kind of like a Secret Sister Eye Message, except it was with her mother instead of her sister. The wink clearly meant: *Princess Polish is not going to stop Sparkle Spa!*

"Aly," Garrett shouted across the room. "What's

the best rock star nail polish color for my thumbs-up man-icure?"

"I'll help him, Aly," Brooke said, walking Giovanna to the drying area.

Brooke pushed her glasses up against her nose. "Well," she said, "I like Guitar-ange a lot, but you have gray eyes, so you might like Heavy Metal or—"

But before Brooke could finish, Bethany, Maxie, and Joelle raced into Sparkle Spa. "HELP! You have to help! Look at what Princess Polish did to us!"

nine

Heavy Metal

What happened? Let me see!" Brooke ran over and took Bethany's hand in hers. It was terrible. The polish, which looked like it had started out pink, was turning into a weird orangey yellow at the edges and peeling away from Bethany's fingernails.

Aly could see tears in Bethany's eyes. "We were done about an hour ago," she sniffed. "And then we all went home, and next thing I knew, I looked at my hands, and *this* had happened. And then I called

Maxie and Joelle and found out their polish was doing the same thing. Valentina's, too, but her mom's trying to fix it at home."

Maxie held out her hands. Her blue nails were peeling and turning green. Joelle's red nails were peeling and turning orange.

Aly pulled Joelle's hand closer and inspected the polish. "I think it's old," she said. "Like, really old. Maybe the stuff that makes the polish work like normal went bad."

"Can you fix it?" Joelle asked. "Please? We never should have gone to Princess Polish, right, guys? We're sorry."

Bethany nodded.

"We're so, *so* sorry," Maxie added. "We just . . . we thought it would be neat to go to a grown-up salon. But Sparkle Spa is so much better."

Aly heard what Maxie said, and she kind of

understood it, but before she could answer, she was distracted by a purple splotch on Maxie's forehead, just under a purple feather that was woven into her hair. She looked at the rest of the purple feathers in Maxie's hair. Every single spot where a feather touched her skin, Maxie had a purple splotch—on her neck, her ears, and her forehead.

"Um," Aly said, "I think your feathers are turning your skin purple."

"*What?*" Maxie ran to a full-length mirror on the closet door and screamed. She turned back to Aly. "You *have* to fix it. All of it!"

Maxie's scream brought Mom running, with Miss Gonzales, the sixth-grade teacher from Auden, behind her. Miss Gonzales put down the bag she was carrying and hurried over to Maxie. "What's wrong?" she asked, just as Mom said, "Is everything okay in here?"

"Take a look for yourself," Aly said. "Princess Polish bought cheap feathers, and now Maxie's turning purple."

"Let me see," Miss Gonzales said, inspecting Maxie's forehead. Maxie tilted her head closer to the teacher. "I think you can get it off with soap and water. It'll be fine. You'll still look lovely tonight."

As Miss Gonzales and Mom returned to True Colors, Maxie pleaded, "Can you get me back to normal, Aly? Please, please, please?"

Brooke stared at Aly over her glasses, sending the Secret Sister Eye Message: *I am still very mad at them.* But Aly shook her head at Brooke. What kind of people would they be if they let Bethany and Maxie and Joelle go to the Fall Ball with messed-up nails and color-splotched skin? They were more professional than that.

"We can do it," Aly answered. "But you'll have to

wait. We have other customers with booked appointments," and she pointed to the group of boys now waiting at the door.

"That's right." Brooke nodded. "You'll have to wait."

Aly handed cotton balls and polish remover to Maxie, Joelle, and Bethany. "And you'll have to help out," she added.

But the girls weren't looking at Aly, they were staring at all the boys in Sparkle Spa.

"What happened to you three?" a lacrosse player named Aiden asked.

"Don't look!" Bethany squealed as she turned around and tried to hide her face in her arm.

Maxie covered her face with her arm too. "Ack! I can't believe that the one day I have purple spots on my face is the same day that *boys* are at Sparkle Spa."

Joelle stood her ground. "We had a feather problem," she told the boys. "But it's going to be fixed." Then she turned to Aly and said, "Thank you for fixing us."

"Thank you," Bethany echoed. "So much. We'll never go anywhere else to get our nails done again."

"Never," Maxie agreed, her face still in her arm.

The boys looked at one another. "Did she say 'feathers'?" asked Lee, who played the trumpet in the band with Lucas.

"She did," Lucas confirmed from the spot where he was waiting for Oliver. "But don't worry. They don't do feathers in here. You're safe."

Aly couldn't help but laugh. Then she returned her attention to Oliver's man-icure.

"This place is crazy!" he said to her as she finished filing his nails.

Aly nodded. "Today for sure," she said. "It's a good thing our dog is home with our dad."

"Sometimes there's a dog in here too?" Oliver asked.

"A little one," Aly said. "Okay, I think you're all done now."

Oliver held up his hands and inspected them. "My hands do look kind of different. My nails are, like, smooth and shiny. Thanks, Aly."

Aly smiled. "Well, you're welcome to come back whenever you want."

Oliver called out to Lucas, and just as they left another sixth-grade girl burst through the door. She had green feathers in her hair and green splotches on her skin. Aly knew what she was going to say before she opened her mouth.

"Do you need us to fix you up before the Fall Ball?" she asked.

The girl nodded.

Aly ran her fingers through her hair. "Okay, just

go talk to Lily—she'll schedule you in." She pointed the girl in Lily's direction.

Soon after that, two more sixth graders came in with the same Princess Polish problems. And just when Aly thought there couldn't be any more surprises, the biggest one of the day walked through the door.

Suzy Davis.

Followed by her younger sister, Heather.

"What are you doing here?" Brooke asked.

They rushed past Brooke, right over to Aly. Suzy stared at the floor, and she spoke so softly, Aly could barely hear her.

"Tonight's my parents' anniversary party, and Heather and I went to Princess Polish. I don't know what happened, but our nails are peeling and turning colors, and Princess Polish won't do anything about it. I know Sparkle Spa isn't as fancy as they are, but, um, I was wondering if maybe you could, um . . . Ugh!" Suzy looked up. "Could you help us?"

Aly thought about all the awful things Suzy Davis had said and done at school over the years. If Aly started from kindergarten, she could probably count up to a hundred. That gave her an idea. One of her better ones, she thought.

"We'll help," she said, "but you have to make me a deal. If we redo your nails, you can't say anything mean to me for the rest of the school year."

"Mean? Who's mean?" Suzy said. Then she rolled her eyes. "Fine, Aly. Whatever. Deal. You just have to fix us."

Deal? Aly couldn't believe Suzy had agreed.

"Okay, then," Aly said. Honestly, she would've fixed Heather's nails anyway, and maybe even Suzy's, but this was fantastic. She wondered if Suzy would keep up her end of the bargain and actually leave her alone at school now. It would be fun to see.

Aly directed Suzy and Heather over to the waiting area, handing them some cotton balls and polish remover to give them a head start. Then she sat down at her manicure station across from Garrett.

"Did Suzy Davis just promise to be nice to you?" he whispered, handing her a bottle of Heavy Metal for his thumbs-up man-icure.

"Yes," Aly said as she dunked his hands in warm, soapy water.

"Is it always this weird in Sparkle Spa?" he asked.

Aly laughed. "No," she said. "Today seems extra weird."

But it was also extra exciting.

Aly looked around the salon. Brooke was giving one pedicure after another, and Charlotte was furiously unbraiding and rebraiding hair. And the bracelet-making area was filled with waiting customers.

Aly and Brooke were grinning from ear to ear as they sent each other one of their silent messages: *This is one of the most sparkly days ever!*

ten

News Prince

Three hours later Sparkle Spa was empty. Only Brooke and Aly were left, sitting in the pedicure chairs, hardly able to move. All their customers were gone, and Charlotte's mom had just picked her and Lily up to take them home.

"*That* was the craziest day ever," Brooke said, flopping back against the seat cushion. "Since it's Saturday, I'd say it's time for us to do each other's nails. I'd been thinking News Prince because of the extra glitter, but maybe tomorrow. I'm all polished out."

Aly flopped against her own chair. "I'm all polished out too. And braided out. And talked out. And
everything-ed out."

"Everything-ed out," Brooke repeated with a sigh.
"That's totally it. I'm everything-ed out. But at least
everyone will look beautiful at the Fall Ball. I know
you said before that we'd be like fairy godmothers
today, but I think it's more like we were Cinderella's
mice, racing around all day. No wicked stepsisters, no
carriage turning into a pumpkin at the stroke of midnight . . . but everyone really will look like princesses."

"Or princes," Aly added, looking around the room
and noticing how much straightening up they had to
do. She slowly got up and started putting polish bottles back in the display.

"You know, Brooke, I wish we could see the whole
thing—everyone all dressed up, the party lights, the
dancing, the fancy food . . ."

"Me too," Brooke said. "Actually, I could use

some fancy food myself right now. Maybe we can clean up later?"

"Food would be good," Aly said. "But let's bring Mom the money from the donation jar first—make sure she'll take it for True Colors so all our work will have been worth it. Can you believe we've been able to keep this a secret from her for so long?"

Before Aly even finished her sentence, Brooke was already heading into the main salon. Aly grabbed the donation jar and followed.

Everyone had left True Colors except for Mom, who was at the reception desk, going through the day's receipts; Joan, who was cleaning up her manicure station; and Mrs. Franklin, one of the girls' favorite regulars, who was zipping up her purse and heading out the door.

"Joanie," Brooke said, "do you have any cookies today? Aly and I are Starvin' Marvins."

Joan tucked some hair back into Brooke's braid.

"Sorry," she said. "I didn't have a chance to bake last night."

Mom looked up from the reception desk and checked her watch. Aly checked hers too: 5:52. "I just have a few more things to do," Mom said, but then she noticed that Aly was holding the Sparkle Spa donation jar. "Why are you carrying the jar, Aly?"

"Mom," Aly began, waving Brooke to her side. "We've decided to give True Colors our donations. We didn't count it, but it looks like a lot."

"Oh, girls," Mom said. She looked like she was about to cry.

Brooke added, "There's a lot more money in there than usual, not only because of all our extra customers for the Fall Ball, but because we came up with suggested donations for our special services today. Please take it. We want you to have it all—to help keep True Colors open."

"Plus," Aly said, "if it weren't for True Colors, there wouldn't be a Sparkle Spa. And we don't want Princess Polish to put both of us out of business."

Mom didn't say a word. Aly couldn't tell if she was angry or happy.

After what seemed like forever, she finally said, "You girls amaze me. But as kind and generous and thoughtful as you are, I can't accept your donation."

"But why not?" asked Brooke. "We did this for you." Now it looked as though Brooke might cry.

Mom pulled Aly and Brooke close and kissed the tops of their heads. "True Colors isn't a charity. And while I'm not happy that Princess Polish has moved in across the street, my business is doing fine. You don't have to worry. But I love you girls more than I can say for caring as much as you do. We'll figure out a different charity to donate the money to—maybe Businesswomen Unite this time? It's a charity that helps women entrepreneurs start their own businesses."

Mom hugged both of the girls again. "How does that sound?" she asked.

"If you think that's best," Aly said. And then her stomach chose that time to rumble.

"You two really are hungry, aren't you?" Mom asked.

Aly was, actually, very hungry. She hadn't eaten lunch today.

"We are!" Brooke answered.

"Why don't you let them run out and grab something from the Sweetery, Karen?" Joan suggested.

Mom pulled a few bills out of her wallet. "That's a good idea," she said. "Here's ten dollars. While you're at the bakery, Joan and I will start cleaning up Sparkle Spa for you."

"You don't have to do that, Mom," Aly said. She

wanted to show her mother she and Brooke were responsible business owners, which meant cleaning up after themselves.

Mom squeezed her shoulder. "Don't worry about it," she said. "But don't get used to it either." And she winked.

"Wow! I haven't been outside all day," Brooke said once the sisters left True Colors. "The fresh air feels good. . . . I think I'm going to get something choco-latey with sprink—" Brooke stopped mid-sentence and tugged on Aly's sleeve. "Look, Aly." She pointed across the street.

Princess Polish was dark. The lights were out.

"It looks like they closed early," Brooke said.

Aly squinted. "I think there's a sign on the door."

The girls walked to the corner and crossed the street to check it out.

CLOSED FOR AN EMERGENCY, the sign read.

"Do you think they *really* had an emergency?" Brooke asked.

Aly shook her head. "Not a real one. I think they used old polish and cheap feathers and ended up with a lot of unhappy customers."

Brooke nodded. "Do you think they'll close for good?"

Aly looked at the sign and peered in through the window. "I don't know," she answered. "Maybe it's temporary, until they get new supplies."

"Well, I hope it's for good." Brooke slipped her hand into Aly's as they kept walking toward the bakery.

"Me too," Aly said. "And I hope no other nail salons open up nearby."

"Just True Colors and Sparkle Spa," Brooke said.

It was funny, though. Aly was thinking that having Princess Polish there did make Sparkle Spa better—it had made them come up with some new ideas, which was always a good thing.

The bells from the church downtown started to ring. Aly counted the bongs. One, two, three, four, five, six.

"When does the dance start?" Brooke asked as they walked into the Sweetery.

"Right now," Aly answered, standing at the back of the line.

Aly thought about what it would feel like to win an On the Ball trophy and how nervous some of the sixth graders must be now. But it was a good kind of nervous, she figured—the way you feel right before you open a present you've hoped for and dreamed about getting.

eleven

Good Knight

After Aly and Brooke ate their treats—a peanut butter cookie for Aly and a rainbow cookie covered with chocolate sprinkles for Brooke—the girls quickly walked back to True Colors.

"Mom, Mom, you'll never believe what we saw," Brooke blurted out. "It looks like Princess Polish might be closing!"

Mom looked at Joan, her eyebrows raised. "Well, that's interesting. Let's see if they open for business tomorrow," she said.

But that wasn't the only news. As Mom and Joan were cleaning up, they had discovered a canvas bag in the back room. "Aly, we found this in Sparkle Spa," Mom announced, holding it up. "Did one of your customers leave it? There are trophies inside."

Miss Gonzales! That bag was Miss Gonzales's! She had been holding it when she ran into Sparkle Spa after Maxie screamed. She was the teacher in charge of the Fall Ball and the awards. Aly gulped. "They're for the On the Ball winners!" she said.

"Oh no!" Brooke cried. "What if they can't announce the winners because there aren't any trophies? Because the trophies are *here*, in True Colors, instead of *there*, where they should be!"

"Where should they be?" Joan asked.

"At school!" Brooke and Aly said together.

"Well," Mom said, "it's almost time to go anyway. I'll drive you over to Auden."

"Go, go," Joan said, shooing all three of them out the door. "I'll lock up here."

On the way to school, Brooke could hardly sit still. "Hey, Aly," she said. "Do you know what this means?"

Aly shook her head.

"It means we get to go to the Fall Ball." Brooke's smile was so huge, it seemed to take up half her face.

Aly grinned. "You're right." Even though she was pretty sure her smile wasn't as big as Brooke's, Aly couldn't wait to see how everything looked.

"I'll wait right here," Mom told them as she pulled up to the curb. "In and out, so we can get home to Dad and Sparkly and dinner."

"In and out!" Brooke said. "We promise." She took Aly's hand, and they scooted out of the car. They ran toward the entrance, straight into Mr. Thomas, the security guard.

"Good evening, girls. Where are you going?" he asked. "I don't think either of you is old enough to be going to the dance."

Aly held out the bag with the trophies inside. "We're making a delivery."

"A very important one," Brooke added. "It's the trophies for the On the Ball winners. Miss Gonzales left them at our nail salon."

"I see," Mr. Thomas said. "That *is* very important. Let me lock the door and escort you in."

Aly, Brooke, and Mr. Thomas walked down the second-grade hallway, past the nurse's office, and into the gym. Aly and Brooke paused in the doorway.

The gym didn't look anything like a gym.

The balloons had covered all the lights, so the whole room had a purple and gold glow.

The glitter on the posters sparkled, and the streamers swayed gently back and forth.

There was also some sort of machine that blew bubbles from under the stage.

And Mr. Mehta, the music teacher, was up on the stage with big speakers and a computer.

"Wow," Brooke said breathlessly.

"Whoa," Aly said. It was even more beautiful than she'd imagined. Then she focused on all the sixth graders. They looked so fancy and grown-up. She spotted Anjuli in her bright purple dress. And Bethany and Mia. Then she saw Jenica in her Good Knight–colored dress dancing with Lee, one of the boys who had come into Sparkle Spa earlier that day.

"Okay, enough looking, we have to go deliver the trophies." Aly said to Brooke.

It felt funny to walk into the ball wearing shorts and a T-shirt, but Aly did it anyway. She looked around the edges of the gym for teachers and finally spotted

Miss Gonzales, then headed straight toward her. Miss Gonzales was talking to an adult Aly didn't know.

"Miss Gonzales, Miss Gonzales," Aly shouted over Mr. Mehta's loud music.

Miss Gonzales looked up.

Aly held out the bag. "I think you left these at True Colors today."

"I—oh!" Miss Gonzales said, taking the bag from Aly. "*That's* where I left them! Thank you so much for bringing them over. I've been going crazy trying to find my bag . . . and trying to figure out where I could find another set of trophies somewhere else in the school."

Aly smiled. "Happy to help."

She was about to turn and leave when Brooke said, "Um, Miss Gonzales, are you announcing the winners soon? Do you think maybe you could do it right *now*?"

Aly couldn't believe Brooke! But it would be nice if they could hear the announcements.

"Actually, it's almost time anyway," Miss Gonzales said. "And now that I have the trophies, I don't think anyone would mind if I sped things up by a few minutes."

She walked up on the stage and spoke to Mr. Mehta. The music got softer, and Miss Gonzales tapped the top of a microphone.

"Hi, sixth graders!" she said.

"Hi, Miss Gonzales!" a few of them answered.

Miss Gonzales held the microphone a little closer to her mouth. "As you all know, winning an On the Ball trophy at Auden is a very big honor. These trophies go to two members of our community—one boy and one girl—who embody the Auden spirit of helping others.

"So many of you sixth graders have worked on wonderful community projects this year, from fund-raising to tutoring to food drives and toy drives. I wish every single one of you could win a trophy.

"But there are two students whose projects stood out as exemplary to all the teachers. And they are: Jenica Posner, for promoting team building and sharing knowledge through Superstar Sports, and Oliver Shin, for focusing on those less fortunate and changing school policy through the Helping the Hungry at Lunch program!"

Along with the rest of the kids at the dance, Aly cheered for Jenica. She cheered for Oliver, too, even though, personally, she would have picked Cute Lucas for his Reading Buddies project.

Next to Aly, Brooke was jumping up and down, yelling, "Yay, Jenica! Three cheers for Jenica!"

Jenica and Oliver walked to the stage, and Miss Gonzales presented them with the trophies. Then Mr. Mehta started playing the school song on his keyboard, and all the kids—including Aly and Brooke—sang along.

The sixth graders grabbed hands and formed a circle that was almost as big as the whole gym. When they got to the last line of the Auden Elementary song—*"And we will always love our community"*—everyone raised their clasped hands in the air and shouted: "Go, Auden!" Then they clapped and cheered. It was one of the coolest things Aly had ever seen.

Even though Aly and Brooke weren't sixth graders, they both felt like they were part of the celebration. After all, a lot of those hands that had been raised in the air a moment ago had been in Sparkle Spa that afternoon. Knowing that they had contributed to the Fall Ball—just in this small way—made them feel proud and a part of something bigger than themselves—their community.

Aly had to admit, it was a pretty magical feeling.

How to Give Yourself (or a Friend!)
a Caramel-Dipped Pedicure
By Aly (and Brooke!)

✳ ✳ ✳ ✳ ✳ ✳ ✳

What you need:

Paper towels

Polish remover

Cotton balls

Clear nail polish

Two colors of polish (I recommend purple and
green; Brooke recommends pink and yellow)

What you do:

1. Put some paper towels on the floor so you don't
have to worry about spilling polish. (Actually, you
might want to do two layers. Once, I
spilled so much that it went through the
first layer. But I don't do that anymore.)

2. Take one cotton ball and put some polish remover on it. If you have polish on your toes already, use enough to get it off. If you don't, just rub the remover over your toenails to get off any dirt that might be on there. (Sometimes there's sock fuzz on your toenails. Gross, I know.)

3. Rip off two paper towels. Twist the first one into a long tube and weave it back and forth between your toes to separate them a little bit. Then do the same thing with the second paper towel on your other foot. You might need to tuck in the paper around your pinkie toe if it pops up and gets in your way while you polish.

4. Start with a coat of clear polish on each nail. (You can do your toes in any order you want. Aly and I like going from big toe to pinkie toe.)

Then don't forget to close up the polish bottle tightly when you're done.

5. Open up the polish color that you want to be the main one for all your nails. Paint it on. (You should be a little more careful with this color than with the clear, to make sure you don't get it on your skin.)

6. Fan your toes a little to dry them a bit, and then repeat step five, adding a second coat. (Remember, be careful! And close the polish when you're done.)

7. Once your toenails are dry, open the second color—the one you want your big toes to look "dipped" in—and wipe the brush on the side of the bottle opening so it's not drippy at all. Then,

very carefully, paint a straight line across the top of your right big toe, then the left. (Try not to let your hand wobble much so the line will be straight.)

8. Fan your big toes, drying them a bit before you apply a top coat of clear polish to all your toenails. Again, be sure to close the bottle up tight.

9. Now you have to let your toes fully dry. You can fan them with a magazine or use a nail dryer if you have one or sit and make a piece of jewelry or read a book or watch TV or talk to your friend. It usually takes about twenty minutes, but it could take longer. (After twenty minutes, check the polish by really lightly touching the stripe on your big toe with your fingertip. If it still feels sticky, let your toes dry longer so they don't get smudged!)

And now you have a beautiful caramel-dipped pedicure! Even after the polish is dry, it's a good idea not to wear socks or closed-toe shoes for a while. Bare feet or sandals are best so that all your hard work doesn't get smooshed. (Besides, that way, you can show people how fancy your toes look!)

Happy polishing!

✳ ˎ ✳ ˎ ✳ ˎ ˎ ✳ ˎ ✳ ˎ ˎ ✳

True Colors

✳ ⋆ ⋆ ✳ ⋆ ⋆ ✳ ⋆ ⋆ ✳ ✳

For my dazzling agent, Miriam Altshuler

With gobs of glittery thank-yous to editrix extraordinaire
Karen Nagel and my team of sparkly writer friends, especially
Eliot Schrefer, who read this one for me super quickly and gave
me wonderfully helpful feedback

one

Not-So-Mellow Yellow

"Give that back!" Brooke Tanner yelled as she chased her puppy around the living room couch and underneath the leaves of a rubber plant. "Sparkly, I mean it!"

But Sparkly didn't listen. With Brooke's glittery Not-So-Mellow Yellow–colored hair band hanging out of his tiny mouth, the puppy raced up the steps and then back down. Brooke was at his heels.

"Sparkly, stop!" Brooke shouted. "Now! Stop!"

"Maybe if you stopped chasing him, he'd stop

running!" Aly Tanner called from the kitchen. It was early Tuesday morning, and Aly was preparing two bowls of cereal for breakfast: a purple bowl for herself, and a pink one for her younger sister, Brooke. Both bowls had granola inside. And blueberries.

"But I want my hair band!" Brooke shouted back to her sister.

"Like I said, if you want it back, just stop running!" Aly yelled into the living room.

"But what if he eats it when I stop?" Brooke sped into the kitchen after Sparkly, who leapt over the girls' backpacks. Brooke leapt over them too, but her sneaker caught in her backpack strap and—*bam!*— she crashed to the ground.

"Ow!" she screamed. "Ow! Ow! Ow!"

Aly went running over. For a minute she wondered if Brooke was fine and just being dramatic, which was the case with Brooke a lot of the time. But tears were running down Brooke's cheeks, and she was holding her arm against her stomach.

"I heard it crack, Aly," she sobbed. "Get Mom."

Now it was Aly's turn to race through the house, ducking under the leaves of the rubber plant, flying around furniture and then up the stairs until she got to their parents' bathroom.

"Brooke fell! She thinks her arm is broken!" Aly pounded on the door, yelling over the sound of a hair dryer.

"What did you say, sweetie?" the girls' mom asked as she cracked open the door.

Aly repeated herself, and then Mom took off, racing down the steps two at a time, Aly right behind her. When they reached the kitchen, Brooke was right where Aly had left her, still on the floor, still crying. Sparkly was whining and nudging Brooke's hair band toward her.

"That won't help anymore, Sparkly!" Brooke whimpered through her tears.

Mom bent down, asked Brooke a few questions, touched her arm in a few spots—which made Brooke yell even louder—and then said to Aly, "I have to take your sister to the hospital. Please call Joan and tell her what happened. She'll have to take you to school today."

As much as Aly liked spending time with Joan— who was the girls' favorite manicurist at their mom's salon, True Colors—she didn't like this plan at all. What if something was *really* wrong with Brooke? What if Brooke needed her? Aly couldn't go to school. She had to be there for Brooke. The sisters were a team.

"Can't I come with you and Brooke?" she asked. "To make her feel better?"

Mom shook her head. "Sorry, Aly," she said. "I don't know what's going to happen at the hospital or how long it'll take. You can go straight to the salon after school. Either I'll be there or Joan will fill you in. You have her number, right?"

Aly nodded. "It's on the refrigerator, just like it always is."

Brooke wasn't crying as hard now, which made Aly feel a little bit better about leaving her. But not all better about it.

Mom ran her hand through her hair, which she hadn't finished drying, and twisted it into a messy bun. "It's times like these that I wish your father didn't travel all week long."

"Do you think he'll come home early?" Brooke asked, sniffling, as Mom carefully helped her up off the floor.

"Let's call him from the car," Mom said.

Once Mom pulled the door shut behind her, Aly called Joan. And when she started explaining what happened, she found herself crying a little.

"I bet that was scary," Joan said.

"It was," Aly said, crying a little more now. "And what if Brooke's really hurt?"

"If Brooke's hurt, the doctors will make her better," Joan said. "Now sit tight, and I'll be right there to take you to school. Get Sparkly's leash on too, so I can bring him to the salon."

All day long Aly worried about Brooke. She had trouble paying attention in class. She kept looking at her purple polka-dot watch to see if it was 3:07 yet, the end of the school day, when she could go to True Colors and find out if her sister was okay. But every time she checked, it wasn't even close to 3:07. Time was moving slower than the snail that Aly and Brooke had watched crawl across the sidewalk the weekend before.

At lunchtime Aly sat with her two best friends, Charlotte and Lily, as usual, but she was too distracted to concentrate on their conversation about the Lewis and Clark project that was due next Monday. She sat, barely touching her bagel and cream cheese, barely even drinking her orange juice, until Lily asked if there were any open appointments left at Sparkle Spa that afternoon.

"Umm," Aly said, "I don't know if we'll even open today."

"But it's Tuesday," Charlotte said. "You're *always* open on Tuesdays for the soccer team's rainbow sparkle pedicures."

Aly clapped a hand over her mouth. "Oh no!" she said. "You're right. It's Tuesday! And Brooke won't be there! And the whole soccer team is coming! And they're going to be in the quarterfinals this weekend! This is going to be a disaster."

Sparkle Spa was a business that Aly and Brooke started in the back room of their mom's nail salon. Kids could have their nails and toes polished and not take up time or space in the busy grown-up salon. Plus, it was more fun when it was just kids. They could pretty much do whatever they wanted, and as long as they were quiet, no one really bothered them.

It was because of the soccer team—the Auden Angels—that the spa had started in the first place. Their captain, Jenica Posner, came to True Colors one day, and Aly—not an actual salon manicurist— wound up giving Jenica a rainbow sparkle pedicure. Brooke had come up with the color combination, and Jenica thought it was really cool.

Jenica scored so many goals in the next soccer game that the whole team wanted rainbow sparkle pedicures too. And they still came every week so that their "sparkle power" wouldn't fade. So far, they were undefeated for the season and had made it all the way to the quarterfinals.

The team insisted it was due to the sparkles. Aly was pretty sure it was because they were awesome soccer players, but she couldn't risk not giving them sparkle power before the quarterfinals, just in case. Even with Brooke gone, Aly would *have* to do the Angels' pedicures this afternoon. She didn't want it to be her fault if they lost this week. But how would she give all those sparkle pedicures without Brooke's help?

Maybe if I make a list, I can figure it out, Aly thought.

Making lists was something Aly did to organize her thoughts and help her solve problems.

She took a sheet of paper from her notebook and began writing.

<u>Ways to Make Sure All the Angels</u>
<u>Get Their Sparkle Power</u>
1. Walk to True Colors as fast as
   possible.
2. Ask Jenica if some players can
   come on other days.
3. Find more manicurists.

Aly stopped writing and looked up at Charlotte and Lily.

"I know this is a ridiculous question, but is there any chance either one of you learned how to polish nails over the weekend?" Aly asked her friends.

Both girls shook their heads. "Sorry, Aly," Lily said.

"But we can help with other things!" Charlotte offered.

"Absolutely," Lily agreed. "We'll both come with you after school."

"I guess that's better than nothing," Aly said, taking a bite of her bagel, even though she was feeling kind of sick to her stomach. "Thanks."

She started to think of a fourth item for her list when she heard, "Is it really, really true that Brooke broke her arm?"

Aly turned. It was Brooke's best friend, Sophie, who had just come in from recess. Her face was flushed, and her dark bangs stuck to her forehead.

"Hi, Soph. I won't know about Brooke until later. Do you want to come with us to Sparkle Spa after school and find out?"

"Please, can I?" Sophie begged. "I'll call my mom from there, if that's all right." She looked as anxious as Aly felt.

"You can help with the soccer team's pedicures, if you want," Charlotte added. "Even if you can't polish."

Sophie's eyes lit up. "I'd be happy to. Anything for Brooke. And for the Sparkle Spa."

The bell rang for class, and as the girls walked together down the hall, Aly thought, *Well, that's three helpers. But not even three people will equal one Brooke.*

two

Red Between the Lines

On the way to True Colors after school, Aly taught Charlotte, Lily, and Sophie how to racewalk. When Aly and Brooke wanted to get somewhere fast and didn't want to—or weren't allowed to—run, they racewalked. It involved lifting your knees high to take very big steps and swinging your elbows to move forward. There was a man in town who had been a racewalker in the Olympics, and Aly and Brooke had learned by copying him.

Aly wondered if Brooke would've gotten hurt
if she'd been racewalking around the house this
morning instead of running. But then again,
Sparkly had been zipping around so quickly, racewalking wouldn't have been fast enough to catch
him anyway.

"Am I doing the elbows right?" Sophie asked
while they sped to the salon.

Aly glanced over and checked. "Perfect elbows,
Sophie," she said.

Aly saw the light-blue True Colors sign up
ahead.

"Thank goodness we're almost there!" she heard
Lily say behind her. "This is hard work!"

Aly didn't think so, but she was glad they were
close. She was really worried about Brooke. And the
sooner they got to the salon, the sooner she could
find out how her sister was doing.

When Aly pushed open the door to True Colors, the chimes jangled loudly. She looked around the salon for her mom and sister, but she didn't see either one. Joan was seated at the reception desk, Sparkly snoozing at her feet.

"Aly!" she said, standing up.

"Joan!" Aly said, flying into her arms. "How's Brooke? Where is she? What's happening? Where's my mom?"

Joan gave Aly a squeeze. Sparkly woke up and yipped, and Aly picked him up.

"Brooke's home resting. She broke her arm and has a cast. She's going to need to rest for a few days, and she won't be able to run around for a while, but she'll be good as new before you know it. Your mom is home with her."

"Whew!" Lily said. "I'm glad that's all it is! I had a broken arm once. Remember that time in kindergarten when I fell off the swings and needed a cast for a while?"

Aly nodded. She did remember now, but she hadn't until that moment. "Did it hurt?" she asked, hoping the answer was no.

"A little," Lily said. "At the beginning. And then it was itchy. And heavy. And I had to wear a sling. But it wasn't as bad as breaking a leg and needing crutches. That happened to my mom once, and it was the pits."

"That happened to me once too," Mrs. Bass said from the drying station. She was a True Colors regular and sometimes gave the girls books that once belonged to her sons. "A broken leg is a disaster. But a broken arm isn't that bad. Tell Brooke that having a broken arm is a great excuse to sit in bed with a good book."

"I'll tell her," Aly said, though she thought Brooke was more likely to draw than to read. Brooke was a talented artist, just like their mother. Since Brooke's drawing arm wasn't the broken one, Aly was sure she would be making tons of pictures while she was resting today.

"Joan," Aly said, "if it's okay with you, I'm going to call Brooke on the True Colors telephone. I promise not to tie up the line."

Aly took the cordless phone through the main salon into the Sparkle Spa, where she, Charlotte, Lily, and Sparkly plopped down on the big floor pillows in the drying and jewelry-making area. Sophie sat at one of the manicure stations and leaned back in the Teal Me the Truth–colored chair.

When Mom answered, she told Aly that Brooke was sleeping but would probably be up by the time Aly got home.

Aly hung up, a little sad that she hadn't gotten to talk to her sister.

"It's okay, Al," Charlotte said. "You'll see her after the Angels' pedicures. Oh, and Anjuli's manicure." Anjuli was the goalie and the only soccer player who needed sparkle power on her hands as well as her feet.

"Right," Aly answered, starting to feel panicky. According to her watch, the soccer girls would start arriving in two minutes, and she hadn't finished her homework yet, which meant she had already broken one of her mom's rules for the Sparkle Spa. She had a feeling that before the day was over, she would break some other rules, too. Eleven pedicures and one manicure all by herself was not going to be easy. Not even close.

Aly took a deep breath and pulled out a piece of paper and a glitter pen from the desk at the back of the room and started a new list.

<u>Other Ways All the Pedicures Could</u>
<u>Get Done</u>
1. A True Colors manicurist could
   help.
2. Sparkle Spa could be open
   tomorrow too, so I could polish
   fewer people each day.
3. Enlist a lot of helpers.

This was good! Aly had come up with great
options!

"I'll be right back," she said to the girls as she ran
out into the main salon.

"Joan!" she said "Joan! I have eleven girls coming
in for pedicures and one who also needs a manicure,
and it's just me because of Brooke's broken arm. I
know it's only a kid salon, but is there any, any chance

one of the True Colors manicurists could help? Just for a little while?"

Joan looked over at Aly, then looked down at the schedule in front of her and shook her head. "I really wish someone here could give you a hand, Al," she said. "But with your mom out, we're already all over-booked, taking care of her clients along with our own."

Aly felt like a balloon that had just been popped. But she understood.

"Okay," she said. "Thanks, Joan."

When Aly got back to the Sparkle Spa, Charlotte said, "What was that all about?"

Aly picked up her list again and crossed out the first option. "I'd thought of a way to get the pedicures done faster, but none of the grown-ups have time to help. Instead, maybe I'll see if some of the soccer girls can come tomorrow," she said, underlining the second item on her list.

"You can't," Lily said. "Remember? We have to do research for our Lewis and Clark project tomorrow after school."

Aly closed her eyes. She had totally forgotten about Lewis and Clark. That left her third and final option: *Enlist helpers.*

She walked over to the polish display wall and grabbed bottles of Strawberry Sunday, Under Watermelon, Lemon Aid, Orange You Pretty, and We the Purple—the colors for the rainbow sparkle pedicures. "In that case," Aly said, "I need someone to be a bottle opener and closer for me today."

"I'll do it," Charlotte said, raising her hand.

"And I can be in charge of the donations," Lily said, picking up the teal strawberry-shaped cookie jar the girls used to collect donations. "I'll make sure everyone contributes before they leave."

"How about Sophie, Aly? Do you have a job for her?" Charlotte asked.

Sophie was quietly painting her nails with Red Between the Lines, a newish color that looked kind of like a mixture of red and gray. She screwed the top back onto the bottle and held up her hands. "Can I be a second manicurist?" she asked.

Aly walked over and inspected Sophie's nails. She'd done a nice job. Not quite as professional as Aly's and Brooke's polishing, but better than most people's. "Whoa!" Aly said. "Good work."

"Brooke and I have been polishing each other's nails," Sophie told her. "It's not perfect yet, but maybe it's good enough to fill in for Brooke, since it's just you today?"

Aly looked at Sophie's hands again. A little polish was on the skin around both of her thumbnails, and she'd missed two spots on the corner of her right pinkie.

And another on the bottom of her left pointer finger. The polish on one of her ring fingers was a little gloppy too.

Aly sighed. "I'm not sure if you're ready yet, Soph," she said. "So first let's see how it goes with just me polishing."

Sophie looked at her own nails, inspecting them the way Aly had. "I see what you mean," she admitted. "I'll keep practicing. For now, I can help with nail drying and filling the pedicure basins. Is that okay?"

"Great," Aly said, and she and Sophie turned to fill the pedicure basins with water. But before she could even flip on the faucet, Jenica came into the Sparkle Spa with Valentina, one of the other soccer players.

"Happy Tuesday!" Valentina called.

Jenica glanced at Aly, Charlotte, Lily, and Sophie. "Actually, none of you look very happy," she said.

"Brooke broke her arm," Lily answered.

"Oh, man," Jenica said. "Tell her I'm sorry. I broke my wrist at summer camp once. I couldn't play sports or go swimming for six weeks after that."

"Wait a minute," Valentina said. "Aly, are you polishing all by yourself?"

"That's the plan," Aly said. "Why don't we get started?"

Two hours and twelve minutes later Aly had done eight pedicures and still had three to go . . . plus one manicure. She was running very, very late. Usually, the Sparkle Spa was closing about now. Her friends were being as helpful as possible, and the soccer girls were being as patient as possible, but Aly could tell they all wanted to get this over and done with. She was also pretty sure she had nail polish smeared all over her forehead—We the Purple, to be exact.

"Okay . . . next," Aly called out. "Sophie, could you please refill the pedicure basin on the right?"

Mia walked over and hopped into the chair. "I hope Brooke's ready to polish again before the dance showcase."

Aly felt the blood drain from her face. "That's *this* Friday?"

Mia nodded. Aly groaned. A group of the girls who attended Miss Lulu's dancing school were in a dance showcase, so they could show their families what they'd been working on all fall, and many of them had booked manicure appointments for Thursday after school.

"I don't mean to be mean or anything," Mia said,

"but unless Brooke is back or you have someone else doing nails, I might cancel my manicure appointment for the showcase. Giovanna and I have been waiting for half an hour for our rainbow sparkle pedicures. And we have homework. If it weren't for the quarter-finals, we'd have left by now."

Aly felt a headache coming on. "I'm really sorry," she said. "I think Brooke will be back by then. I promise the wait won't be as long on Thursday."

Mia nodded. "Okay. I really *do* want a manicure before the showcase. I want shiny nails to go with my shiny costume. We're dancing to a song called 'Stop! In the Name of Love,' and we have red leotards with white trim and white leg warmers—all covered with sequins and glitter."

"That sounds awesome," Charlotte said as she uncapped a bottle of clear polish. "And it's cool that you do soccer and dance."

"They're both fun," Mia said, easing her feet out of the warm pedicure water.

Just as Charlotte opened the Strawberry Sunday, Joan rushed into the Sparkle Spa. "The drain snake! The drain snake!" she yelled. "Aly, where's that twisted metal thing that snakes down the drain to clear out clogs?"

"I saw that before!" Lily said, hurrying to the back closet and retrieving a wiggly metal contraption. "Here!"

"Cookies for you," Joan told her. "I'll bake you a whole batch."

Joan's delicious cookies were famous all over town. Receiving an entire batch was one of the best presents ever.

"Running a salon by yourself isn't all it's cracked up to be, huh, Al?" Joan said before zipping back into True Colors.

Aly sighed. It was definitely better to run a salon as a team.

"Charlotte," she said, "ready with the polish?"

Charlotte nodded.

"Okay," Aly said, "here we go." But as she polished Mia's toes, she worried about what in the world she would do on Thursday if Brooke wasn't back at work by then. With fourteen dancers on the schedule, there was no way Aly could polish that many fingers alone.

thʀee

We the Purple

The next thing Aly knew, Joan was saying, "Wake up, sleepyhead. You're home."

Aly barely remembered closing her eyes, let alone falling asleep on the ride to her house.

"That was some day, huh, Al?" Joan said.

Aly got out of the backseat of the car with Sparkly and walked over to Joan's window. "I don't know what I'm going to do if Brooke can't polish on Thursday," she told Joan. "Going to school all day and then spending so many hours at the salon is exhausting."

"I hear you," Joan said. "But Brooke and your mom might be out for the rest of the week, Aly. Both of us had better be prepared to be busy."

Aly's stomach fell. Brooke might be out the whole week? That couldn't be. Aly needed her there on Thursday. "Are you coming in?" she asked Joan.

"I think I need to go home and relax, just like you do. But please tell your mom to call me if she has time later. Stay strong, kiddo."

"You too," Aly said. "Thanks for the ride. I have to work on a Lewis and Clark project tomorrow, so I probably won't see you. But I'll stop by afterward if I can."

Joan nodded and scratched Sparkly behind the ears. "Give Brooke a hug for me."

"I will," Aly said, and then she and Sparkly started walking up the driveway.

By the time Aly reached the house, Mom was

there, opening the front door. "Brooke's sleeping again," she whispered, "so be quiet when you come in. Keep Sparkly quiet too."

Sleeping again? Aly couldn't believe it. "No problem," she whispered back, covering Sparkly's mouth with her hand. Aly walked in, put Sparkly down, and slipped off her shoes. She dropped her bag on the floor and fell into her mother's arms. "I'm so tired," she said. "And hungry. Going to school *and* going to work is hard!"

Over two tall glasses of milk, peanut butter and jelly sandwiches, and a plate of celery, Mom and Aly talked about both salons, Brooke's arm, and Dad's schedule.

"Joan said you might be home with Brooke all week," Aly said. "Is that true? Because I need her in the salon."

"I'm not sure," Mom said. "We'll have to see how she feels."

Aly nodded. She hoped Brooke would feel better super fast. But even if she didn't, Aly thought Mom should go back to True Colors to help Joan and the rest of the staff. "Why can't you call a babysitter or ask Dad to come home if someone needs to stay with Brooke?" she asked.

"I'd hate to leave Brooke with a sitter if she's not feeling well. And Dad's trying to change his plans," Mom answered, "but he's not sure he can. He'll definitely be home earlier than usual on Friday, though."

Aly nodded. Dad traveled a lot for work. He was usually gone from Monday afternoon until Friday afternoon. Sometimes he even got stuck places because of bad weather or bad airplanes or late meetings and got home on Saturday.

"So how did everything go at the salon?" Mom asked.

"Oh, Mom, it was crazy!" Aly said, leaning back in her chair. "I was the only one polishing in the Sparkle Spa, and I had to do eleven pedicures and one manicure, and my friends helped, but mostly, it was all up to me to get it done."

"That's what happens when you're the CEO of a business," Mom said, smiling a tiny bit.

"The what?" Aly asked. She had no idea what Mom was talking about.

"CEO," Mom said. "Chief executive officer. It's another name for the boss—the person who's in charge of everything at a company. Sometimes when you're the CEO, you have to jump in and take care of things—do more than you thought you would have to—because it's your business. You want it to succeed."

Aly nodded. That's how she'd felt this afternoon at the Sparkle Spa. She couldn't let the customers down. But then she thought about Joan running True Colors today and taking care of the clogged drain. "Are you the CEO of True Colors?" Aly asked her mom.

Mom nodded. "President and CEO is what my business card says."

"What about Joan? Does she have a title?"

"That's a good question," Mom said. She took a bite of celery and thought for a minute before she spoke. "Joan's my only senior manicurist, so she's second in command at the shop. When I'm not there, she takes over."

"Just senior manicurist?" Aly asked. "If she's in charge when you're not there, shouldn't she have a more important job title than that? One with initials, like yours?"

"You know, Aly," Mom said, "I think that's actually a very good idea. I've been thinking about hiring a COO, a chief operating officer. That person's job would be to manage the day-to-day organization of the salon. Then I can work more on getting new customers and maybe even starting a second shop. I'll talk to Joan about that."

"Joan watches Sparkly and bakes all the time and was great today at taking care of a broken pedicure basin, no problem," Aly said. "I bet she'd be a good COO. As long as she still gets to do manicures. I know she likes that part. Oh, and also—I just remembered: She said to call her tonight when you have time."

"Thanks for the message," Mom said. "I'll give her a call when we're finished with dinner."

"Are there other jobs?" Aly asked. "With initials like CEO and COO? For a business, I mean?"

Mom nodded. "Businesses can have a chief finan-cial officer—"

"CFO?" Aly asked.

"Yes," Mom said, after swallowing a bite of sand-wich. "And sometimes a chief marketing officer, a chief creative officer, a chief security officer, a chief digital officer, a chief legal officer . . . there are a lot. You can have someone in charge of every part of a business. Bigger companies have all those positions and more. Smaller companies sometimes just have a CEO."

Aly licked a drop of jelly off her thumb. "Will True Colors get all of those?"

"Maybe one day if I open lots and lots of salons and we need a team to run all of them."

"Is that what you want to do?" Aly asked. "Open lots of True Colors salons?" She hadn't known that was her mom's plan, but now it seemed like maybe it was.

"Just dreaming," Mom said. "I'm just dreaming. Far into the future. For now, we've got one salon and one broken arm to look after."

She pushed her empty plate forward. "Anyway, as the co-CEO of the Tanner household, I've made an EMD—an Executive Mother Decision." Mom grinned and continued: "Brooke has to rest and recuperate. I don't want the two of you jumping around. So I've moved some of your clothes and your sparkle pens and a few pieces of your favorite purple paper into the office upstairs. While Brooke's in pain, I think it's better for you to move in there. At least for a few days."

As Mom brought their dishes to the sink, she added. "And tomorrow, can you please pick up Brooke's homework assignments and any other schoolwork she'll miss?"

"Sure," Aly said, her brain quickly switching from True Colors to her sister. "But . . . what if Brooke needs someone in the middle of the night? I should be there to help her."

"I left the cordless phone with her," Mom said. "She'll call my cell if she needs something. Besides, if she doesn't feel well in the middle of the night, I don't want her to wake you. Don't forget, you have school tomorrow."

Aly was not happy. She didn't like the idea of sleeping in the tiny office. And she didn't like not being with Brooke, either.

"Can I at least go check on her?" Aly asked.

Mom nodded. "Just don't wake her if she's sleeping."

"I won't," Aly said.

She tiptoed up the steps and slowly pushed open their bedroom door. She poked her head in and saw Brooke, her arm wrapped in a big white cast, asleep in her bed. Sparkly was curled up at her feet. Her stuffed animals were next to her.

"Hi, Brooke," Aly whispered. But Brooke didn't budge. Aly sighed. Hopefully, Brooke would be up the next morning before Aly left for school. She'd see then if Brooke would be able to polish with a cast on. Because Aly really, really needed her to be ready to work in the salon by Thursday!

four
Traffic Coney Island

The next morning when Aly looked in on Brooke, she was still sleeping. Sparkly hadn't moved from the end of her bed. Her stuffed animals had fallen to the floor.

"She had a rough night," Mom said when Aly walked into the kitchen. "Her arm really hurt. I'm glad she finally fell back asleep."

Aly had not planned on this.

"But I need to know about the polishing!" she

cried. "We have *fourteen* manicures for the dance showcase tomorrow!"

Mom sighed. "I'm sorry, honey. But I wouldn't count on Brooke being able to help. Think about it, Al. Would you be able to polish with one arm in a cast or a sling?"

Aly hadn't really considered that. She held her left arm against her stomach and realized that, without it, she wouldn't be able to open any bottles, file fingernails, keep a customer's hand steady, or polish well at all.

She closed her eyes. What was she going to do tomorrow afternoon? Aly already knew she couldn't ask one of the True Colors manicurists to help. And there were no days available to reschedule anyone before the showcase because of her research project.

Aly popped a few banana slices into her mouth

and grabbed her backpack. She would have to think of something while she was at school.

During gym, while the rest of her class played volleyball, Aly tried and tried to come up with a plan, but other than finding kids who could polish as well as she and Brooke could to work at the salon, she couldn't come up with anything. And really, no other kids she knew could polish like she and Brooke could.

After the final bell rang, Aly went to the library to work with Charlotte and Lily on their Lewis and Clark project. Half of their fifth-grade class was in there with them, and Ms. Abbott, the librarian, was going from group to group helping everyone out. In between researching, Aly and Lily and Charlotte talked about Brooke's arm and the fact that she wouldn't be able to work tomorrow.

"I wish I were a better polisher," Charlotte said.

"I wish I could polish at all," Lily added. "But you remember what happened last time I tried?"

"Orange pinkie toe," Charlotte and Aly said together. Then the girls giggled, in spite of the seriousness of their conversation.

Aly knew she would have to find a solution that didn't involve Lily painting people's entire pinkie toes orange. Because that would absolutely not be good for business at the Sparkle Spa.

When the girls finished their research and Ms. Abbott had to close the library for the day, Aly decided to stop by True Colors quickly to see if Joan needed anything. With Mom gone, Aly knew it would be crazy at the salon. And sure enough, she was right.

"Oh, thank goodness you're here! Can you pitch in with the usual stuff?" Joan asked the moment Aly entered the salon.

"Absolutely!" Aly said. She quickly took care of the jobs she and Brooke usually did at True Colors—went to the bank to turn twenties into singles, organized the polish wall, and refilled the rhinestones at Carla's, Jamie's, and Joan's stations.

When that was all done, Aly sat down to take a breather with Mrs. Franklin, one of the girls' favorite regulars, who was under the nail dryers.

"Where's your sister?" Mrs. Franklin asked. "I brought a new photograph of Sadie I know she would love to see." Sadie was Mrs. Franklin's dog, a famous dog model—or, at least, she was a little bit famous. She was in magazines and was the official spokes-dog for the Paws for Love animal shelter in town. Brooke especially loved seeing pictures of Sadie dressed in silly outfits from her photo shoots.

"She broke her arm chasing Sparkly," Aly replied. "But I'll tell her that you have pictures."

"A broken arm!" Mrs. Franklin said. "Well, that's too bad. But I think I might have something more than pictures to cheer her up. Would you mind unzipping the side pocket on my purse?"

Aly did as she was asked, pulling out a gold pencil case and opening it to find paw print stickers inside.

"Why don't you take a couple of those for Brooke to put on her cast?" Mrs. Franklin suggested. "It's Sadie's autograph."

Aly smiled. Brooke would love the stickers. "Thanks so much, Mrs. Franklin."

Mrs. Franklin nodded. "Of course, dear. And please tell your sister I hope to see her back in the salon soon."

"I will," Aly said.

Aly noticed Joan putting some paper on a clipboard and attaching a pen to it with a ribbon. "What's that?" she asked.

"Lately, there have been so many walk-in customers, in addition to our regulars," Joan explained. "There just isn't enough room, with all these people crowding here. So I made a chart: name, cell phone number, time of arrival. I'll call people five minutes before we're ready for them so they can run other errands and not clog up the salon while they're waiting."

Aly glanced around at the customers in the waiting area. Most of them looked a little impatient, checking their phones or reading magazines. Joan was right. They could probably put the time to better use running errands rather than sitting around until a manicurist freed up.

"Nice plan," Aly said. "Do you think my mom will like it?"

Joan massaged her forehead. "If she doesn't, she can discontinue it when she's back. But as long as I'm

in charge, we have to keep business—and people—
moving."

Aly nodded. She'd never seen Joan so serious
about something salon-related before. Usually, she
was the fun one who made cookies and hosted pizza
picnics while Mom took care of salon business.

"Sounds great," Aly said. Then she looked at the
clock. She really should head home now and see how
Brooke was doing, but then she spotted a familiar
face poking through the front door.

"Sophie!" Aly said. "What are you doing here?"

"My mom is at the Sports Palace with my
brother—buying him new sneakers. She said I could
come here until they're done. I wanted to ask Joan
how Brooke's doing."

"Big brother or little brother?" Aly asked.

"Big," Sophie said. "Sammy is at home with
NaiNai." Sophie had two brothers, one in seventh

grade and one who was three. Her grandma watched the three-year-old a lot. "I thought you had to work on Lewis and Clark today?"

"I did," Aly said. "But I stopped in here afterward for a little bit. I'm going to go home to see Brooke soon. My mom said she had a bad night, but I don't know how she's been today."

Sophie nodded. "Maybe I'll give her a call when I get home," she said.

Aly thought that was a good idea. "As long as she's not sleeping, I bet she'd like that."

Sophie nodded again, but she didn't leave the salon. "Um . . . ," she said. "Since you're here, there's something I wanted to show you." She held out her hand for Aly to see. "I practiced polishing a lot last night. Look."

Aly inspected Sophie's fingers. They were close to perfect. Not a drop of color on her skin, and every part of every nail was polished.

Aly grinned at Sophie. She really *did* need help tomorrow, and if Sophie could polish, that might fix Aly's scheduling problem. And even if she did a terrible job, the thing about polish is that it's easy to take off.

Aly looked at Joan's clipboard list. Then she took a big breath. "Sophie," she said, "I'm making an ESSD—an Executive Sparkle Spa Decision: You're now an official Sparkle Spa manicurist. Can you come in and polish tomorrow afternoon?"

Sophie beamed. "Absolutely!" she said.

For what seemed like the first time since Brooke broke her arm, Aly exhaled with relief. She put her arm around Sophie's shoulders. "Welcome to the team," she said.

"Aly!" Joan called from the reception desk. "Your mom is on the phone. She said you should head home now."

"I'll see you tomorrow," Sophie said, still smiling, and she walked out the door.

Aly got her backpack and started to head out too. But before she did, she stopped at the reception desk and blurted out, "Joan, just like you, I made a big decision today: I hired a new manicurist for the Sparkle Spa. Sophie. And now everything's going to be okay tomorrow."

At first Joan was silent. She stared at Aly for a few seconds, then finally said, "Aly, you're in charge of the Sparkle Spa. If you think that's the right thing to do, you should do it. But you have to take responsibility for this decision—no matter what happens."

Aly gulped. "I know," she answered. "I know."

five

White Christmas

When Aly walked through the door, Brooke was curled up on the overstuffed chair in the corner of the kitchen. Sparkly was at her feet.

"It feels like I haven't seen you in a *year*," Aly said, speeding over to her sister.

"More like three hundred years," Brooke answered. But she didn't sound like her usual bouncy self.

"Hi, Aly," Mom called from the laundry room. "I'll be up in a second!"

"She's transferring," Brooke said. "Washer to dryer."

Aly nodded. "So how does your arm feel?" she asked, studying Brooke's cast.

In the light it was really bright, like the White Christmas polish at the salon.

"It hurts," she said. Her face started to crumple. "And I can't polish nails. I can't go to school or to the Sparkle Spa. I never get to see anyone—not you or Joan or Sophie or anyone."

Aly sat on the arm of the chair and stroked her sister's head. She almost started crying herself because Brooke was so sad. This was definitely not the time to worry her with Sparkle Spa issues. Besides, Aly had fixed everything by hiring Sophie. She'd tell Brooke all about it later.

"You'll feel better soon," she said. "You'll go back to school and polish nails, and I'm here right now. I even brought your homework home. Besides, it's only been two days. Not even."

Brooke didn't stop complaining there, though.

"I didn't like the hospital either," Brooke said, snuggling her head against Aly. "It smelled funny. The doctor had to give me a shot, and I had to wait for a hundred million years. It was so boring . . . and a little scary."

"But you made it through," Aly said. "And you don't have to go back, right?"

"Wrong," Mom replied, coming up the steps into the kitchen. "You have a doctor's appointment in two weeks."

"When can everything get back to normal, Mom?" Brooke asked. "I can't wait."

"Remember what we talked about?" Mom answered. "Salon on Saturday. Your arm will feel much better by then. And school on Monday. You just need some time for the swelling to go down."

"That's too long," Brooke grumbled. "I *hate* having a broken arm."

Aly almost wanted to say, *Then you should've listened to me and not gone racing around the house after your hair band,* but she kept it zipped inside. Instead, she said, "I have a present for you. From Mrs. Franklin." Aly pulled the paw stickers out of her pocket.

Brooke smiled for the first time since Aly got home. "They're to decorate your cast."

Brooke looked at the fiberglass on her arm. "I can decorate it?" she asked.

Aly shrugged. "Mrs. Franklin seemed to think so."

"Mom," Brooke said, a little louder, "can I decorate my cast?"

"Sure," she said. "No reason why not. But after dinner."

"I'll cut your chicken tonight, Brookester. But don't get used to it," Aly offered, and gave her sister's braid a gentle tug.

After dinner, homework, and a quick conversation with Dad during which Aly begged him to come home—*now!*—Aly went back to the office to sleep on the couch, and Brooke got to stay up late decorating her cast.

Aly had unscrewed the tops of six different polishes—and had peeled up the edges of a bunch of stickers so it would be easier for Brooke with her one hand. But Aly wasn't allowed to stay up to help Brooke decorate.

Brooke had slept for so much of the day that she didn't have to go to bed yet. Plus, she could sleep in tomorrow because she wasn't going to school. A definite broken-arm perk, as far as Aly was concerned. One she was trying hard not to feel jealous about.

Aly got into bed, but she couldn't get comfortable. She couldn't stop thinking about all the dance show-case manicures scheduled for tomorrow. Sophie would be a good second manicurist, but Aly knew she'd be slow, slow, slow, just like Aly and Brooke had been at the beginning. She had to figure out a way to make the afternoon go as smoothly as possible.

Aly climbed out of bed and tiptoed over to her mother's desk. She quietly wiggled the mouse on the computer to see if it was on. The screen lit up.

On it were the words *Joan West, COO, True Colors,* along with the salon's address and phone number, plus a cool picture of a bottle of nail polish the same exact colors as the sign on the salon. It looked like the layout for a business card. Mom must have been working on it today. *Neat,* Aly thought.

She opened up a new document and started typing a list.

Ways to Speed Up Sophie's Polishing

1. Ask someone else to open and close

   bottles for her.

2. Have someone else or the customer

   remove any old polish.

3. Ask someone else to set up her station.

Lists always made Aly feel better and more pre-pared. Reading over it, she realized she'd added "someone else" to each item. If that "someone" wasn't Aly, who would it be?

Then the answer came to her. *Of course,* Aly thought, and typed:

4. Ask Charlotte and Lily if they'll also help.

With her mind a bit quieter now, she climbed back into bed. But just as she was about to fall asleep, Aly

sat up with a start. *Oh no!* She never told Brooke—
or Mom—about hiring Sophie. Or that their other
friends had helped out on Tuesday.

Although she hadn't meant to keep it from Brooke,
Aly also didn't want Brooke to feel bad about not being
able to work at the salon this week, so maybe it was
a good thing that she'd forgotten to tell her. Besides,
Aly decided as she snuggled back into bed, Brooke
wouldn't mind anyway. Charlotte and Lily had helped
out in the Sparkle Spa before, and Sophie *was* her best
friend after all.

Six
Copperfield

After school on Thursday, Aly, Sophie—*and* Charlotte and Lily—sped to True Colors. At some point they gave up racewalking and started running, so they were all a little out of breath by the time they ran through the salon's front door.

"Carrots are in the fridge!" Joan said as the girls rushed in. "Water, too."

Mom usually had snacks waiting for the girls when they arrived after school. Aly was happy that Joan had remembered. She was starving.

"Oh, and Lily, there's a bag of cookies with your name on it," Joan called after the girls.

Once they were all in the back, Aly read from the list she had written during lunch that she'd titled "Jobs":

> Lily: Set up the manicure stations
> Charlotte: Open and close polish
> bottles and help people choose colors
> Sophie: Second manicurist

Lily asked, "*Sophie's* polishing?"

Aly nodded.

"High five!" Lily said, holding her palm out to Sophie. Sophie smiled and slapped it.

Charlotte was happy with her job too. But then she looked around, like she was searching for something. "Color of the Week!" she said. "What is it?"

Aly's eyes popped open. Choosing the Color of the Week was usually Brooke's job, but without her here, Aly had totally forgotten. "How about one of the new Presto Change-o shades?" she suggested. "Arnold, the delivery guy, brought them yesterday, and they look like two different colors, depending on how the light hits them. Do you want to pick one, Charlotte? They're on the bottom shelf of the display, on the right."

Charlotte picked Copperfield, the gold and red shade. "How about this?"

"That's good," Aly said, nervously looking around. "Did I miss anything else? The dancers will be here any second."

"Well," Lily said, sounding a little nervous herself, "you know how the Sparkle Spa has special treatments? Like the rainbow sparkle pedicure for the soccer team and the thumbs-up man-icure for guys?

437

Should you create something special for the dancers?"

Lily was right. But Brooke usually thought up those, too. "How about . . . ," Aly said. "How about . . ."

"How about a heart on the dancers' pinkies, painted in a different color?" Sophie offered. "That way, everyone can show the audience how much they love dancing."

Aly nodded. "Good plan, Soph," she said. "Let's call it . . . 'I Love Dancing'! So, Charlotte, everyone has to pick two colors if they want the special I Love Dancing manicure. And we need to get some of those tiny nail art brushes my mom keeps in the closet."

"Got it," Charlotte said.

"Okay, everyone. Now we're ready," Aly announced.

But Lily corrected her. "The donation jar!" she said. "Aly, you *always* forget the donation jar. I'll be in charge of that, too."

"It's all yours, Lil," she said. "And *no* walk-ins. Scheduled dancers only. Sophie's not as fast as I am yet, so any walk-ins will have to come back another day. No exceptions."

"Yes, boss," Charlotte said, and everyone started laughing.

Aly thought about how lucky she was to have such good friends. She might not even need Brooke this week with them around.

A few minutes later the first dancers arrived.

Sophie was definitely slow—Aly could finish almost two manicures in the time it took Sophie to do one—but she was good. She chatted with the customers and didn't seem nervous at all. She did mess up once, but luckily, it was on Mia—and since Mia was a regular and had gotten to know Sophie at the Sparkle Spa, she didn't mind so much.

"It's your first day on the job," Mia said to Sophie.

"Don't worry. You're doing better than *I* could ever do."

Aly was leading a girl named Maisy over to the drying station when Charlotte's twin brother, Caleb, peeked into the salon.

"Um," he said, "how's it going? Charlotte said you might need some help, and, well, I finished up at baseball practice in the park. Mom said it was okay if I came."

Aly grinned. Caleb was probably the nicest boy in the whole fifth grade. "I think we're okay," she said. "It's busy, but it's not that bad."

Caleb pointed at Lily. "What's going on over there?" he asked. She was organizing Sophie's manicure station with one arm while the other was hugging the big teal donation jar.

"She's doing two jobs—donations collector and station resetter," Aly explained.

Aly could barely hear Caleb when he spoke: "I

can do one of them, if you want. I mean, probably the donation jar, because I don't know about setting up, um, what did you call them? Stations?"

"Great idea," she said. Then she turned to Lily. "Caleb's going to help with the donations for a bit."

Lily darted over and handed him the ceramic strawberry. "Thanks," she said. "But just so you know, collecting donations is *my* favorite job, so I'm going to want it back."

Caleb scrunched his eyebrows. "Sure," he said. "No problem." Caleb parked himself and the giant strawberry by the Sparkle Spa door. "This way, I can do security, too, just like my dad," he said. Caleb and Charlotte's dad was chief of security for one of the largest buildings in town.

"I don't know if we need security," Aly told him, "but we do need someone to tell walk-ins that we're booked up." Aly handed Caleb the appointment book.

"All the dancers who are scheduled for a manicure are written down in here. Don't let anyone else in, okay?"

Aly was in the middle of an I Love Dancing manicure for a girl named Zorah, with Golden Delicious fingernails and Copperfield pinkie hearts, when she heard Caleb say, "I'm sorry. If you don't have an appointment, I can't let you in."

Aly stopped mid-polish. And groaned. It was Suzy Davis.

Ever since Aly fixed Suzy's messed-up manicure and hairdo before the Sixth-Grade Fall Ball a few weeks ago, Suzy had been nicer to her than she used to be. But Suzy was still Suzy. That meant she still had some mean inside her.

"I need a manicure. Now," Suzy demanded. "And it looks like Sparkle Spa is open today. So I'm coming in. It's a free country."

Caleb stood in the doorway. "Even in a free country, there are private places where people get to make their own rules. The rule here is that you need an appointment to come in. At least for today. No walk-ins." He looked over at Aly for confirmation.

"I'll be right back," Aly told Zorah. Usually, Brooke was the one who stood up to Suzy, but today Aly had no choice. She walked over to the door.

"What's the problem, Suzy?" she asked.

"I just cracked my thumbnail. I need a manicure. This minute." She shoved her broken nail past Caleb into Aly's face. Aly winced. It looked like it hurt.

"Suzy, I can't take care of that right now—we're too busy today with the dance showcase—but I can give you a nail file. You can fix the cracked part yourself."

"This is a nail salon," Suzy answered, her voice growing louder. "Not a do-it-yourself place. This is ridiculous!"

All of the dancers in the salon stared at Suzy.

Caleb cleared his throat. "If you don't leave, I'm going to get Joan."

"What is your *problem*?" Suzy said. "I mean, all I want is a manicure!"

Caleb didn't budge. "Bye, Suzy," he said.

Suzy glared at him. "You stink big-time, Caleb Cane," she huffed, and left.

Charlotte beamed. "Isn't my brother awesome?" she said.

"He sure is," Aly agreed, walking back to her station. "Zorah, let's finish up your fingers."

By five thirty Aly had done nine manicures and Sophie had done five. "Nice work, team! I couldn't have done this without you," Aly said. Even though she missed Brooke, she was super happy she'd gotten through the day without any major disasters. Well, not counting Suzy Davis, but truly, because of Caleb, that had been only a minor mishap.

And right then and there, Aly made the biggest ESSD of all: She offered everyone jobs at the Sparkle Spa.

Lily would be the CFO; Charlotte, the COO; Caleb, the chief of security; and Sophie, a manicurist.

Aly was delighted with her new Sparkle Spa team. She knew Brooke would be too. At least she hoped so.

Seven
Silversmith

Aly didn't have to wait long to find out how Brooke felt.

She arrived home to two surprises: a happy Dad, who had managed to return one day earlier and . . . a furious Brooke, who had just gotten off the phone with Sophie.

"Sophie is a Sparkle Spa manicurist? And she polished nails today instead of me? And you let Charlotte pick the Color of the Week? Who made you the boss of the world?" Brooke shouted. She stomped up the stairs and slammed the bedroom door.

Sparkly started yapping and whimpering.

Mom and Dad exchanged looks.

Aly felt her face turning the color of Ruby Red Slippers nail polish. It wasn't exactly the response she was expecting.

"Aly, sit down," Mom said firmly. "And, Mark, why don't you go check on Brooke?"

Sparkly followed Dad upstairs while Aly and her mother sat across from each other at the kitchen table.

"Is what Brooke said true?" Mom asked.

"I had no choice, Mom," Aly said. "Remember how you said that the CEO has to jump in and make decisions and take care of emergencies? Without Brooke and you around, I had to make sure the Sparkle Spa customers were taken care of."

Mom didn't answer, so Aly continued. "Isn't that what the leader of a business does, Mom?"

Her mother smiled. It was a small one, but it was a smile.

"You're right, Aly. That is what the person in charge has to do. But I think you may have forgotten that your sister is your partner. She works with you, not for you. She shouldn't have heard the news from Sophie. In fact, she should have been part of the decision."

Aly felt her stomach drop a little. She couldn't argue. Mom was right, and Aly had overlooked that point, but still, she thought her decisions were pretty good ones. "Everything happened so quickly," she started to explain. "And I didn't want Brooke to worry about not being around to help during such a busy week. I just wanted to do what was best—for our customers and for Sophie and Brooke and everyone.

Charlotte and Lily and Caleb helped out too. If they hadn't, it would've been a disaster at the Sparkle Spa, and we've worked so hard to build it. I didn't want it to fall apart just because of Brooke's arm."

Mom looked at Aly for a long moment. Then she got up and gave Aly a hug from behind, resting her chin on Aly's head. For a second Aly kind of wanted to cry. "Why don't you wait until Dad comes downstairs, and then you can apologize to your sister," Mom finally said.

"I will," Aly told her. She knew she had to. She knew it was the right thing to do—plus, she hated it when Brooke was mad at her. But she knew that in addition to apologizing, she was going to have to tell her sister about giving the other kids jobs at the Sparkle Spa too. If Brooke was already upset about them working there for a day, she was *not* going to be happy about the longer-term arrangement. "First, I'm going to make a peace offering, though." Aly thought making Brooke's favorite snack might help out a little. It was worth a try.

As Aly made a heart-shaped cream cheese and jelly sandwich for Brooke, she and her mom talked about the new Presto Change-o colors that had arrived while Mom was home with Brooke—how some shades looked muddy, but how the metallics, like Silversmith, seemed popular.

When Dad came back into the kitchen, Aly quickly took the sandwich and a glass of chocolate milk upstairs. "Brooke?" she called, knocking on their bedroom door. "Brookester?"

"I'm not talking to you," Brooke answered.

"You just did," Aly said. "And I'm sorry. I'm so sorry. And I'm leaving you a present."

Then Aly went to the office—she figured it would take Brooke a little while to come around, and she still had some reading to do for her Lewis and Clark project. Once she was finished sticking flags on the book Ms. Abbott had given her about Sacagawea, noting that Lewis and Clark would probably have gotten lost and not been very good explorers without Sacagawea's help, Aly sat down at the computer. After clicking around for a bit, she found the new business card Mom had made for Joan. She copied it and pasted it into a new document over and over, then started typing new wording into each little rectangle. In just a few minutes she'd made Sparkle Spa business cards for everyone on the team—Sophie, Lily, Charlotte, Caleb, and herself—so she could give them out tomorrow at school. She pressed print and watched the pages pile up.

She'd have to cut the thick paper to the right size, but the cards looked pretty good. She especially liked the purple star she'd added in place of the polish bottle Mom had on Joan's card. It had little lines around it to make it look like it really was sparkling. Once Brooke was talking to her again for real, she'd make one for Brooke, too.

Aly picked up the sheets of paper.

"What are those?" Brooke said, standing at the door.

Aly jumped and the pages went flying. "You scared me!" she said. Aly bent down to pick up the papers. "They're Sparkle Spa business cards."

Brooke adjusted the strap of the sling on her shoulder. "For us?" she asked, her eyes growing big. "Is that another way besides the sandwich that you're apologizing to me? Because that's so cool!"

"Well, they're Sparkle Spa business cards, but they're not just for us." Aly swallowed hard. She knew she had to say it, but the words stuck in her throat. "They are for our friends," she finally continued. "Sophie wasn't the only one who helped out. Charlotte, Lily, and Caleb worked there today too, so I gave them all jobs at Sparkle Spa."

Brooke blinked once. Then twice. Aly was afraid Brooke would cry. But she didn't. She yelled. "You did *what?*"

"They're our friends. And I needed help. Fourteen dancers were booked, and there was no way I could give them manicures all by myself." Aly was trying to defend herself, but it sounded like a bad excuse, even to her.

Tears ran down Brooke's face. "Sparkle Spa is *our* thing, Aly. *Ours.* And you're acting like it's only *yours,*" she sniffed.

"You left me, Brooke!" Aly said. "You left me all alone, and I had to do everything myself. We're lucky our friends offered to help; otherwise, I would've had to cancel everything. All the girls who were counting on us for manicures for their showcase would've been so upset. That would have been terrible for Sparkle Spa business."

Brooke crossed her unbroken arm over her broken one. "You could've talked to me about it. It's like you didn't even care I wasn't there. Did you at least give me a good job on my business card?" Brooke asked, her voice quivering.

"I didn't give you one yet," Aly muttered. "But you can choose your own. Right now Lily's in charge of money, and Charlotte's in charge of the schedules and how things work, and Sophie only wanted to be a manicurist, not in charge of any—"

"What about you?" Brooke asked.

"Um, I'm . . . I'm CEO," Aly whispered.

"What does that mean?" Brooke demanded.

"Well, it kind of means I'm in charge of everything," she admitted. But then she quickly added,

"But we can share the title. Or—or you can have it if you want it, and I can be something else."

Brooke started crying now for real. "You didn't even think about me! I broke my arm, and you forgot all about me and took away the Sparkle Spa. I don't even want to be your sister anymore." She ran out of the office, down the hall.

And before Brooke slammed the bedroom door for the second time that night, she yelled out, "And don't worry about giving me a job, Aly. I quit."

eight
Blue Skies

Friday was usually one of Aly Tanner's favorite days of the week: No school for two whole days, Sparkle Spa for one full day each weekend (not just a weekday afternoon), and she and Brooke always polished each other's fingernails first thing on Saturday morning so they would look fancy all weekend long.

But this Friday, Aly floated through the day, barely talking to anyone or noticing anything. She gave Charlotte, Lily, Caleb, and Sophie their new business cards, and she wished the dancers luck for their showcase that night, and she stopped by True Colors right after school to see if Joan needed any help, but the whole time, she was thinking about Brooke and how she'd quit their whole Sparkle Spa business. No matter how many lists Aly tried to make, she couldn't figure out a way to fix things.

When Aly got home, Brooke was sitting in the overstuffed chair in the kitchen reading *Tales of a Fourth Grade Nothing*. She didn't even look up when Aly walked in.

Mom and Dad were busy preparing dinner and didn't seem to notice that the sisters weren't on speaking terms. Aly knew she could ask her parents for advice, but she wanted to try to fix the problem herself.

After a quiet dinner, Aly went to the office, took out a sparkly pen and a piece of purple paper, and started to write.

Dear Brooke,

Please come back to the Sparkle Spa.

It won't be the same without you.

You are my sister, and we started
the spa together. I should have
thought of that before anything else.

No one can ever take your place.

I'm so, so sorry.

Love, your sorry sister,

Aly

Aly slipped the note under their bedroom door,
along with a Sparkle Spa business card that she'd
made for Brooke that named her co-CEO. Aly realized that she should have given Brooke that title from
the start. The sisters were a team, and she'd never forget that again. If only Brooke would agree to come
back to the Sparkle Spa. . . .

✳ ✳ ✳ ✳ ✳

Early Saturday morning Aly was awakened by
Sparkly's lick, followed by a hug—a hug from
Brooke.

"I forgive you, Aly," Brooke whispered in her sister's ear. "Let's get ready for work."

Brooke needed help getting her cast through the
armhole of her T-shirt. And with the straps on her
sandals. And with brushing her hair, too. Aly even
put toothpaste on Brooke's toothbrush for her—but
she drew the line when Brooke asked if Aly would
brush her teeth for her. So Brooke did that herself.

"Broken arms are the pits," Brooke said, after she
spit out her toothpaste.

Aly nodded. "But you'll be better soon."

"Six weeks!" Brooke answered as she handed her
hair elastic to Aly. "That's forever."

"Not even close to forever," Aly said.

* * * * *

An hour later Mom was driving the girls to the salon. Sparkly was spending the day with Dad.

"The whole team will be there today," Aly warned Brooke.

"I know, I know," Brooke said. "It's fine. I'm glad they helped keep the Sparkle Spa in business."

When the girls walked through the front door of True Colors, all of the manicurists made a big deal over Brooke being back. Each one wanted to sign and decorate her cast. Meanwhile, Aly headed to the Sparkle Spa, where she was surprised to see Charlotte, Caleb, and Lily already there. Sophie was there too, sitting at the second manicure station, ready for work.

"Look what I did," Charlotte said as soon as Aly walked in. She pointed to three sheets of paper attached to the wall in a row, with a pen dangling from a string taped next to each sheet. Charlotte had made photocopies of the pages from the Sparkle Spa appointment book for next Tuesday, Friday, and Sunday.

"This way," she said, "customers can sign up for appointments themselves while they wait."

"Oh." Aly said. She sort of wished Charlotte had asked her first, and she was a little worried about what Brooke would think.

But before she could respond, Charlotte added, "And I made these signs for the front window of True Colors." She held up one that read: KIDS, COME TO THE BACK! SPARKLE SPA IS OPEN! And another that said: SPARKLE SPA IS CLOSED, BUT CALL TO MAKE AN APPOINTMENT. She'd left space underneath to include a phone number.

"I think we should get a business cell phone so people can leave messages," Caleb said.

"No cell phones allowed," Aly said quickly. "But thanks for thinking of it." She was starting to feel a tiny bit uncomfortable about all these new suggestions.

"And, Aly, look at the new donation box," Lily said. "The old jar could break, so I brought in this safe, which even has a combination lock." Lily practically shoved the box in Aly's face.

"Oh," Aly said again. She didn't want a new donation box. She loved the sparkly teal strawberry Mom had made in art school. And she knew Brooke did too. But what could she say? Lily was only trying to do her job as CFO.

A few seconds later Brooke walked in, her cast covered with rainbows and hearts.

"Brooke!" Sophie squealed, standing up. "I'm so glad you're back!"

Brooke squinted at her. "What are *you* doing in *my* manicure chair?" Brooke hissed.

Sophie's face paled. "I, um, I'm a manicurist now, remember? This is where I was sitting on
Thursday . . . ," she said quietly.

Brooke looked around. "What's that on the wall?
And why isn't the strawberry donation jar on the
side table?" she said, clearly growing more upset at
each new change she noticed.

"Charlotte made us sign-up charts, since she's
the COO now," Aly said nervously. "What do you
think?"

Brooke didn't answer. Instead, she focused on
Caleb. "He won't be here all the time, will he?
Everything will be different if there's a *boy* in
the Sparkle Spa! Aly, you're ruining everything!
Again!" She turned around and ran back into True
Colors.

Aly's stomach flip-flopped. "I'm really sorry,
everyone," she said. "I think Brooke is just a little

surprised. It's my fault. I should've explained things better to her. I'll go get her."

But before Aly had a chance to follow her sister, two sixth graders from their school, Uma and Aubrey, came in for manicures and pedicures. Aly had totally forgotten about them, but they'd made appointments on Monday and were right there in the book. Aly poked her head into True Colors and saw Brooke talking to their mom.

"I picked my colors," Uma called out.

"Me too," said Aubrey. "Which are we doing first? Fingers or toes?"

Aly looked at Brooke one more time and then sighed. "Toes," she said to Aubrey and Uma. "Let's get started."

The day was busy with both regulars and walk-ins. Sophie was improving, but she was still pretty slow.

Charlotte kept coming up with new ideas every hour, from where to move the stations to what colors to paint the walls. Caleb pretty much sat near the door, checking out his sneakers. And Lily kept counting the donations over and over. Nobody asked about Brooke at all. But Aly was thinking about her all day long. She couldn't believe no one else was.

Even without Brooke, everything was going along smoothly. Aly was putting the top coat on Keisha's fingers—she was a second grader Aly knew from the library—when Charlotte said, "Aly, I think we should have two Colors of the Week, not just one. And three on special occasions like Halloween and the Fourth of July."

And that's when Aly snapped.

She waited until Keisha left and there were no customers in the salon. Then she exploded. "Charlotte, you have to stop asking me so many questions about colors and appointments. Lily, please stop rattling the coins in the box. And, Caleb, you haven't gotten off that chair all day!"

They all just stared at Aly.

No one said anything for close to a minute.

"Are you feeling okay?" Charlotte finally asked. "Did we do something wrong? We're just trying to be helpful."

Oh, boy. What had she done? Aly felt terrible. Really terrible. "No, it's me. Not any of you. I'm so sorry," she said. "I think I just miss Brooke."

Aly absolutely needed all her friends' help, but she *really* missed Brooke.

She missed their Secret Sister Eye Messages and Brooke pushing up her glasses and tugging her braid. She missed Brooke's awesome ideas. She missed Brooke's color combinations and the way she knew which new polish everyone would like best.

And if she was being perfectly honest, Aly had to admit that having all these new job titles at the Sparkle Spa had kind of added a few too many bosses to the mix. Did she *have* to accept every single one of their suggested changes now that Charlotte, Lily, Sophie, and Caleb were part of the team?

Being CEO was hard. And without Brooke, it was even harder.

The rest of the afternoon was fine, and the only one who seemed bothered by Aly's outburst was Aly. She made sure she was extra nice to everyone because of it, even though she hated the safe that Lily had brought and liked the manicure and pedicure stations exactly where they were.

"Thanks, everyone," Aly said as her friends were getting ready to leave. "Really. You all did a super job, and I'm sorry again for getting upset earlier."

"No problem, Aly. We know you miss Brooke. See you at school on Monday," Charlotte said, waving good-bye.

Sophie was the last to leave the spa. "I'm sorry I'm so slow, Aly, but I really love being here and polishing nails," she said quietly. "I just . . . I just wanted you to know that."

"Sophie, you're a great manicurist." Aly sighed. "I didn't mean to be mean today."

Once the Sparkle Spa was empty, Aly went on a hunt for Brooke. She found her sitting with Mom on the sky-blue bench in front of True Colors. They were both eating ice cream. With sprinkles. Aly didn't say a word, she just stood there listening.

Brooke was chattering away, too busy to notice her sister. "They changed things," she said. "While I was gone, Sophie took my spot and Charlotte made new signs and Caleb is a boy."

"Joan had new ideas too," Mom said. "For True Colors. I wish she would have asked me first, but sometimes being part of a team means letting other people do what they want to make a project or a game or a business the best it can be."

"I don't know if our friends love Sparkle Spa as much as I do," Brooke said, staring at the roses that Joan had drawn on her cast.

"You might be surprised, Brookie," Mom said. "They're just trying hard to make it even better than it already is."

"I guess," Brooke said. "But I liked it better when the team was just me and Aly, and we did everything together, just us."

Aly took a deep breath and finally spoke up. "I liked it that way too, Brooke." Then she sent a Secret Sister Eye Message that said, *I miss you so much.*

And when Aly felt tears forming in her eyes, she saw them in Brooke's eyes too.

nine

Forget Me Not

All day Sunday, Aly and Brooke talked about what had gone right and what had gone wrong after Brooke's accident. That way they could learn from what had happened.

They each made a list.

How to Fix Aly's Mistakes
1. Talk to Brooke before you make any Executive Sparkle Spa Decisions! She's your partner.

2. ESSDs should sometimes be discussed with Mom.

3. Think before you make big decisions, like hiring all your friends to work.

4. Don't yell at your friends in the Sparkle Spa. They're just trying to help.

5. Try not to be mean like Suzy Davis.

How to Fix Brooke's Mistakes

1. Watch out for backpacks that are lying on the floor.

2. Don't chase Sparkly through the whole entire house.

3. Don't get mad at Caleb for being a boy.

4. Sometimes it's okay when there
   are changes at the Sparkle Spa.
   People are just trying to make it
   even better.
5. Try not to be mean like Suzy Davis.

And when Charlotte, Lily, Sophie, and Caleb showed up for work at the Sparkle Spa on Tuesday, Aly folded up her list, stuck it in her back pocket, and apologized to them. She apologized again for her outburst on Saturday. She apologized for giving them all jobs without talking to Brooke first. And she told them that they could keep their jobs at the Sparkle Spa for as long as they wanted, but they had to understand that Brooke and Aly were the ones in charge. And they would make decisions together, just like Lewis and Clark. Even though those explorers needed help from their friends too, like Sacagawea.

"We know you're in charge," Charlotte said. "But we do love being here. We just want the Sparkle Spa to be the best kids' salon in the world."

"Yeah, it's been okay, but just so you know, I don't think I can hang out here all the time. I've got sports, too, you know," Caleb said.

Aly nodded and looked at Brooke, who was biting her lip to keep from smiling. Then Caleb took his post by the door, and the girls started to get ready for the Auden Angels' rainbow sparkle pedicures. Since Brooke couldn't polish, she decided her job was going to be standing near the polish display and talking to people. It really was the perfect job for her.

When the pedicures were done, all the players lined up to decorate Brooke's cast. Jenica grabbed a bottle of bluish-purple Forget Me Not polish. "Quickly," she said as she dipped the brush in and painted a star on Brooke's cast. "Because we have to get down to the field for practice for the semifinals on Saturday. You're coming to cheer us on, right? Rainbow sparkle power helped us get there."

"We'll be there," Aly said.

"Wouldn't miss it," Brooke added.

Lily and Charlotte nodded in agreement.

Caleb did too.

After the team left, Lily started counting the day's proceeds in the teal donation jar. The first thing Aly and Brooke had decided as co-CEOs was that the safe was out and the strawberry-shaped jar was back in. Their mom had made it after all, which made it extra special.

Lily handed Caleb a stack of bills and a handful of change. "Can you remember thirty-three?" she asked him.

He nodded.

Lily counted out some more money and handed that to Caleb too. Then she stood up.

"Ahem," she said. "This week the Sparkle Spa made exactly one hundred and seven dollars and— what was the number I told you, Caleb?"

"Thirty-three," he said.

"Thirty-three cents!" Lily finished. "That means it's time to contribute to a charity, right? Whichever one you choose?"

"Yep, every hundred dollars, we donate," Brooke confirmed.

Charlotte and Brooke had just finished organizing the polish wall and sat down on the floor near Caleb and Lily. "So are you guys going to pick a place to give the money to now?" Charlotte asked the sisters.

"We should," Aly said, turning to Brooke.

She saw Brooke looking around at Charlotte's sign-up sheets, which Aly and Brooke had decided could stay. And then her eyes traveled to Sophie, who'd made it possible for Sparkle Spa to stay up and running while her arm was healing.

Finally, Brooke looked at Aly and gave her a Secret Sister Eye Message: *Let's make it a team decision.*

Aly nodded in agreement, so Brooke asked, "What do you guys think?"

Everyone thought for a while.

"Puppies?" Charlotte suggested.

Aly glanced at Brooke, who shook her head.

"Great idea," Aly said, "but we already donated to the animal shelter."

"Dancers?" Sophie asked.

"Are they a charity?" Lily said.

"No, I guess not," Sophie agreed.

Then Brooke jumped up. "I know!" she said. "We should donate to kids who are in the hospital's emergency room—especially in the waiting area. It's so boring there and sometimes scary. The hospital can use the money to make a library, maybe—or at least some magazines and comic books to start. And then maybe people from all over town can donate books they don't want anymore. We'll tell Mrs. Bass that we'll take any of her sons' books that we can get!"

"I like that idea a lot," Aly told Brooke, beaming. Then she whispered in her sister's ear, *"But should we let everyone vote?"*

When Brooke nodded, Aly said, "Everyone who agrees with this choice, raise your hand."

Everyone raised their hand.

"Nice teamwork," she said with a smile.

Aly knew that for as long as she and Brooke needed them, Lily, Charlotte, Sophie, and Caleb would be there to help. But she and Brooke would still be in charge, just the two of them. Because that's how they liked it best.

ten

Diamond Jubilee

"May I have another slice, Joanie?" Brooke asked. "This pizza is delicious!" Her arm may have been in a cast, but that didn't stop Brooke from eating three slices of extra-cheese pizza.

True Colors and the Sparkle Spa were celebrating Joan's promotion to COO with a pizza party. She worked so hard and could always be counted on—and she came up with some great ideas while Mom was gone, proving that she had a good head for business. No one deserved this promotion more than Joan, Aly knew. She was so happy for her.

"Come on, Brooke. We'll be late for the game," Sophie said. Aly and Brooke had agreed that they should invite all their friends to Joan's party too, since they were part of the salon team now. "I don't want to miss kickoff."

"Okay, okay. One more bite and we'll all go," Brooke answered.

"Run, Jenica, run!" Brooke yelled.

"Get it to the goal!" Aly shouted.

"Kick it!" Lily screamed, jumping up and down.

"She's *fast*!" Caleb said.

Aly couldn't believe how quickly Jenica was moving as she bolted down the field. She was faster than anyone—and her hair was flying all over the place as she ran. The other girls were coming up behind her in different spots on the grass.

It was cool to see how the whole team worked together and knew how to play the different positions.

Jenica passed the ball to Bethany, who kicked it to Mia.

Aly watched Mia's Diamond Jubilee fingernails flash in the sun, with little Silversmith hearts on her pinkies. Sophie had polished her nails for the dance showcase over a week ago, and they were still holding up. "Your manicure's looking good out there, Soph," she said.

Sophie smiled.

Mia kicked the ball toward the goal, but a girl from the other team blocked the shot and sent it in the other direction. Bethany got there first, then kicked it. *Hard.* The ball went *flying, flying, flying* past the goalie's hands, right into the top left corner of the net.

GOAL!

The Angels won their semifinal match! The team ran cheering onto the field.

Aly heard Jenica scream, "We did it! We did it together!"

I wonder if rainbow sparkle power really did help them at all, Aly thought.

Brooke cheered. "They're a team, just like us," she said.

And that's exactly how Aly felt about the new crew at the Sparkle Spa. It hadn't been easy, but they'd done it together.

"So," Brooke said to Aly, Lily, Charlotte, and Caleb, after they'd congratulated all the Angels, "I heard the soccer girls are celebrating with ice cream. I think we should celebrate too. Not just because they won the game, but because we're a great team, just like them."

Aly smiled and threw her arm around her sister. "That," she said, "is one of your best ideas yet."

How to Give Yourself (or a Friend!) an I Love Dancing Pedicure

By Aly (and Brooke!)

✳ ⋅ ⁕ ✳ ⋅ ⁕ ⋅ ⁕ ✳ ⋅ ⁕ ✳ ⋅ ⁕ ✳ ⋅ ⁕ ✳

What you need:

Paper towels

Polish remover

Clear polish

One color polish for the base

(we suggest silver)

One color polish for the hearts

(we suggest copper)

Toothpicks

What you do:

1. Put some paper towels down on the floor so if anything spills, no one will get mad at you. (This

is very important. This one time we got Tickled Pink on our grandma's white rug. She was not happy at all.)

2. Rip off another paper towel, fold it up, and put some polish remover on it. If you have polish on your toes already, make sure you get it all off. If you don't, just rub the remover over your nails once to remove any dirt that might be on them. (Dirt makes polish look lumpy, and that is the absolute pits! No one wants lumpy polish!)

3. Rip off two more paper towels. Twist the first one into a long tube and weave it back and forth between your toes to separate them a little bit. (This will help keep polish off the skin of one toe when you're painting the one next to it.) Then do the same thing with the second paper towel on your other foot.

You might need to tuck the end of the paper towel under your pinkie toe if it pops up and gets in your way while you polish. (You can also use tape if you need to—but you probably won't need to.)

4. Open your bottle of clear polish and apply a coat on each nail. Then close the clear bottle up tight. (You can go in whatever order you want, but our favorite is big toe to pinkie on your right foot, then big toe to pinkie on your left foot. It's easy to keep track that way. But whatever you do, make sure you get them all!)

5. Open the silver polish (or whichever color you chose for your base; we like metallics for this pedicure). Apply one coat on all toenails. Close the bottle up tight.

6. Fan your toes to dry them a little, then repeat the fifth step. (If you don't do a second coat, the polish won't look as bright. Some people like to do a third coat, but we think that's too many. Plus then it takes even longer to dry.)

7. Fan your toes a little again. (You should actually fan them for more than a little while. We recommend singing the whole alphabet song three times in a row. Aly likes to show off and sing it backward, but I do it forward, and that's just fine.)

8. Open your copper polish (or whatever accent color you chose). Wipe the brush on the sides of the nail polish bottle and then balance the brush upside down so the polish doesn't drip anywhere.

Dip a toothpick into the polish and use it like a tiny paintbrush to draw a heart. (You will probably need to dip a few times to get the whole heart drawn.) Then repeat on the other pinkie toe. (Your pinkie toenail is smaller than your pinkie fingernail, so you may want to switch and put the heart on your big toe instead. Either way, it looks beautiful.) When you're done, close the bottle up tight.

9. Fan your toes again (one alphabet song should do the trick—forward or backward, it's up to you) and then open your clear polish. Apply a top coat of clear polish on all your toenails. Close the bottle up tight.

Now your toes have to dry. You can fan them for a long time (like, at least fifteen alphabet songs), or you can sit and make a bracelet or read a book or watch TV or talk to your friend until they're all dry. Usually, it takes about twenty minutes, but it could take longer. (After twenty minutes you should check the dryness by really carefully touching the nail of your big toe very lightly with your fingertip. If it still feels sticky, keep waiting! Patience is the most important thing—otherwise, you might smudge your pedicure and have to take it all off and do it all over again, which, let me tell you, is a very grumpy-making process. This one time that happened to me twice in a row, and I was ready to pull my braid out of my head, I was so mad about it!)

And now you should have a beautiful I Love Dancing pedicure! Even after the polish is dry, you probably shouldn't wear socks or closed-toe shoes for a while. (And make sure no one steps on your feet—not even your dog!) Bare feet or sandals are best so all your hard work doesn't get smooshed. (Besides, then you can show off your beautiful toes!)

Happy polishing!

* . .* * . . * * . .* * . .* * . .* *

JILL SANTOPOLO is a big fan of sparkles. She's also a big fan of sisters. And spas. And writing. In addition to the Sparkle Spa books, she's the author of the Alec Flint Mysteries. You can find her online at www.jillsantopolo.com. Or you can find her in person in New York City, where she likes getting her nails painted with Good as Gold nail polish.